A NECESSARY SIN

THE SIN TRILOGY: BOOK I

GEORGIA CATES

Sign-up to join the monthly newsletter for Georgia Cates. You will get the latest news, first-look at teasers, and giveaways just for subscribers.

Editing Services provided by Jennifer Sommersby Young

Interior Design by Indie Formatting Services

Photograph by Nera Strand, Black Beach Studios

ISBN-13: 978-1505391190

ISBN: 978-1-63452-376-9

To J, F, and M.
You are my dream come true.

PROLOGUE

STELLA BLEU LAWRENCE

AGE SEVEN

I'M WEARING MY PRETTY PINK PRINCESS APRON AND CHEF HAT WHILE DOING MY most favoritest thing in the world–baking chocolate chip cookies with my mama. I inspect the shiny plastic roll of dough, studying the picture of the white fluffy pastry boy on the package before turning it around for her to see. "Mama, look. He's wearing a puffy hat just like mine. Except mine's prettier." Everything is prettier when it's pink.

My mama sprays the pan we're using for our cookies. "He sure is, Bleubird. And I think you're right. Yours is much prettier. Did you know only the best chefs in the world wear hats like yours?"

Wow. This hat makes me one of the best chefs in the world so that means these cookies are going to be the most delicious I've ever baked.

"It's your favorite song," I squeal when "Amanda" begins to play. Mama says Boston sings that song just for her. I think she could be right since Amanda is her name.

We always listen to music when we're cooking so I've heard this song a million times. I know every word by heart but I don't understand what it means. Mama says it's all about grown-up stuff and I'll understand one day. I'm not sure I ever want to understand. Grown-up stuff makes my mama cry. A lot.

I'm singing my guts out because it always makes her crack up. I love seeing her laugh because it means she isn't crying. She's too pretty to cry so much.

She holds the plastic roll of dough to her mouth and pretends it's a microphone. She sings so pretty. Everything about Mama is pretty. I hope I grow up to be just like her.

The song gets to the part where there are no words, only guitars, so she puts her pretend microphone on the counter and slices into it with a sharp knife. She always does that part because she says I'm still too little to use knives. My job is to roll the dough into little balls. I'm not always great at it, though. Some come out big, some little. But she always tells me I've done a great job–even when I know I haven't.

"Can I have a bite of dough?" She's making her "no" face. "Please … with lots and lots of sugar on top."

I can't remember why she said it's okay to eat the cookie dough after it comes out of the oven, but not before. "Hailey's mama lets her have cookie dough."

"Maybe one little bite will be okay, but we're not going to make a habit of this, little lady." She pinches off a tiny ball and I almost jump up and down because I'm so happy. I've always wanted to taste it because Hailey says it's delicious.

I miss cooking with Mama. We used to do it all the time but that was before she started her new job. She works at night so she has to leave me with our neighbor. Amelia's nice to me but she's old, smells funny, and never wants to play. All she does is sit in her chair with her feet up and watch that news show where the same stories repeat over and over. It's sooo boring.

I finish my tiny ball of cookie dough and immediately want more. "Another? Please, with sugar on top." That worked the first time.

"No, Stella. I said one bite and that's what I meant so don't ask again." I knew she'd say no but it was worth a try.

I line the balls of dough on the pan and she puts them in the preheated oven. "We'll check them in ten minutes." She sets the timer on the stove because we don't want to burn them. We love our cookies gooey. "What do you want to do while we wait?"

I look at the roll of leftover dough in the roll. "Umm … eat cookie dough?" I grin and bat my eyelashes, as if that's going to get me what

I want but she doesn't budge. I only succeed in making her laugh, which is better than making her mad since I asked again after she told me not to.

I sit at the table in our kitchen, tortured by the smell of baking cookies. "They smell sooo good. How much longer?"

I'm not sure why I asked. I can plainly see the timer counting down. "Five more minutes."

I huff and blow my hair out of my face and prop my chin on my hands. "I wish they'd hurry up. I'm ready to taste those ooey-gooey cookies."

"Good things come to those who wait." She tells me that all the time but I don't understand why good things can't come sooner instead of later. I hate waiting. "Do you want milk with your cookies?"

"Yes!" I run to the fridge and swing the smaller side open. I hope we have mugs in the freezer. I love that milky ice that forms in the glass.

The doorbell rings and Max, our ginormous German shepherd, barks as he runs toward the door. I bounce up from the kitchen table to follow him. "I bet it's Hailey wanting to play."

Mama puts her hand out and catches me by the back of my shirt. "That's not Hailey. Her mother wouldn't let her come over this late." She goes up on her tiptoes and spies through the peephole. She jerks back and twists to look at me before placing her finger to her lips. "Shh." She tiptoes to me and takes my hand. She grabs Max by the collar and takes us down the hallway.

She goes to her knees so we're face to face and holds both of my shoulders when we are in my bedroom. "Listen to me very carefully. We're going to play a little game. I want you to hide under your bed and be very, very quiet. Stay there until I return and tell you it's okay to come out. Do you understand, Stella?"

I nod, afraid and confused, but I do as I'm told and crawl under my bed.

"Max, stay," she commands. I see him obey, his butt sitting on my carpet, but he doesn't understand that he's supposed to be quiet. He's whining the way he does when he wants to disobey. "Don't come out no matter what you hear," Mama says.

I watch her feet leave my room and she pulls my bedroom door shut. I lie silently on the floor beneath my bed, waiting for her to return so I can come out. This game is not fun.

The music gets super-duper loud. Loud enough that I'm sure the neighbors will call and complain to Mr. Johnson.

It's another song I know by Boston. "More Than a Feeling." The guitar is screaming so I know we're going to get in trouble with the landlord. Our neighbor, Mr. Benson, likes to turn us in every chance he gets. He doesn't like us much and I don't know why.

The carpet is making my cheek itch so I lift my face to scratch it. In the process, I bump the back of my head on the railing of my bed. "Oww." I put my hand over my head and rub it where it burns.

Max gets up from where he's sitting and scratches at the carpet, trying to get out of my room. He whines louder and begins barking as he paws at the door. "Stop, Max. You're gonna make Mama mad if you scratch the paint."

I hear a bang, the loudest noise I've ever heard in my life, and my heart beats faster than I can ever remember. "Mama?" I whisper but stay put because it's what she told me to do. Don't come out until I say it's okay.

What was that loud sound?

I smell the burning cookies. Mama wouldn't let our cookies burn.

I think something bad is happening.

Max howls, now clawing to get out, and I press my face into the carpet so I can see between the floor and my bed skirt. I think about letting him out so he can go to Mama.

I don't have time to do it before my bedroom door opens slowly. Max backs away and then lunges for the leg of the person coming into my bedroom.

I hear that same bang again, this time even louder, before seeing Max fall to the floor.

Red. It's splattered all over my beige carpet and I know what it is. I want to scream at the top of my lungs but I can't. My breath is gone and it feels like there's a person I can't see covering my mouth with a hand to quiet me.

I want to squeeze my eyes shut but I can't because I'm watching the big, black shiny shoes come toward my bed. It's a man and his pants are torn where Max bit him. He's bleeding.

His feet go still next to my head. I hold my breath so he won't hear me but I can't do it for long. It feels the same as when I've been under water too long. My body forces me to take a breath. It's louder than I intend. I hear it so I'm scared he did too.

His feet don't move and then the bed skirt next to my head lifts. "I see you under there," he says and I recognize his voice. He's that man that talks funny.

My mama has never let me meet him but I know it's him–the man who comes here to see her at night after I've gone to bed. She calls him Thane. "You can come out, wee darlin'."

I squeeze my eyes and scoot away. "Mama told me to stay here until she comes back."

He crouches next to the bed. I still can't make out his face but I see the bloodstain getting bigger on his pants where Max bit him. "She says it's okay. Your mum sent me to your room to get you."

I don't believe this man. He's bad. He killed my dog. "No."

"How old are you, toots? Six? Seven?" he asks.

I back away until I'm pressed against the wall.

He doesn't say anything for a moment but when he does, it's loud. "Fuck! Why did that wench have to go and have a bairn in the house?" he yells in a growly voice as he kicks my bed. I'm shaking because I'm scared. I squeeze my hands over my ears because I don't want to hear him yell.

He reaches beneath my bed and grabs my ankle, yanking me from the safe place. I have nowhere to go so I curl into a ball and wrap my arms around my head. I know what comes next. I've seen what bad men do. They hit.

"Oh, toots. I really don't want to do this but I have no choice."

I squeeze my eyes tighter and wait for the pain to come. But that isn't what happens. He flips me to my back and presses something soft and feathery into my face so I can't breathe.

I kick, struggling for air, but he presses it harder. I fight with every ounce of strength I have but it's no use. He's a grown-up and I'm only a little girl. I don't have the strength to make him stop and I'm afraid. I'm about to die.

Then everything goes black.

CHAPTER ONE

BLEU MACALLISTER

MEMPHIS, TENNESSEE

JUST AS A ROSE IS UNABLE TO CHANGE ITS COLOR, IT ISN'T POSSIBLE FOR US TO alter the past. It's only once you realize this that you'll be set free. This sounds really lovely, like it should be a quote in a book, but what happens when you can't break the chains clutching you to a devastating and life-altering event? No one likes to talk about that kind of ugliness.

Events in our lives shape us. There's basically two categories–good or bad. I'm not going to touch on the praiseworthy since I'm not a motivational speaker. I want to address the ugly.

This isn't a perfect world. Bad things happen to good people. True evil exists and it walks this earth in the form of a well-suited man wearing expensive shoes. He speaks with a charming Scottish accent and smells of liquor and sweet tobacco. My mother's killer.

Most children are too naïve to recognize the moment they are being ruined for the rest of their lives. I wasn't that lucky. I remember everything about that dreadful day and the memories often replay in my head–the bitter aroma of burning cookies, the smell of gunpowder floating in the air, even the vision of seeing Max's brains splattered onto my carpet. I wish the amnesia I claimed to have would've stolen those gruesome memories. Maybe then this unquenchable demon with a thirst for hunting and executing wouldn't have been spawned inside me.

That was the day Stella Bleu Lawrence died. And Bleu MacAllister was born.

I can barely recall a time in my life when I wasn't obsessed with finding our attacker. I've spent years imagining the different ways he might beg for mercy as I hold a gun to his temple. These were the aspirations in my head when my mind would drift from memorizing presidents and state capitals. I never had innocent, childlike thoughts. My dreams weren't of becoming the doctor to discover the cure for cancer or becoming the first female president; they were consumed by dark, vengeful thoughts.

For eighteen years, every aspect of my life has revolved around retaliation in one form or another, with the exception of the two pleasures I allowed myself: photography and playing violin.

Other kids took karate lessons for fun. I took Muay Thai for strength and defense skills. Girls my age enrolled in gymnastics because it's what all their friends were doing. I became a gymnast to learn balance and agility. My fellow ballerinas liked wearing tutus. I became a dancer to master grace. I wasn't naturally the brightest student so I excelled to the top of my class by becoming the most studious. Why? I've always known being the smartest person in the room would one day be my greatest tool. An intelligent person has a chance at outwitting another using a gun in place of his brain.

How does a person live this way without going mad? It wasn't easy. But I had a confidant—my dad.

I was twelve years old when I sat Harry, my adoptive father, down and told him it was time for a talk. No, not about the birds and bees. I'm certain that would've been much more preferable. Instead, I described my memories of the dreadful day my mother was murdered and how I was suffocated with a pillow and left for dead.

I'd spent the previous five years claiming to have no memory of the horrid event. To say Harry was shocked to learn the truth would be an understatement. But that didn't hold a candle to what came next. Telling him I intended to hunt and execute Thane Breckenridge was the straw that broke the camel's back.

Harry wasn't delighted to learn that this little girl he saved was planning a murder. I'm certain no father wants to hear that his daughter's aspiration in life is to grow up to be a killer, especially when he's an FBI special agent sworn to uphold the law. That's why I had to give him an ultimatum. Some might call it an ultimatum he couldn't refuse–either teach me how to kill or watch me attempt it on my own without any training.

It was a hell of a bomb to drop. I can't imagine the despair he must've felt while hearing such a declaration. For that I've always been sorry. But I must have been convincing since he agreed. I suspect he went along with it in the beginning to pacify me. He probably believed a twelve-year-old girl would eventually change her mind or lose interest. Neither happened.

Once Harry saw my determination, he took precise care in teaching me how to safely blend with monsters. That's how I plan to do it–infiltrate Thane Breckenridge's world of organized crime.

Although I was tutored in the art of facade from an early age, Harry couldn't prepare me for everything. Together, we decided I should briefly work as a police officer before applying for the FBI academy. He was once an instructor at Quantico so he knew all the right moves to expedite my acceptance into the program as soon as I turned twenty-three and had the proper credentials. It was a good decision since it furthered my education. Although brief, the most beneficial was the hands-on training in undercover work. I regret I wasn't able to obtain more experience.

Being an agent taught me to think of no one as more than a profile, even myself. I'm Stella Bleu Lawrence MacAllister, former special agent for the Federal Bureau of Investigations, Memphis division. I'm a twenty-five-year-old Caucasian female with chestnut brown hair and light blue eyes. I'm five-six, weigh one hundred fifteen pounds. I'm considered attractive by most men's standards. I lack an interest in relationships, both romantic and social. I'm emotionally cold, detached, and often display narcissistic characteristics. I'm very well aware of my thick skin and completely unapologetic for it. I'm simply inclined to not make connections or friendships with people, with three exceptions: Harry, Julia, and Ellison.

Harry trained me to be a chameleon. I can easily adapt to any situation—except the one happening right now. Julia, my adoptive mother, is gone. Cancer claimed her two years ago. Now Harry has it as well and the treatments aren't working anymore.

I haven't recovered from losing Julia and now I face the same prognosis with the only father I've ever known. Losing two parents to cancer only a few years apart isn't fair. I'm bitter and angry but this is different from my mother's death. I can't avenge losing them because an intangible illness is the villain to take them from me.

Harry and I sit in my living room with the soft sound of Violin Concerto in D Major playing in the background as we comb through years of records. The final arrangements we're making aren't for Harry's death. They're for Thane Breckenridge's. The files scattered before us concern him and his criminal organization known as The Fellowship.

We thought I'd get a few years of FBI undercover experience before I walked directly into the lion's den but Harry's illness is forcing my hand prematurely. We planned for four years of experience. Instead, I got seventeen months. We're forced to finalize the plan because he insists I do this while he's still alive—and lucid. He says he can't die in peace unless he knows I've put all this behind me.

We've had eyes on them for years. I've memorized everything in these files about the Breckenridge gang and the people within his circle. It's all in my mental vault, etched on my heart for good measure.

Lounging on my sofa with feet propped on the coffee table, I chew my pencil as I look through the worn file and mull over my options. I already know how I want to do this but my plan has Harry and me butting heads.

Thane's son, Sinclair Breckenridge. He's presently finishing his traineeship with the law firm, Hendry-Irvine, so he may be groomed to replace Rodrick Lester, the present attorney for the brotherhood. The older Breckenridge son is a twenty-six-year-old Caucasian male with dark brown hair and brown eyes. Height is six-two, weight approximately one hundred eighty-five pounds. He's very attractive, highly intelligent, and studious—hence, Thane's decision to make him the organization's next criminal defender.

Harry doesn't like the idea of me infiltrating the brotherhood through the son. He's afraid Sinclair will have a strong attraction for me. In other words, he fears I'll allow the lines to blur because he's handsome and charming.

A snowball in hell has a better chance than me allowing myself to develop anything less than hatred for a Breckenridge.

The younger son, Mitch, is a no-go. At twenty-two, he's too immature and not in an optimal position within The Fellowship. "I've looked at this from a lot of different angles and I still believe the older son is my best way in."

Harry shakes his head while scouring a section of the file in his hand. "And the most dangerous," he counters, never looking in my direction. "These aren't the kind of people to welcome a stranger into their fold. You have to penetrate lower on the totem pole and gradually move your way up to not rouse suspicion. It's far too dangerous to start at the top."

Beginning at the bottom takes time, a luxury we don't have. Harry's cancer has already proven to be a hungry little bastard. "Going straight to Sinclair Breckenridge will save weeks, possibly months."

"I shouldn't have to remind you that the long road is safest with these people. The more they know you, the better they trust you. Shortcuts get you killed."

Harry's oncologist says he has six, maybe up to eight months left. After my experience with Julia, we can probably only expect three of those to be good.

There's not a single minute to be wasted but I won't argue or remind him why our timetable is short. I'll concede for now and then do what I must when the time comes. "You're right." I thumb through the papers and find the profile for Sinclair's friend, Leith Duncan. "What do you think of worming in through his friend, the bar owner?"

"Remind me again who he is."

"One of Sinclair's best friends, owner of the bar where they all drink. He's the son of a somewhat insignificant—a grunt responsible for carrying out tribute."

"You're determined to get to Thane through his boy." He's reading me like a book. He knows I may start at Leith Duncan but it'll be short-lived when I move on to the son. "That doesn't have anything to do with his pretty face, does it?"

He knows I've never been a sucker for a pretty boy. "Don't make me hit a sick, old man."

He laughs while stretching to reach for the profile. "I know you won't toy with this Leith for long but let me take another look at him."

I give him a minute to review the file before making my suggestion. "With the exception of Thane and Abram, the brotherhood members frequent this bar on a regular basis. I'd be in contact with all of them at one point or another so that broadens my options. They all like pretty girls in short kilts to serve their drinks." I hold up the surveillance photo of the bar. "I'd look pretty good in the Duncan Whisky Bar uniform."

"I'm not crazy about ruthless men ogling you in that tiny skirt."

"It's a kilt."

"It's a nearly nonexistent scrap of plaid. I'd rather you didn't walk around wearing it for all of The Fellowship members to see." He sighs. "But I guess it's a solid idea." He peers at me over his reading glasses. "Although we both know I'm aware of what you're going to do." He means me skipping through the chain of command and going straight for Sinclair.

"You know I'm careful." Being an undercover agent was the perfect job for me. I was very good at it. But I should've been. I'd been trained for it since I was twelve.

"I can't help it. You're my daughter. It's my job to protect you."

Elli is the one he can coddle, not me. She's the princess so she eats that shit up.

We're parent and child by choice, not blood. Harry is the one who saved me that day. He was off duty and visiting family in my apartment building when he heard the gunshot. I was unresponsive without a heartbeat—or any sign of life—when he got to me. The doctor said the only reason I lived was because Harry performed CPR and kept oxygen circulating to my vital organs until the EMTs arrived and shocked my heart into beating again.

We also share a secret, forging a bond between us that my sister will never understand—and can never know about. She thinks Harry loves me more because we spend so much time together. She often feels excluded, but of course, he loves her equally. She isn't able to see it and for that, I'm truly sorry. I regret making my sister feel less loved.

Harry views us in different light, as he should. Ellison and I are very different. I'm strong and resilient while my sister is soft and delicate. She's the epitome of Daddy's little princess.

They have a normal relationship. My sister is his and Julia's biological child, and Julia was the only love he's ever known, so of course he loves Elli with all his heart. I sometimes envy the ease of their relationship but that's my own fault. I ruined any chance of father-daughter normalcy when I asked him to teach me how to kill.

"Okay."

"Okay, what?"

"You're getting your way. You'll go in through Duncan's Whisky Bar." Yes! "But when this is said and done, I'm afraid you'll not find the peace you think it'll bring. Serenity is the last thing you're going to experience. I fear you'll find yourself in a new kind of hell."

He's still trying to convince me I shouldn't go through with this. "I've killed before and slept soundly afterward."

"You killed because it was your job and you were given no choice. You went for the arrest but it turned into kill or be killed. This is different. You're going to exterminate an unsuspecting man."

Thane Breckenridge is not a man. "He's a monster. He deserves to die."

"When the time comes, you're going to feel differently about killing an unarmed person. You shouldn't be surprised if you're not able to go through with it."

"I'll be able to do it." I've never been more certain of anything in my life.

"Are you still hell-bent on not using an alias?"

"Yup."

I don't have the help of the FBI on this one so I think it's best to go in simple. They'll have no reason to suspect I'm there for any reason other than the one I give—unless Thane believes I'm a ghost who's risen from the grave.

CHAPTER TWO

SINCLAIR BRECKENRIDGE

EDINBURGH, SCOTLAND

"Thanks for coming, Sin. I really appreciate it."

I've known Hewie since I was a bairn but I didn't come to court to act as moral support. I was sitting in as Rodrick's assistant so I could observe the way he bends the law to the brotherhood's favor. He's a master, well known by all for his ruthless measures, as I will be when I take his place as solicitor for The Fellowship. This means I'll be Hewie's defense attorney in the future, but not today.

"You were stupid and sloppy. Will you do us both a favor and make smarter moves when I step into Rodrick's shoes?" And more importantly, when I take my father's place as leader.

"This won't happen again."

"Good. See that it doesn't." I'm certain there won't be a recurrence after Abram and my father are finished with him. "Atonement is scheduled for tomorrow."

Hewie unknowingly brought an undercover agent into The Fellowship but we were lucky. Intent to sell heroin is the only charge they were able to bring against him. It could've gone much worse had the agent made it deeper but he was an anxious rookie, ready to jump on a bust.

"Whatever Thane and Abram choose as my punishment will be

better than spending another night in that jail. The walls felt like they were closing in around me."

Everyone knows Hewie has a thing about small spaces so I'm guessing he'll get to spend the night in a tight, dark space after he takes a merciless beating. "I'll come back for you at seven in the morning. Tell your wife you have a job and you'll be gone a few days." The last thing we need is her reporting him as missing.

Sterling brings the car to a stop in front of Hewie's flat. "I'll be ready when ye return."

Dumb bastard. He's never paid retribution so he has no idea what's in store for him. I guess that's a good thing.

———

I have Sterling drive to Duncan's Whisky Bar so I can meet up with my two best mates, Leith and Jamie, for a drink. The three of us are as close as any three pals can be. We've known one another since we were bairns and share far more than our involvement in The Fellowship. Together, we're the future of the coalition. But we aren't equals. I'm the one who will step into the role of leader.

Leith snaps his fingers at his head server, Lorna. "Bring Sin his usual."

"How'd it go with Hewie?" Jamie asks.

"In our favor, as always. The prosecution didn't have shit, thanks to some dodgy police work. It should never have gone before the High Court but we all know how it made it through." The authorities believe they can take The Fellowship down bit by bit, no matter how small the piece. "All the charges were dropped so Hewie's legal problems are over, but he has atonement in the morning."

"Who's his enforcer?" Leith asks.

"Sangster." He's the meanest son of a bitch in The Fellowship. He finds entirely too much pleasure in carrying out punishment. I strongly suspect he's a sadist.

"He can do some real damage. I don't know why Thane and Dad keep him on as an enforcer. It seems more hurtful to have him damaging our men, rather than punishing them," Jamie says.

I know why Abram and my father keep Sangster on. "They think the threat of being maimed will make the brothers more aware of their actions and careful to avoid mistakes."

"Sangster crippled Potinger while carrying out his atonement last month." I'm sure Jamie knows firsthand the damage that enforcer can cause since he was the one to initially treat him. "I had to send him to a therapist but it isn't helping. I think it's permanent nerve damage."

"It's a damn shame. Potinger will be useless if he never walks right again." Leith quickly turns to look at me. "You know I didn't mean that the way it sounded."

"Of course not." I shrug it off. I don't want this conversation to turn into one about my injury so I steer it back toward Hewie. "I think he'll go easier this time since he knows the elders are watching."

"I hope so—for Hewie's sake," Jamie says.

"Geneen came in last night with McLain," Leith informs me. "You gonna do something about that?"

They know I don't give two shits about Geneen but they find it disrespectful for her to come into the bar with another brother. We had a few fucks over a couple of weeks. He's welcome to my leftovers. "She'll tire of this game once she realizes I don't care."

Leith waves his hand toward the back of the club where the barmaids pick up drinks. "Lorna's working late tonight. You should take her into the storage room if Geneen comes back. That would show her you're not concerned with her anymore."

I stopped tasting Lorna's nectar years ago. Since then, she's been passed around by almost every brother in this place, so I have no interest in ever having her again. I prefer a woman who hasn't had every dick in the room inside her.

I admit it. I'm a selfish bastard. Even if I'm not interested in a woman for the purpose of a relationship, I don't want any of the brothers to have had her before me. What she does afterward is not my concern. "I'm looking for something a little fresher."

"Leith has something fresh—an American lass." Jamie laughs. "She definitely hasn't been touched by any of the brothers."

Leith slams his hand on the table. "No one puts a finger on her. If anyone gets a piece of that fit arse, it's going to be me."

"Good Lord, Leith! An American?" This isn't good. Dad and Abram won't be pleased. "You can be such a dobber sometimes."

Leith knows he's to only hire local girls within our circle. Taking in a stranger we know nothing about is a foolish move since members of the brotherhood frequent this bar. "I can't believe you've brought in an outsider. The elders won't approve."

"Don't worry. The lass is in Edinburgh on a temporary basis. Her employment won't be long-standing." And her life may not be either, thanks to him.

"You have to get rid of her," I argue.

"She can be very persuasive."

"Persuasive, as in she had sex with you?"

"Not yet."

"Did she promise you sex?"

"No."

Damn fool. "Tell me you were steamin' when you hired her."

"She needed some quick cash. I can pay her under the table and she'll move on in a few weeks. No worries."

No worries, my arse. "There's a reason you only hire a lass with a connection to The Fellowship. This one could become a problem for the brotherhood. If that happens, she'll be sleeping with the fish. You've done her no favor by employing her. She's been placed in the middle of a dangerous situation and has no idea."

"You'll understand why he hired her when you see her sweet arse," Jamie says.

"I don't care how fit the American is." Leith should know better than to think with his dick.

"There she is," he says. I look over at the barmaid's station and see her from behind. Her chestnut brown hair is pulled into a messy pile on top of her head. She's wearing the typical Duncan uniform—a short plaid kilt and tight white blouse tied above her waist.

She spins around while holding a tray of whiskies over one shoulder and smiles at Leith. She doesn't give me so much as a glance when she walks by to deliver drinks to the table behind us. "Good-looking, eh?"

She's definitely bonny. I can't debate that. "No woman is fit enough to put yourself on Dad's and Abram's shit lists."

He looks at the American as she bends over to pick up a napkin that blew off her serving tray. "I don't know about that, buddy. Her bum is nice."

I watch her skirt ride almost up to the cheeks of her arse and then back down again when she stands. "She's easy on the eyes, mate. I won't argue that point but I can say with confidence that you've made a problem for yourself with the elders."

"If I get between those legs, it'll be worth the fallout with Thane and Abram."

"Whatever." Leith can't be trusted to make the wisest decisions when it comes to The Fellowship. It's a good thing he's in charge of this bar and not within the inner circle where the big decisions are made. I'm certain Dad and Abram wouldn't put up with his bullshit.

The American lass passes by our table on the way back to her pouring station. Leith reaches out to catch her around the waist. "Come here. I want you to meet my other best mate." He snakes his arm around her and grasps her hip, pulling her close. He's being a wanker. "Meet the infamous Sinclair Breckenridge."

"The infamous, huh?" She smiles and holds out her hand. "Hi. Bleu MacAllister."

Bleu MacAllister. I repeat her name in my head five times as I look at her face so she'll be etched in my memory. It's probably unnecessary. I highly doubt I could forget her unusual name or bonny face. "It's a pleasure, Miss MacAllister. May I ask what brings you to Edinburgh?"

"My Aunt Edy, who was really my grandmother's best friend, fell ill. Cancer. I was quite fond of her. She was like family so I came over to care for her during her last days."

"Then she's already passed?" I ask.

"Three weeks ago."

"And you're still here?" I point out.

"I'm the only one in the family who has the flexibility to stay and settle Edy's estate."

"Is that a more dignified way of saying you don't have a job?" I sound rude—exactly the way I intend.

"Stop cross-examining her," Leith warns. "You'll have to excuse him, Bleu. He's near finished his training to become a solicitor and he takes it a little too far sometimes."

I don't need Leith to apologize for my actions. "I'm not taking anything too far. I'm making conversation about why a grown woman would not have a life or profession to get back to."

"I never said I didn't have a life or profession." She places her hand on her hip.

"Then you have employment?"

"I'm a photographer—mostly babies and brides. I'm the owner of a private studio so I have more freedom in my job than my father or sister."

"Yet you're working in a bar as a wench?"

"I'm a visitor, and as a lawyer, I'd think you'd be aware that I don't have a work visa. Because I can't be legally employed, I'm very grateful Leith hired me as a wench since Edinburgh isn't a cheap place to live."

I do believe Miss MacAllister is a firecracker. "Did your aunt not leave you an inheritance?"

"Yes, hence my reason for staying to settle her affairs. It's time consuming, as I'm sure you understand, being that you're in the legal profession." She turns away from me to Leith. "Is your friend always this disagreeable?"

Leith slides his hand from her hip to her arse. "Unquestionably."

She moves his hand off her bum. "You don't pay me enough for that privilege."

"I can give you a raise." Leith laughs.

"I'm sure you can, boss," she calls out over her shoulder as she walks away.

"That lass is something, eh?"

She's beautiful and charming. I hope that doesn't backfire on my pal. "My gut tells me she's something all right, but what, I'm not certain."

"You're always so paranoid."

He's right. I suspect everyone but paranoia keeps me alive, so I'm perfectly fine with it.

The next hour is much the same. Leith looks the part of a prick as he flirts with the American each time she walks by. She seems receptive to his advances but I'm not so sure that's a good thing.

I wonder how long she'll be here. I hope not a minute longer than it takes to settle her business since Leith is too stupid to see this is a train wreck waiting to happen. Perhaps I should offer her legal assistance so I can hurry along the process. Private law concerning inheritance settlement isn't my specialty but I know enough to advise her.

"She's back." I don't have to turn around to know whom Jamie means. It's Geneen. "And she's brought McLain with her again."

I turn around and Geneen smirks, looking proud to have me see her with another man. It's laughable for her to think she could make me jealous.

"You're a tube if you don't go over there and beat him until he pisses himself."

I despise that bitch for coming here with him but Jamie's right. She's forcing my hand or I'll appear weak in front of the brotherhood. I can't have that. "I will, but not before Geneen gets a penance fuck for doing this." I'll get far more satisfaction from that than slamming my fist into McLain's face.

I get up from the table and go over to her. She's sitting on a barstool next to her new man. I grab her arm and squeeze. "To the back. Now." I look at McLain. "And not a fucking word out of you."

She grins because I'm guessing she thinks she knows what going to the back means. Too bad for her, she's mistaken.

I know her kind. They think they can win my heart with hot sex but she couldn't be more wrong. I'll use her up and toss her aside, just like the rubber I'll wear when I fuck her.

I lead her into the storage room and reach under her dress. I roughly yank her knickers down her legs and shove her back against the shelving unit. I'm sure it's uncomfortable but we aren't doing this for anyone's pleasure but my own.

The fleeting thought of pleasure causes me to change my mind about how we're going to do this. If I fuck Geneen, I'll be giving her exactly what she wants, so I decide she'll suck me off instead.

I step away from her. "I changed my mind. Get on your knees." She steps forward and tries to kiss me but I shove her away. Her mouth will never touch mine. "I said, get on your knees."

She lowers herself to the floor and unzips my trousers. She's reaching inside for my knob when the door swings open. Leith's new American barmaid barges into the room and stands with her hands on her hips. "Can you move over, please? You're blocking me from what

I need to get."

Is she serious? "No. I'm busy. Come back after we're finished."

"Kenrick sent me to fetch a bottle of Ballantine's and you're in my way."

This girl would never speak to me like this if she was from here and knew who I was. She'd show me respect. "Can't you see what's happening here?"

"Unfortunately, it's something I can never unsee." She points to my left. "I'm certain she can still give you a first-class blow job eighteen inches in that direction."

Neither of us makes a move and she huffs. "Look, all the leaves on my give-a-fuck tree have fallen. It's been a long day. I've been grabbed and fondled by strange men for the last six hours. Some old geezer slipped his hand up my skirt and I had to smile and kindly encourage him to remove it … instead of breaking his face with my fist. I'm tired. I just want to finish my job so I can go home and have one or a dozen glasses of wine and then pass out. I'm not asking for much."

This lass's behavior is absurd—and highly entertaining. I shove my cock back in my pants and step out of her way. "You heard Miss MacAllister. We're in her way."

Geneen laughs but not because she's amused by this American called Bleu. "Oh, hell no. I'm not moving," she says, arms crossed and still kneeling.

"Then you should probably expect this to be hugely unpleasant," Bleu says.

"Really?"

I'm caught completely off guard when Bleu punches Geneen directly in the center of her face, knocking her to the floor, and then kicks her in the gut. She doesn't give her another glance as she reaches over her crumpled body. I watch her grab a bottle of whisky and inspect it. "I believe this will do nicely." She sashays toward the door, calling back over her shoulder, "Carry on."

I burst into laughter as I help Geneen from the floor. "The girl must be certifiably crazy, but my God, that was the most entertaining thing I've seen since … ever."

"Are you kidding me?" Geneen touches her face. "I think that bitch broke my nose."

I look at her and confirm her suspicion. Her nose is definitely no longer in the center of her face. "I fear you're right. Looks broken to me."

"I'm kicking her arse," Geneen growls as she starts for the door.

I grab her arm but not because I fear for Bleu's safety. I'm certain she can do a right nice job of protecting herself. "There will be none of that, I'm afraid."

Bleu has greatly lifted my mood so I'm feeling far too generous to give a penance fuck or start a fight. "Get out of here. Take McLain with you and never come back."

CHAPTER THREE

BLEU MACALLISTER

I'M SERVING ALE TO FOUR OF THE FELLOWSHIP MEMBERS WHEN I SEE SINCLAIR return from the storage room. My back is to him but I watch his reflection in the mirror behind the bar as he returns to the table to sit with Leith and Jamie. I eye him carefully, not allowing him to see I'm observing him, but I read his lips: "I handled Geneen. She won't be coming back here again."

Jamie and Leith respond but I can't see their mouths.

I return to my station and watch Sinclair's mouth from afar. "That American you hired is passionate about her job." He recounts the events in the storage room and their laughter reverberates through the bar. Good. I'm glad they find me amusing.

They drink until all the patrons are gone and only employees remain. Lorna is instructing me in the last of the closing duties when Leith comes over to send us home for the night. "About finished, lasses?"

"Close enough," Lorna says. "I'll show you the rest tomorrow."

We go to the tiny hole in the wall called a break room and fetch our things.

"Can I get a ride home, Leith?" Lorna asks. "My car is in the shop." I get the distinct impression that a lift home isn't the only thing she's talking about.

"I was going to take Bleu home since it's her first night."

There's no way I'm getting into a car with Leith Duncan. He's put his hands on my ass no fewer than a half-dozen times. If he does it again, I'm going to kick the shit out of him and I doubt it would be well received for me to whip my boss's ass on the first day. Plus it would jeopardize the connection I'm trying to make with Sinclair. "Thank you for the offer but I'm fine. It's a short walk, not more than ten minutes at most."

"I want to take you home," he insists. Right—and then come up for a nightcap fuck? No, thank you.

"Another time, boss." I put my bag on my shoulder and walk toward the exit, my signal to let him know this discussion is over. "See you tomorrow."

I go out the door and walk in the direction of my faux late-aunt's house. It's really the furnished flat of a woman who recently died but it's what I'll call home for the next two to three months.

The flat was a nice score. Every once in a while, the moon and stars align perfectly. And this was that one time for me. The flat's owner was a terminally ill elderly lady with no living relatives. She once lived in Tennessee, two cities over from my grandparents. If her life is investigated by The Fellowship, everything they'll find will lead them to believe I'm telling the truth.

I'm no more than two minutes into my walk when a black luxury sedan creeps alongside me. The windows are tinted darker than night so I can't see inside. I suspect it's Leith making one last attempt to drive me home.

The back passenger window lowers and luck is with me. It's Sinclair. "Get in."

This guy is used to getting everything he wants so I think it's time I make things interesting. "Thanks for the exceptionally courteous invite, but no thanks. I'll walk."

Do I think Sinclair Breckenridge gives a shit if I make it home safely? No. Do I think he wants to know where I live so he can ransack my place while I'm not there? Absolutely. And he can knock himself out trying to discover a hole in my story but he won't find one.

I spin to walk away but hear him call out behind me. "Get in.

Please." He sounds as though it pains him to say that word. Good. He should learn a little humility. It would serve him well.

I hesitate for a moment, as though I'm thinking it over before I get into the car with him. "I couldn't decline your invitation since you said please."

"I'll need to remember that in the future."

This will be a short drive. We won't have much time for talk. "I don't live far, just six blocks ahead on the right."

"I'd like to apologize."

"For which incident? Questioning me as though I was a belligerent witness or refusing to move after I asked you nicely to get out of my way?"

He laughs. "Both, although I'm not exactly sure your request was polite. I seem to recall you sounding a wee bit on the bossy side."

"Then I apologize for being rude while interrupting your blow job." I read his lips when he told Leith and Jamie he was going to give her a penance fuck. It's unfortunate for his sex life that being with another woman doesn't fit into my plan to make him fall for me. I'll be cock-blocking him at every opportunity.

"You broke Geneen's nose." Good. It'll keep her from getting in the way.

I shrug. "I probably shouldn't have done that but I rather enjoyed it after she got smart with me."

"Would you have broken my nose as well if I hadn't done as you asked?"

I shrug and laugh. "Maybe."

"Ahh … another thing to remember for the future. Who taught you to throw a punch like that?"

I hold up my hand and flex it as though it might be in pain. But it isn't. I know the proper way to hit someone without injuring myself. "My dad. He wanted me to be able to protect myself." Total truth. It's likely the only time he'll get that out of me.

"Mission accomplished. He did a quality job."

"That's not all. Per his instruction, I also do an exceptional job of grabbing a man by the balls and forcing him to his knees."

He's amused again. "Then I should worry about the wallopers at Duncan's instead of you?"

"Indeed." I point to my building. "This is my flat on the right."

His driver pulls to the side and turns off the car's engine. I think that's a sign he expects his employer to come in. "Thanks for the ride."

"Anytime."

He trails behind and attempts to follow me inside so I put my hand to his chest and stop him. "Good night, Mr. Breckenridge." Women fall at this man's feet. They literally go to their knees for him whenever he says so my plan to win him over has to be different. I must capture his heart in a new and unfamiliar way. I have to be a challenge, a conquest he's desperate to conquer.

"Mr. Breckenridge is my father. Please, call me Sin."

"Then good night, Sin."

He takes my hand and kisses the top. "Good night, Bonny Bleu."

Damn, he's a handsome and charming villain.

I spy on him through the peephole as he returns to his car. He stops before getting inside and I'm certain he's taking note of my address. I have no doubt that 114 Lansbury Way will fall under scrutiny by tomorrow's nightfall. Good thing I'm prepared for his probing. Still, I'm calling Harry. One last run-through of the plan never hurts.

I work an eight-hour shift at Duncan's with no sign of Sinclair. I already know he doesn't come in every night, but I'd hoped yesterday's events would've sparked his interest enough to bring him around. Guess not. That means I must do better.

I'm walking to my flat after declining a second insistent offer from Leith to drive me home. He's becoming more aggressive and I can see it developing into a problem if Sinclair doesn't declare me his soon. That's an impossibility when I don't have contact with him.

This is a race, not a sprint. I can't expect Sinclair to fall at my feet on day one. That's why I must bet on the long play.

I get to my flat and gloat when I see a black Mercedes parked on the street. I've memorized his plates so I confirm it's Sinclair but I don't allow myself to appear as though I've noticed. I go about my business as I would if the car weren't parked there.

Once inside, I peek through the curtains down at the street. Why didn't he get out when I walked by? Did he not see me?

"Aye, that's my car."

Shit. He's already inside.

"Shit!" I spin around and appear startled because that's what normal people do when they find an uninvited guest in their home. "You scared the hell out of me." I place my hand to my chest. "What are you doing in here?"

"You didn't ask me in after I drove you home so I thought I'd extend an invitation to myself tonight."

He wants to have me believe he can get to me any time he likes, with or without my permission. It's a scare tactic and I have to make him believe he's succeeded. "You can't come into my house like this. What if I had a gun and shot you … or something?"

"I can leave if you like, since I certainly don't want to be shot … or something." He's laughing at me.

I need him to stay. Spending time together is the only way we'll connect. "You can stay if you agree to not give me another fright."

"I make no promises." His voice is husky. I think he means to make me uneasy. He's succeeding.

"I'm going to have a drink." I go to the cabinet I've stocked with liquor, including his favorite—Johnnie Walker. "Would you care for one?"

"Sure. I'll take something dark and neat. Pour it tall. It's been a dreadful day."

I hand him his drink and sit on the opposite end of the sofa. "Want to tell me about it?"

"It's a case I'm working so I can't discuss it."

"Client confidentiality?"

"Something like that."

He takes a long drink, like it's water. "Mmm … that's good stuff."

"Nothing beats JW."

He places his drink on the end table and twists slightly to face me. "How was day two on the new job? I trust you didn't break anyone's nose today?"

I damn sure wanted to. "No, but I'm thinking of breaking a few grabby hands."

"That isn't wise, Bleu."

"Then what am I supposed to do? Let those men put their hands up my skirt? That's what some of them do. And they act like they have the right and I'm supposed to allow it."

"It's what they're used to doing because the other lasses let them." He's laughing at me again and it pisses me off. It's not okay for any woman to have to put up with that on the job.

"I'm not like the other girls. I don't allow random men to put their hands on me. I would've told Leith that had I known it was going to be an issue." I put my hand to my forehead, as though stressed. "I really need the money from that job but not at the expense of degrading myself."

He takes another gulp of whisky. "I'll take care of it tomorrow. It'll be made clear that they aren't to touch you again."

That's unexpected. "I don't want to put you in a predicament."

"You're not. No more worrying. They'll only bother you for another drink from now on."

"Thank you." He turns up the last of his whisky and I've only taken a few sips of mine. We need more time together.

I get up to collect his glass. "You need a refill."

"No, thank you. I must be going. I have court early in the morning."

I walk him to the door the way any good hostess would. "Will I see you tomorrow?" I smile sheepishly, flirtatious, just the way I intend. He needs to see a side of me other than the tough girl who can throw a punch.

"Maybe." If you're lucky. Those are the words I imagine when I see the grin that spreads across his face.

I stand in the doorway and watch him go to his car. "Good luck on your case," I call out.

He gives me a smile and a nod. And then he's gone.

The first thing I do once I'm alone is study my flat. I'm certain he scoured the place while he was here but for some reason, I want confirmation. I need it.

It only takes a couple minutes for me to notice the only deviation. A picture frame holding a photograph of me is missing from the bookcase. That's not what I was expecting.

How peculiar. He doesn't need that photograph to run a facial recognition analysis. Any of his grunts could've taken my picture if he'd ordered them to. The FBI consistently wipes any trace of the true Bleu MacAllister from the Web so the only one he'll find is the identity Harry and I created.

Nothing else is out of place, although he snooped through my things. That's fine—I was prepared for such. All the appropriate measures have been set into motion. There isn't a single thing out of place in this carefully orchestrated life I'm living, so I'm certain Sinclair and I will be removing any trust issues between us sooner rather than later.

It isn't call day but I want to talk to Harry. This is so much harder than I imagined. I need to hear a comforting voice.

I'm not certain the flat hasn't been bugged since last night so I take a walk and use my burner to phone my dad. I assure him all is well before I tell him about tonight's events. "Sinclair was in my apartment when I came home tonight."

"Does that surprise you?" His voice is steady, without alarm—exactly what I need to hear.

"Not a bit."

"Good. I'd be worried if it did. I hope you put on a good front."

"A bang-up job, as always."

"Perfect. This is good; it means he's investigating you. We knew he would. It's always best to get it out of the way early so you can move into the trust phase. I assume everything was in place?"

"Of course."

"Good job, girlie." I still love hearing Harry's praise.

"How did he explain being in your apartment?"

Uh-oh. Here we go. "He said he was inviting himself inside since I didn't the previous night."

"What the hell was he doing at your place the night before?"

"Relax. He drove me home after work, but I turned him away at the door."

"He's going to try to get you into bed." Harry's voice isn't so calm now. "You know that, right?"

"I completely expect him to try." No way I'm telling him about Sinclair taking the photograph. He'll freak.

"I know how badly you want this but don't compromise yourself in the process. It isn't worth it. I've seen it happen in the field a hundred times. Believe me when I say you'll hate yourself afterward." He trained me to be a killer, yet he still sees me as an innocent little girl.

"No worries, Dad. I'm not going to give myself to a Breckenridge. They've taken enough of me already." I hate lying to Harry but I can never tell him the truth. He'd be furious if he knew what I was planning.

"Sometimes being strong is about following your heart. There's no shame in not going through with this. If at any point you want to stop and come home, don't hesitate. We'll never speak of it again."

That's my plan—to never speak of it again, but only after the job is done.

CHAPTER FOUR

SINCLAIR BRECKENRIDGE

I RECLINE IN MY DESK CHAIR AND STUDY THE PHOTOGRAPH I TOOK FROM BLEU'S flat. It seems fairly current since her appearance is relatively the same, with the exception of her hair length. It's a few inches shorter in the picture. I'm guessing this was likely taken several months ago.

She's standing by a business front and the writing on the glass reads Bleu Mac's Photography. I do an Internet search for her business and its demographics, quickly finding her website and all the social media she uses. By all appearances, she seems to have a thriving business, so it seems unlikely that she'd go along with being plucked from her livelihood to come here and pose as an impostor for any of our rivals.

Unlikely, but not impossible—if they're paying her enough.

If she was selected by our adversary to invade the brotherhood, they chose poorly. They should've gone with a woman willing to go to bed with the brothers. This one doesn't budge an inch. She has respect for herself and body and expects those around her to as well.

Bleu's story holds water with me for now. I'll allow her to continue working at the whisky bar unless she gives me reason to suspect she's anything other than what she claims to be. I'll personally monitor her and won't hesitate to immediately extract the lass if I suspect a problem.

I place a call to Seamus so I can make good on the promise I made to Bleu. "Aye, boss?"

"There's a new lass working at Leith's. An American."

"I know the one you're talking about." I'm not surprised he's already aware of her presence. I would expect my men to talk about a fit lass like Miss MacAllister.

"No one's to touch her. Anyone who does risks losing his hand." My men know I don't put out warnings unless I mean them.

"Got it, boss. Will that be all?"

The further the girls allow the men to go, the better their gratuity is at the end of the evening. I know how these things go. It's not as though I haven't seen the girls getting fucked against the building in the back alley to ensure a good tip at the end of the night. "Make sure the brothers understand that she's hands off but that doesn't decrease her tips. Encourage them to be … generous."

"Aye, sir."

I end the call and examine the photograph of Bleu. I'm not sure why I took it. It has no place in this office, yet I don't want to put it in the drawer. I want to be able to see it.

I place it on the corner of my desk. It looks strange and feels out of place. I've never had a photo of a woman within the four walls of my office—not even one of my own mother—but I admit it's a beautiful first. I could get used to looking at her.

I don't have to weigh my options of home versus Duncan's when I leave the firm. I want to see how work is going for the bar's new wench since my orders to the brothers to keep their hands off.

I sit at the table everyone knows belongs to the trifecta—me, Leith, and Jamie. Lorna notices me and immediately comes over, ready to take my drink order. "What's it going to be this evening?"

"I want the American to be my barmaid."

She looks at the station where Bleu loads a tray with drinks. "She already has a full load."

"It's not a fucking request, Lorna. But since you were stupid enough to argue instead of doing as I say, you can take all her tables and yours while she only serves me."

I look at Lorna, daring her to do anything but agree. "As you wish."

"Damn right. And she still gets her tips. All of them."

"Of course, Sin. Anything you say."

Bleu comes to my table after she's relieved of the tray of drinks. "Lorna says I'm your personal server and she's going to take all my tables."

"That's right."

"Why?" Her expression is confused. She has no idea I can make anyone in this place do whatever I demand, whenever I like.

"Because it's what I want."

She looks around, worried. "Is Leith going to be okay with this? I'm here to serve customers—plural, not singular. I don't want to make him angry and end up fired. I'm earning good money here."

"The tips have been generous?"

"Yes, remarkably so."

Good. The brotherhood listened. I'd expect no less. "I'm glad to hear that."

"What can I get for you?"

"Whatever you're having."

I can see I've bewildered her further. And I thoroughly enjoy it. "I can't have anything. I'm on the clock."

"I want to buy you a drink, so choose what you'd like and I'll have the same."

She smirks. "Whatever you say."

A few minutes later she returns with two girlie drinks and pushes one my way. "What the hell is that supposed to be?"

She's grinning. "It's sex on the beach."

"You brought me a drink with a slice of pineapple and a fucking flower in it?"

"You told me to choose something for myself and you'd have the same. This is what I wanted."

"I expected you to have a whisky."

"I wanted to have sex on the beach. I thought you'd enjoy it as well." She's grinning bigger, probably feeling quite clever.

I sample the drink and discover it's exactly as I expect— sickeningly sweet. It's definitely a cocktail for a lass, so I push it back in her direction. "You don't like sex on the beach?"

"I like the actual thing very much, but not this drink."

"Would something tall, dark, and neat be more preferable?"

"Aye."

"You're going to put your trust in me again?" she asks.

"Allow me to be clear about one thing, Bleu." I motion for her to lean forward and I do the same until we're nearly nose to nose. "I trust no one until they've proven themselves to be trustworthy."

"I get the distinct feeling we're no longer talking about choosing a brand of whisky." If I didn't know better, I'd think that was a challenge.

She's a smart one, this lass, so I don't wish to get into a battle of wits. "I'm the only customer you're serving. I shouldn't be thirsty."

Bleu goes to fetch my drink and Leith slips into one of the chairs next to me. "Lorna told me what you ordered her to do. Why the hell are you claiming Bleu as your own personal barmaid while Lorna takes a double load?"

"Someone has to validate this lass's motives since you were too careless to do so."

"You're going to tell me that monopolizing her as your own is a way of investigating her purpose for being here?"

"Having her one-on-one so we can talk does a far better job than your hands running up and down her arse every time she walks by."

"Don't worry, Sin. No one's putting their hands on her now."

He acts as though he's a toddler and I've taken away his favorite toy. "She didn't like the way she was being manhandled."

"And you know this how?"

"She told me."

"When?" he asks.

"Last night."

Leith looks pissed off, which means he's putting the pieces together. "Then I guess it's safe to assume you didn't have this conversation at the bar?"

"No." As his superior, I don't owe him any explanation. "I needed to do a sweep, to be sure Bleu is who she claims to be. I was going through her things when she came home and found me inside, so I had to act as though I was there to talk."

"How very convenient." He's right. I could've sent my people to do the search but I wanted her to come home and find me there.

"What's your verdict?" he asks.

She's clean as far as I can tell. For now. "I believe she's telling the truth."

He slaps his hand on the table. "I fucking knew it."

"You didn't know shit, Leith. Like always, I'm the one out doing the dirty work."

"Sure. Keep telling yourself that being alone with Bleu at her flat is dirty work and maybe you'll eventually believe it." He's calling bullshit, and we both know he's right. I wanted to spend time with her.

Bleu returns with a glass of something much more preferable and Leith leaves without another word. "Something wrong with him?"

"He has business to tend to."

She places the drink in front of me. "Johnnie Walker. Black Label."

"Seems you are capable of making good choices."

"See? I can be trusted." That still remains to be seen but we're off to a good start.

"Are you having a better day?"

"Absolutely." She's beaming. "Almost all the ass grabbing has stopped."

Almost? "There's still men in this bar putting their hands on you?"

"Yeah. There's one guy who won't leave me alone."

I put out an order to not touch Bleu and one of the brothers isn't heeding my word. That's outright defiance, something I don't tolerate. "Lorna looks overwhelmed. Maybe you should take your customers back."

"Sure."

I stop her before she gets up from the table. "Do you remember when you told me you wanted to break grabby hands and I told you it wasn't a good idea?"

"Yeah." She laughs.

"I've changed my mind. Do as you please if he touches you again. Bring him to his knees if you like."

Bleu returns to work and I stay put to see which brother will reveal himself as her harasser. I don't have to wait long before a young member, Duff, reaches out to run his hand up the back of her thigh. He's forearm-deep up her skirt so there's no way he's not touching her knickers. Plus some.

She's bent over serving drinks at the neighboring table when his hand assaults her from behind. Mother. Fucker.

She whirls around and places her hand on top of his, the one reaching up her skirt. Without a moment's hesitation, she hyperflexes his wrist, pushing his hand down toward his inner forearm. He immediately comes out of his chair onto his knees.

"Aww … fuck! Let go, bitch!" he yells.

Bleu is enraged when her eyes meet mine but she manages to maintain self-control. I can't say I'd be able to do the same. Kudos to her for that, but I know what she wants to do to the little bastard. She's questioning me with her expression, looking for my approval. But I can't give it to her. My brothers will see that as choosing her over them. I'm already flirting with disaster by allowing her this sanction.

I get up from my chair and go to her in case Duff has it on his mind to attack when she releases him. "That's enough."

Bleu does as I tell her and steps away before I place my hand on her shoulder. "No one touches her again. No. One." I announce it loud enough so everyone can hear and there's no confusion.

I look at Leith across the bar and the fury flashing across his face can't be mistaken. But he won't question or defy me. I'm his superior.

"Penance was carried out by the wronged individual," I announce. "Continue as you were."

Drinking, talking, and laughing resumes. The escapade with Duff no longer captures the attention of the crowd so I lean over and whisper in Bleu's ear. "I want you to come with me."

I lead her to Leith's office since I figure it would be in poor taste to take her to the room where she found me with Geneen on her knees only a couple of days earlier.

I shut the door and say nothing as I look at her. I'm trying to figure her out. "Did I do something wrong … or misunderstand your directions?"

"No, you were perfect." I move closer and capture her face with my palms. "Tell me how it made you feel when you brought a man to his knees in pain after he wronged you."

I feel her trembling beneath my hands. "Powerful."

"Do you feel guilty about it?"

She shakes her head. "Should I?"

"No. Not at all."

"How did you feel watching me do it?" she asks.

"I liked it. A whole-fucking-lot." I step closer and graze my mouth along her jaw until my lips are next to her ear. "A total turn-on." I lower my hands from her face and skim them down the sides of her body until I reach her perfect arse. I cup both cheeks with my hands and crash her body against mine as I suck her earlobe into my mouth.

"What happened to no one touching me?"

Does that mean she doesn't want me to touch her?

I release her and straighten to look at her face. "Do you want that to apply to me as well?"

"I want things to be very clear so there's no misunderstanding between us. I won't give my body to someone who'd fuck me in a storage room or on a desk in the office of a bar. I want to enjoy the pleasure that goes along with great sex, so I will only sleep with a man who is eager to please me. I must be able to trust that you aren't in it only for yourself. I'll demand more of you than any other woman ever has, and for that, I'm completely unapologetic."

"Allow me to be clear with you. I only do what pleases me and that, Bonny Bleu, is what you can trust."

I'm still holding her so close, we're nose to nose. "Then I believe we've come to an impasse that will bring neither of us any pleasure."

There's a loud knock at the door but our eyes remain locked. "Go the fuck away."

"Sin," Leith calls out from the other side of the door. "Your father is here to see you."

The timing couldn't be worse.

"Fuck!" I yell loudly. I release her and move away to adjust my cock. "We'll finish this later."

She whirls and starts for the door. "Not likely."

I beg to differ. I don't believe for a second that either of us will be satisfied with an impasse.

CHAPTER FIVE

BLEU MACALLISTER

I ONLY GET A GLIMPSE OF MY MOTHER'S KILLER BEFORE HE AND SINCLAIR LEAVE the bar. I have no recollection of seeing his face when he attacked me. I must have squeezed my eyes shut out of fear but I've seen countless surveillance photos of him. His face will be forever etched in my brain, yet I find he differs from the way I've visualized him. He appears ... human, not at all the monster I've come to imagine.

It's closing time and neither Thane nor Sin have returned. I'd hoped the pair would come back so he might introduce me to his father. I'm anxious to embark this ship of deception that will bring me into the Breckenridges' inner circle.

I'm walking home when Sinclair's black sedan eases alongside again. "Get in."

He doesn't get to give me orders like I'm one of his Fellowship members. "No."

"I said get in."

"And I said no." It's my job to teach him how to treat me early on.

"Please, Bleu. I'd really like to take you home." He's almost making this too easy.

I look at him for a moment, as if I'm considering his proposition, but I already know I'll get in. "Okay, but only because you asked nicely."

I wait for him to lead the conversation but he says nothing—so I don't, either—during the two-minute drive to my flat. We're angry at one another. Well, he's mad and I'm pretending to be.

I'm the first to speak when Sterling parks in the usual spot. "Thanks for the lift." Sinclair doesn't reply as he opens his door to get out. "What do you think you're doing?"

I sit in the car with folded arms like a juvenile. He opens my door and puts his hand inside to help me exit. "I'm coming in with you."

I take his hand and allow him to help me out. "What makes you think that?"

"We were interrupted earlier, and I'd like to finish where we left off." Yeah, I'm sure he would.

I stop him at the door, placing my hand on his chest to let him know it's a no-go. "We want two different things, and I won't settle for less than everything I deserve."

"What if I told you I thought about it and changed my mind? What if I want to try it your way?" He's coming around but not quite there. He needs more time to simmer so he can see things my way. Completely.

"Mmm … no." I say it like a spoiled brat.

"What do you mean, no?" He sounds like a brat too. I think he's truly shocked he isn't getting his way.

"You don't get to … try me out. That's not how this works."

"Then how would you like this to go?"

"You told me earlier that you only do what pleases you, so you'll need to convince me that you want to make it good for me."

"You want this to be all about your pleasure." He laughs.

"Mmm … not completely. Just mostly."

"My God, woman. You've enchanted me. Now I'm desperate to find out what being with you is like."

Fucking perfect. "You'll have to work for it. And after you do, I might not agree if I feel you didn't work hard enough to suit me." Wow. I sound like a total bitch. I may have taken it too far.

"All right. I agree to your terms." I cannot believe he just agreed to those stipulations.

What have I gotten myself into? I knew there was a possibility I might have to get into bed with the enemy, but I had no idea I'd be this electrified about doing so.

It makes me feel dirty. But I like it. And I shouldn't.

Two days have passed since Sin's been into the bar. Nor has he come by to give me a ride home. I'm afraid playing hard to get isn't the way to go since it seems to be backfiring.

He's accustomed to a quick fuck with a willing Fellowship groupie. He never takes anyone to his home or a hotel. I had hoped something fresh and different would catch and hold his attention. I thought a girl from the outside, untainted by the members of The Fellowship, would be the key. I guess I was wrong. Maybe I need to consider another approach.

It's closing time and I go to the back to get my things. Upon opening my locker, I find a single red rose accompanying a folded note on top of my bag. I sniff the rose and read the message.

I'm taking you out tomorrow night. Seems I have something I must work for. Be ready at 7:00.

— S

Oh, wow. He's been at the bar and I didn't even know. Maybe my plan isn't dead in the water after all.

One problem. I'm supposed to work tomorrow night. Has he taken care of this with Leith?

I stop by the office on my way out. The door is open, Leith sitting at his desk working on the computer. "Hey, boss. You got a minute?"

"Sure."

I feel sort of weird asking about a change in my schedule when we haven't discussed it. "Am I still working tomorrow night?"

"No. Sin moved Greer to work in your place."

"Hmm." I'm not at all surprised by this, but I make an expression as though I am. "Then I guess you know he's taking me out."

"I suspected as much since he's making changes to your shift."

"I don't want it to be a problem."

"It's not." He returns to punching numbers into the computer. "I'm used to Sin getting whatever he wants and saying to hell with everyone else."

Yup. He's bitter. Probably best I don't say anything else. "Umm … I guess I'll see you Sunday, then."

"Bleu, Sin is one of my best mates but he can be a son of a bitch. You're a nice lass and I'd hate to see him hurt you."

That's not a possibility but I can't tell him that. "Thanks, Leith. I'll be careful."

I'm not surprised when the black Mercedes creeps alongside me. "Good evening, Miss MacAllister. It would be an honor to take you home, but the real question is would it please you for me to do so?"

This is going to be a fun game. "Your company would please me very much."

We arrive at my place in a matter of minutes. "May I come in?"

I ponder what an invitation to come inside will mean to him after our last conversation. "Bleu, if I'm to earn the privilege of taking you to bed, I must be given the opportunity to perform your prerequisites for proving myself."

He's got me there. I can't back out or I'll lose my footing. "Yes. I'd love for you to come in."

Once inside, I kick off my shoes by the door. "God, that feels so much better." I pull the tie out of my hair and shake it until it flows freely, my scalp sore from wearing my hair up all day. "I'm gonna change into something more comfortable. Help yourself to a drink. You know where the whisky is."

I opt for tight black yoga pants and a fitted white T-shirt. It's one of those outfits that isn't intentionally sexy, yet it is.

I return to the living room and find that Sin has poured JW for two. Tall and neat, waiting for me on the end table.

I sit in the spot he's chosen for me since I figure there's motive, but he completely surprises me when he moves to the floor at my feet. "Hard day, Bonny Bleu?"

It seems I have a nickname. It's sweet. Score: one, Sinclair.

"It was rough but it's much improved since you did whatever you did to make the grabby hands leave me alone."

"No one's bothering you?" He reaches for my right foot and rubs.

Shit, that feels good. I think I may orgasm.

I shake my head. "Not anymore."

"I could do a better job if I had lotion or oil. Do you have any?"

"Umm … yeah. I think it's on the bathroom counter."

He disappears down the hall, then reappears with my favorite body lotion and sits at my feet again. He squeezes a generous amount into his hand and begins his sweet seduction of gliding his palms over my feet. "You were telling me about your day."

I can barely concentrate enough to put a coherent sentence together. "It was okay."

"Just okay?" He sounds a little disappointed.

"It got better once I found a beautiful red rose and invitation for a date tomorrow night. Thank you, by the way. It was a lovely surprise."

"Is that an affirmative?"

Really? He's asking after he rearranged my work schedule? "I don't recall there being a question anywhere on the note. Only instructions to be ready at seven."

"Please, bear with me, Bleu." He stops massaging, so I open my eyes. "This is new to me."

He looks so sweet sitting on the floor … serving me. "I can see that and I also know you're trying. Please know it doesn't go unnoticed. I appreciate your effort."

"Let me try this again because I want to get it right." He clears his throat. "Will you please join me for dinner tomorrow night and perhaps dancing afterward?"

How in the world can I say no to that? "Yes. I'd be happy to."

He applies more lotion to his hands and works his way up my calves.

"You haven't been to the bar in a couple of days."

"I've been working on a really important case."

"Oh." I'm glad to know his reason for not coming wasn't his choice.

"Did you think I wasn't showing up because I wasn't interested in seeing you?"

"Maybe."

"Were you disappointed?"

I think I should throw him a bone. "Maybe."

"Damn, you don't give much away."

He's right. I have to make myself more vulnerable. "Most men don't appreciate hearing the word no when it comes to sex, so I thought you were skipping out on me." I shrug. "I must confess it was a huge letdown to not see you for two days. I wondered if my demands might have been too much for you to handle or maybe I was a turnoff."

"It's the opposite for me. I've never been more turned on."

"I'm calling bullshit." As much as I hate to admit it, that damn Geneen was stunning—until I broke her nose. "I've seen the women at the bar. Some are gorgeous and have bodies to die for. There's no way I'm the biggest turn-on you've ever had."

"Bleu. Those women are beautiful until you know them and understand their motives for being at Duncan's. Every last one of them wants to be claimed, and they're willing to do whatever it takes to make that happen."

Claimed. I remember reading about this in one of the files. The Fellowship has this bizarre practice of laying claim on women they aren't married to. "I don't understand what you mean by claimed."

"You don't understand because you aren't like them. And I like that very much."

"I want you to tell me what it means. Is it a Scottish thing?"

"Another time, Bonny Bleu."

CHAPTER SIX

SINCLAIR BRECKENRIDGE

BLEU AND I WILL BE DINING IN THE FINEST RESTAURANT IN EDINBURGH. IT'S A place I visit often, but never with a companion. I know the owner and manager well so I've called ahead and confirmed our seating at the table I desire–the one for two hidden in the back corner where lighting is low and foot traffic minimal. I've chosen this with an ulterior in mind. I want to talk to her with as few interruptions as possible. I want to find out who Bleu MacAllister is. I know the basics but those things aren't enough to satisfy my curiosity. I want to learn what makes her tick. What—or who—has made her so sexually demanding? Most importantly, I want to confirm that what I'm working toward will be worth my effort.

I wait until our dinner is ordered and drinks are served before I begin digging. "What made you want to be a photographer?"

"It's sort of strange so you can't laugh."

"I won't."

She grins. "I love to capture feelings."

It sounds like an art-minded response.

"People don't realize the things they say without uttering a word. Something as simple as the lift in the corner of one's mouth can reveal thoughts and emotions better than any voice. Body language—it's nature's crafty trick, second only to falling in love."

"Aye. It's a shan."

"A shan?"

"Americans would probably use the word shame."

"Oh. You sound like you know from experience."

I have no experience. I'm far too intelligent for such nonsense. "When one falls in love, that person makes the decision to become vulnerable. It's not a path I'd ever willingly choose so, no. What about you? Has Bonny Bleu ever been in love?"

"I've tried dating but it never matters what I do. I'm always what's wrong." She's nervously twisting the ring on her thumb. "I'm able to capture other's emotions in photos yet I can't get a grip on my own. I avoid connecting with people. I make myself an island so it gives me an excuse to remain alone." She sighs and looks embarrassed. "Wow. That sounded like a psychological profile ... or something."

She's sharing intimate details. I didn't expect that. "What about brothers and sisters?"

"One sister. Ellison. She's an ER nurse. What about you? Any siblings?"

"One younger brother, Mitch. He's still in college. And then there's the two numpties, Leith and Jamie. We're as close as brothers."

"The whole thing at the bar is sort of confusing. Everyone knows one another. It feels more like a private club than a public bar." That's a pretty accurate description. "It sometimes feels like there's a secret everyone's privy to except me."

This girl has it all—brains and beauty. I hope she isn't too smart for her own good. "How long do you think you'll stay?"

"Not sure. I'm trying to get everything finished up as soon as possible. The business at home waits."

Basing my judgment on the flat where Bleu is staying, her aunt wasn't a wealthy woman, so she can probably be done within the next couple of weeks. "I believe that should be doable."

"Tell me about your parents."

This is where my story can go sideways quickly. "My mum and father are still married. I guess you could call Dad an entrepreneur. He owns a few businesses. Mum doesn't work. What about yours?"

"My mom passed away two years ago. My dad won't even consider dating. He says he loved her too much to be with another woman."

I can't imagine having parents who tolerate each other, let alone love one another. It's completely foreign to me. And I'm destined to be just like them.

With a fair amount of certainty, I don't believe I'll ever be able to love.

I send Sterling into the club for a look around before we enter. I need to make sure it's clear. The last thing I need is an altercation with a rival in front of Bleu. "All clear, boss."

"Perfect. Thank you, Sterling. That will be all."

"What was that about?" she asks.

"Nothing for you to worry about."

It's Saturday night, so the dance floor is bouncing. We opt for seats at the bar. "What do you want? Sex on the beach?"

"No." She laughs. "I did that because I thought it would be funny to see you with a girlie drink. Your reaction was priceless."

"Would you take a Johnnie Walker Black Label instead?"

"You thoroughly enjoy JW, don't you?"

"Aye. It's good stuff."

"Suits me fine."

We get our drinks and go down the stairs into the cave where the best dance floor is. "This is an unusual place."

"Not bad, right?"

"It's great. We don't have anything like this at home."

We move toward the dance floor. "Do you like to dance?"

"When I have a good partner."

There's a new Sia song playing. "Want to kill these so we can get out there?"

"Sure. On three."

We click our glasses and count, "One. Two. Three."

We down the dark liquid. "This stuff is never disappointing. If anything in this world suffers from the tragedy of perfection, it's some motherfucking Johnnie Walker," I say.

"Agreed."

Glasses abandoned, we move to the floor. The song isn't really a slow one, but Bleu moves close and puts one arm over my shoulder while clasping my hand. "I really love this song."

I listen to the lyrics for a moment. "Fire, meet gasoline?"

Bleu sings a few verses and shrugs. "Sorry. I know I can't sing worth a damn but it doesn't stop me."

Several couples hit the dance floor all at once, forcing her to move closer. "It's getting crowded."

This is nothing for this place. "It's a popular club but it's still early. It'll be mobbed in another hour."

"Won't be able to stir 'em with a stick."

"What?"

She laughs. "It's an expression we say in the South. Means a place is really crowded."

She's hasn't told me where she's from but I already know from when I did the online search for her photography studio.

A new song picks up where Sia left off, and we'll have to scream at one another if we want to continue any kind of conversation. "Another drink?"

"Sure. It's hot in here."

I lead her from the dance floor toward the downstairs bar. "Want the same?"

She shrugs. "Suits me."

Getting our drinks takes longer than I'd like. "A table just opened up in that little alcove. I'm gonna grab it while you're waiting for our drinks."

I order doubles since I'm in no hurry to stand in line for drinks again. Three is probably plenty for Bleu anyway. I'm guessing she's a lightweight based on her size. I probably outweigh her by seventy pounds so it's not fair to expect her to keep up.

I move through the crowd toward the table where Bleu's waiting when I see one of my worst adversaries sitting next to her. Lloyd Buchanan, an officer who's been after The Fellowship for years, is cozying up and talking into her ear. She's leaning away, which means she doesn't like the things he's saying. "Move the fuck away from her."

"What a lovely American lass you have with you tonight, Mr. Breckenridge."

Perfect. He's going to be an arse. "Leave her alone."

"Since when did you start branching outside of the brotherhood?"

Things could become very unsafe for Bleu if he keeps talking. "Shut the fuck up."

"Aww, she's doesn't know who you are. You haven't told her you come from one of the most notorious families in Edinburgh. No … make that in Scotland. She has no idea your father is a sadistic crime lord and one day you'll be his replacement."

Buchanan strokes his finger down Bleu's bare arm. "Sweetheart, the man you're with is a deplorable criminal. He lies, steals, and kills. And that's just the shortlist."

I hate hearing him say those things to Bleu but I hate seeing his hands on her more. "Don't touch her."

Bleu looks at his hand and then at his face. "I'm giving you a warning and then an entire second to take your hand off me before I break it."

"You just threatened the deputy chief constable of the organized crime unit." Buchanan's hand moves down Bleu's arm to her leg. "I could take you in for that alone."

He's threatening Bleu. I'm sure she's frightened but I'm not. I move toward him, prepared for what might happen next. "I said, take your hand off her."

I don't take a full step toward them before Bleu goes for his balls. I see the rotation of her wrist and know exactly what's she's doing. Buchanan yells out in pain and drops to his knees. "Take me in if you like. I'd rather enjoy hearing the tale you'd weave about how a young American female tourist came to have your balls twisted in a dance club."

I don't take another step because I see that my assistance isn't necessary. Bleu's totally got this.

"Let go!" he hisses through clenched teeth.

Bleu releases him and he falls against the floor into the fetal position. She swings her legs around and steps over him as she gets out of the booth. "I believe I've been delighted by his presence long enough."

She loops her arm through mine as we exit the club. It's surprising. She seems to be taking the news of my crime-family background rather well, as she isn't running away. Maybe she thinks it's bullshit.

We're driving to her flat and I'm waiting for her to bring up the things Buchanan said. She doesn't disappoint. "Is that stuff true? Are you part of an organized crime family? Or organization? Or whatever that jackass was talking about?"

I guess I could lie. She knows no one in these parts so she'd probably never be privy to the reality but I find I prefer to tell her the truth. Nothing about her is typical so I'm curious to see her reaction. And test her. "My father is the patriarch of our family and an organization called The Fellowship. Some people call us a gang. We've been referred to as mobsters or Mafia. I don't care for any of those names. We're Scotsmen—not Italians—so clan or kinship is much more fitting."

"Do you do those things he accused you of? Lie? Steal?" She hesitates before saying the last. "Kill?"

"I'm in the business of boundaries and limits. I'm aware of what mine are and how far I'm willing to go to get my job accomplished. It can include lying and sometimes stealing." I wait a moment for driving the last nail into the coffin. "And perhaps the occasional killing."

"How do you feel when you do those things?"

"Powerful." I purposely choose that word because it's the one she used to describe how she felt when she brought Duff to his knees. I want her to see just how similar we are.

She watches out the window for a minute before speaking again. "Do you like the way it feels?"

I can't lie. I get a high from it. "Very much."

Another minute passes. "Okay."

What? "Just … okay?"

"Would you like me to be horrified?" she asks. "I can do that if it would make you feel better or improve your opinion of me."

She's no fucking Pollyanna. So I guess there's no reason for her to pretend to be. "No. Okay works for me."

I'm not sure if I should be disturbed by her lack of appall. It feels like a double standard to be shocked by an absence of dismay.

My God, has the pot met the kettle? "I wish I could get inside your head."

"No, you don't," she says. "My mind is a dark place to be."

I think I may have met the perfect woman. In her eyes, I'm not a monster at all.

CHAPTER SEVEN

BLEU MACALLISTER

I STOP WHEN WE REACH MY FRONT DOOR. MY HAND PRESSED AGAINST SIN'S chest is my signal for him to understand he won't be coming in. "Thank you for tonight. I had a very good time."

"Again?" He sighs and rubs his hands down my arms. "I'm not invited to come inside?"

I grin while shaking my head. "You aren't ready."

"I suspect it's you who isn't ready because I know for damn sure I am." He's going to kiss me. I know he is. "I promise I'll make you feel good."

He's trying so hard. It's sort of sweet in a way, even though he is trying to get me into bed. "I have no doubt you will, but it won't be tonight."

"I want to kiss you." He comes closer, invading my personal space. "That's something I never have a desire to do."

I suppose one kiss won't hurt. It's probably a good idea to throw a dog a bone, even if it's a small one.

I hold up one of my fingers. "One bite of the apple. That's all you get."

The corner of his mouth turns up and a small dimple appears. I've not noticed that until now. It's sexy as hell.

My God, he's a handsome devil.

His eyes are beautiful, like melted dark chocolate.

His hands go to my waist and pull me tightly against him. Our mouths are impossibly close yet not touching. We make a sport of it, almost like tug of war. One advances, the other retreats. We alternate until his lips finally brush mine and it's a game to me no more. I want to taste him.

I move my hands up his arms, over his broad, muscular shoulders. His lips meet mine and I open my mouth, inviting his tongue inside. They're soft and wet gliding together. He tastes likes whisky. And I love it.

His hand moves to the hem of my dress and creeps up my thighs. That's more than the one bite I promised, so I grab his wrist. "You're being a very bad boy."

"The only thing that's bad is how much I want to touch you."

I push his hand away. "I know you do—and you will—but not until you come to understand full circle what it is I want and need."

"Bonny Bleu, I can make you feel so fucking good if you'll just let me." His hand is back to working its way up my dress. "Isn't that what all of this is about? Pleasuring you?"

I let his fingers skim my silky panties before forcing his hand away. "It most definitely is but if you understood anything about what I need, you'd be able to predict that I don't want it while standing outside my front door for all of my neighbors to see."

He growls in frustration. "Then let me come in."

"Says the big bad wolf."

He steps back and clasps his hands over the top of his head. "Your game confuses me. You act as though you want to be properly fucked but you have all these stipulations to go along with the manner in which it's done." He moves his hands down his face. "It's fucking exhausting," he growls.

He's becoming annoyed. I'm losing him. I think he's growing tired of the waiting game so I have to reel him in again. "Being properly fucked is worth the wait because when it's good, it's very good."

I need to step up my plan, force his hand.

Sin doesn't take women to his home—ever. It would be a huge concession for him to do so. He needs a really good reason to want to take me there. "It sounds silly but the truth is that I sort of get creeped out thinking about having sex in Aunt Edy's flat since it's where she passed away."

"No storage rooms. No offices. No flats where dead people could be walking around. Should I be aware of any other places you can't have sex?" He's laughing at me again. Good. I prefer that over annoyance.

"If I asked you to take me to your bed after our next date and make love to me, would you?"

"I don't take women to my house. And I don't make love."

"Would you if it pleased me?" I want to plant the idea that taking me into his bed will conquer half the battle.

He doesn't answer immediately but I can tell he's thinking it over. "I might be able to find a way to make an exception this one time."

I'm surprised he gave in so easily. "Good. I'm off Thursday and Friday."

"Fuck, no! That's five days from now."

I shrug, pretending I don't know what the problem is. "And?"

He's shaking his head. "No way. That's entirely too long to wait."

Really? Five days is nothing. "Anticipation is one of the best forms of foreplay."

I'm certain he doesn't agree, based on his expression. "Ugh!" he groans. "Mmm ... I'm going to kiss the hell out of you right now and you're not going to tell me I can't."

He doesn't give me the opportunity to refuse. I'm yanked into his arms, my body slamming against his. His mouth devours mine, consuming me from the outside inward.

His hands are on my ass, squeezing my cheeks, almost painfully so. He's borderline lifting me, the tips of my toes barely grazing the ground. I think he'll have me lifted with my legs wrapped around him at any minute. But then he releases me. And I'm disappointed. I liked what he was doing.

"You better be worth all this work and waiting." He nips my bottom lip and gives my ass another painful squeeze before turning to walk to his car.

Anticipation—it builds excitement and suspense. The brain really is a sexual organ, even for men. Sin is going to spend the next five days and nights fantasizing about what it'll be like when he finally has me beneath him. Waiting is something he's never had to do so this is another way of setting me apart from the others before me. It proves I'm worth the wait and far more than just fuckworthy.

This is happening much faster than I anticipated. It's coming down to the wire and I have to mentally prep myself if I'm going to be ready to do this in a mere five days.

He thinks our only reason for coming together is for sex, but it's going to be about so much more. I need him to feel a bond. It's something I've never had with a man before so I'm not sure I can pull it off.

As one would expect, making yourself an island prevents you from forming emotional and physical connections. That translates into me never having had an intimate relationship with a man. I'm a twenty-five-year-old virgin and my first sexual encounter is going to be with the son of my mother's killer.

It's sick, but all part of my plan to make him fall in love with me.

I've convinced him I'm some sort of sexual butterfly but I wonder what he's going to think when he realizes he is the first man to ever have me. I anticipate it going one of two ways: either he'll be pissed and storm out because I'm not the experienced woman he's expecting, or he'll be so taken by being the one and only that he'll do everything in his power to keep it that way.

I'm hoping for the latter.

The days are closing in quickly and I'm growing increasingly nervous about my approaching deflowering. I sort of know what to expect, yet I don't. I can only think of one person in this world I can talk to about sex—my sister.

"Oh God, Bleu. I'm so happy to hear from you. I wasn't sure if you'd be able to get away to call or not." She understands it isn't always possible for me to call home.

"I'm so happy to hear your voice. You're good?"

"Yeah."

"How's work?" I say.

"The golden child got the day shift, so I'm still stuck on twelve-hour nights. But I expected it, so I'm not too disappointed." Elli had put in for days just before I left. I'm bummed for her that she didn't get it.

"At least it's never boring." It's my attempt at being positive.

"Right. The freaks come out at night, especially in the ER. A dude came in last night—he'd shoved a bag of coke up his ass when he got pulled over. Retrieving that was a load of fun. I promise you I do not get paid enough for that shit."

My sister's wit and charm is effortless. She makes everyone laugh and is adored by all. I wish I were more like her.

"I know you can't tell me anything about your assignment but are you at least enjoying wherever you are?"

"I am. It's beautiful here."

"Tell me you're on a tropical island, mingling with beautiful male criminals who wear togas and feed you grapes while you lounge in the sun."

We always play this game. "Yes. I'm in Hawaii investigating a rich, handsome man. I'm staying with him at his extravagant beachfront home where I have servants at my beck and call but I mostly lie on the beach all day."

"Ahh … being pampered by criminals is so much better than digging in their asses. I want your job instead of mine. Is it too late for a career change?"

There's no way Princess Ellison could hang with my kind of criminals. "You should definitely look into it."

"Seriously, is everything okay? You don't sound like your usual self." She knows me so well.

"No, but is it ever?"

"Can you tell me what's wrong or is it top secret?"

I can give Elli a portion of this story. The other part will have to be fictitious. "I've met someone."

"Bleu! You have to tell me everything! Is he handsome? Rich? When did you meet him? And how?"

"Yes. Yes. Not long ago. And in a bar."

"Ooh … exciting. Tell me more."

"He's Scottish."

"Shut up! You're in Scotland?"

"I didn't say that." This job isn't FBI-related so I think I can divulge a little more information than usual. "But yes, I am."

"Oh … you're in love with a Scotsman." I did not say I was in love. "Do you orgasm every time he speaks?"

"Almost."

"Does he wear anything under his kilt? I hear real Scotsmen don't." Leave it to Elli to ask something like that.

"Sorry. No kilt."

"Well, that's disappointing."

Tell me about it. I'd probably have an orgasm and die if I saw Sin wearing one. "I've only seen him in a suit. But he looks hotter than a freshly fucked fox in a forest fire."

"Ooh, sista … that's some serious hot." She has no idea.

"So … I sort of have a reason for calling."

"You're gonna do it with him, aren't you?" She giggles. "Or are you already doing it?"

God, she sounds like a teenager. "Gonna."

She squeals loudly enough, I have to take the phone away from my ear. "Then I know you are seriously crazy about this guy if you're finally giving it up." Well, not exactly.

"I'm scared." That part's no lie.

"Does he treat you well?"

He's been good to me for the short amount of time we've known one another. One might not expect that from a man like Sin who's accustomed to using women only for his own pleasure. "So far. He's patient, kind, and very eager to please me." The eager to please isn't exactly voluntary.

"Then he'll take care of you in bed." She's right. I've worked it out so this will probably be the best first-time experience anyone could have.

"What should I expect?" I feel so juvenile.

"It's been a while but I remember it was sharp at first and then it ached, almost like a cramping sensation. It didn't really feel too good but you have to remember that my first time was with Chris. He didn't know shit from Shinola."

"I'm positive Sinclair will know shit from Shinola."

"Ooh … you're gonna be getting it on a with a Scotsman called Sinclair. I think I'm jealous."

"Everyone calls him Sin."

"Even better."

Elli had quite the blossoming romance before I left. "Tell me about your doctor friend."

"Yeah … that's not gonna be working out."

"Why?"

"Because I didn't want to join him with his … partner."

What does that mean? "Partner, as in the one from his medical practice, or partner, as in he had another girlfriend?"

"Neither."

"Ohh."

"Yeah. I was never down with a threesome but I didn't think much of it when he asked. I was unconcerned because I thought most guys had fantasies about being with two women at once. I found out it wasn't a woman he wanted to bring in and it made me start suspecting if the threesome was really a twosome and I was the spectator. So I told him to fuck off."

Wow. "I'm sorry."

"I'm mostly sorry because I have to see him at work. It's awkward. I'm afraid he's gonna tell somebody. He's afraid I'm gonna tell everybody. I'm thinking of transferring out of the ER so I don't have to see him anymore."

"You shouldn't have to give up a job you like because of him."

"It has less to do with him and more to do with me being burned out."

"Then you should look for another job."

"It's not just my job. I'm tired of Memphis in general. I'd leave if Dad weren't sick."

"I talked to him a couple days ago. He sounded like he felt good." But I can never tell over the phone.

"He's doing well. Looking good. Says he feels better than he has in weeks."

I feel so guilty for not being with him but at least everything is going okay. "He has a burner. Use it to contact me if anything happens."

"I will."

"I'm not kidding. Don't hesitate to call. Something happens and

I'm on the first plane back."

"I know you will be."

"I've gotta run." I have to be at work in an hour. "Thanks for the talk. I feel much better."

"Go get 'im, tiger." Elli growls.

My sister has no idea I'm more like a tiger than she thinks. I'm a predator and Sin is my prey. And I'm gonna get 'im good.

CHAPTER EIGHT

SINCLAIR BRECKENRIDGE

It's been two days since I saw Bleu and I crave her company. My work performance is suffering because she's the only thing on my mind. That's why I'm going to the bar tonight instead of doing research for my case. My desire to see her is a fixation I can no longer control.

I'm already seated at my table when her eyes meet mine from across the room. Her expression transforms from one of boredom to what I perceive as happiness. I think it's a sign we're equally delighted about seeing one another.

She doesn't take her eyes from mine as she closes the distance. "Good evening, Mr. Breckenridge. How may I serve you?"

"I can think of quite a few ways but they're all rather naughty. I'd better keep them to myself since I still have to wait three days until I can convince you to perform them." I place my foot on the chair across from me and push it away from the table. "Sit with me a while."

"Delayed gratification, Breck. It's something you know nothing about—but you will. You won't soon forget the satisfaction it's going to bring you."

Breck? That's a new one.

I once took great pleasure in taking a woman to bed but my accident stole that indulgence from me years ago. I settle for quick fucks because I'm forced to hide a secret no one from my world can know. But Bleu isn't a part of this life.

She's going to discover this thing I hide when I take her into my bed. I have no idea how she'll respond. I only know I want to find out.

"May I bring you some instant gratification? Maybe a JW?"

I nod. "I'll take it if that's all I can get."

She laughs as she gets up to fetch my whisky. "You're worse than a child."

I'm watching the sway of her hips when I hear Leith's voice. "Why don't you fuck her already and get it over with?"

I force my eyes away from Bleu's arse. "Who says I haven't?"

"You're still interested. It's a dead giveaway."

He knows me so well. "She's making me wait." I laugh.

"What the hell are you talking about?"

Leith is only one of two people I'd tell about my arrangement with Bleu. "She won't give me a quick fuck."

"Then find one who will."

That's exactly what I usually do but there's a problem with that plan. "I don't want to move on. I'm obsessed with having her and she's going to give herself to me … but on her terms."

"Which are?"

I give Leith the short version of where Bleu and I stand. "Don't be stupid. You've kept this on the down-low for six years. Take her to bed and it's a secret no more. She could tell anyone."

She's not conspiring against me or The Fellowship. "She's alone in Scotland. She has no one to tell."

"One person. That's all it takes."

Bleu returns with my drink, ending my debate with Leith.

"We'll finish this conversation another time."

"Whatever." Leith waits until Bleu leaves to finish. "I came over to tell you there's a girl here to see you. She's waiting in my office."

"Who is it?"

"Declan Stuart's sister."

"Her brother's atonement is scheduled for the mornin' and I'm his handler." And I know why she's here—to offer sex in exchange for her loved one's punishment.

I down my whisky. "Do me a favor. Make sure Bleu doesn't find her way into your office while I'm with Miss Stuart."

"Sure."

I go into Leith's office and the female version of Declan is sitting on the leather sofa—the exact spot where I've fucked so many just like her. "Mr. Breckenridge. I hope I'm not disturbing you."

"Well, you are."

"I'm Christie Stuart, Declan's sister. I've come to talk with you about my brother's beating that's scheduled for tomorrow."

A beating? I think she's trying to be dramatic. "It's called atonement. It's retribution for his wrongdoing. He stole from The Fellowship. I'm sure you're aware that isn't tolerated."

"It isn't his fault. He took the drugs and sold them because I needed money. He did it for me so I could attend the dance academy. It's been my dream since I was a little girl to be a ballerina."

"I don't care why he stole from me, twinkle toes."

"I have the money." She takes a stack of bills from her handbag and places them on the desk. "Will you take it back and call off the atonement?"

"I'll gladly take back what was stolen from me but your brother will still be punished." Returning the money must feel like a stupid move now. "No one wrongs the brotherhood and walks away unscathed."

"Please, don't hurt him. It's my fault he stole from you."

"Doesn't matter."

She reaches for the hem of her shirt and pulls it over her head, baring herself from the waist up. She isn't wearing a bra but she doesn't have to. Her tits are perfect. "Maybe we could settle his debt another way."

And here we go.

This isn't the first time someone's sister, girlfriend, or wife has offered to fuck in exchange for a lesser punishment or dismissal. I've done it countless times—taken them up on their offer only to inform them once it's over that the punishment will continue as planned.

I'd do it again today if I weren't opting out for my upcoming delayed gratification with Bleu. I've put too much work—and waiting —into her to jeopardize it now with a quickie. "Sorry. It's nonnegotiable."

"Please," she begs.

"Put your shirt back on and leave." Before Bleu comes back here.

She unzips her skirt and lets it fall before she comes toward me. "I'll let you fuck me any way you want and I won't make a sound."

Shocking. I'm not the least bit turned on by this woman's advances. It doesn't do it for me when Bleu's offer holds far more promise of satisfaction. "I'm not doing this. Put your clothes back on."

The door to Leith's office bursts open without warning and Bleu comes in like an angry tempest. "Really, Sinclair? We're back to this again?"

Fucking perfect!

"This isn't what it looks like." Well, that's not entirely right. It's exactly what it looks like except I told her no.

"I'm not stupid, despite what you might think." She storms away but calls out over her shoulder, "You can forget our plans for later this week. I'll find someone else who can give me the things I need. Leith seems pretty eager to try."

Not happening. No one touches Bleu but me.

"Put your clothes on right now. After you're dressed, go out there and fix this or I'll make sure your brother dies tomorrow."

"You can't kill Declan for stealing."

She obviously doesn't know me. "I've killed for much less," I say. "Have Bleu come back to the office after you're finished fixing the shit you've stirred."

"Yes, sir."

Five minutes pass. Then ten. Bleu doesn't return to the office so I call the front. "Is there a blond woman still talking to Bleu?"

"No, sir. She left a while ago but Bleu's here. She's sitting at your table with Mr. Duncan."

She has another thing coming if she thinks she's going to replace me so easily. "Tell her I said I want to see her in the office right now."

"Aye, sir."

A moment later, she's standing in the doorway, arms crossed. "You wanted to see me?"

"Come in and shut the door." She gives me a sharp look and doesn't move. She's a stubborn one, that Bonny Bleu. "Please."

A moment later she does as I ask. "And lock it. Please."

She looks at me with narrowed eyes. "There's no need."

"We'll require a moment of privacy so we may discuss what just happened."

She pushes the lock on the door. "You mean you want to talk about me finding you with a naked woman in a compromising situation?"

"I was not compromised. It was all her. She's the one who took off her clothes and tried to get me to fuck her."

"I made the decision to let you have me. It wasn't one I took lightly so excuse me if I'm offended by your less than stellar behavior."

Her brow is creased, eyes cast downward. I think her bottom lip may even be slightly protruding.

My God, she's pouting. I hate when women do that, except her. It's beautiful, and it's all for me. "Do I need to remind you it was an attempt—an unsuccessful one?"

"I believe you but we should be clear about one thing. I want no further misunderstandings. You'll share your body with no one as long as I'm giving myself to you."

Ahh … she's a possessive little vixen. It's hot. "I don't know if I can wait three more days to have you."

"Keep imagining how good it's going to be when you finally do. The taste of the remaining apple will keep you going."

I drive Bleu home from work and we're kissing like crazy at her front door. I glide one of my hands under her work blouse and cup her lace-clad breast. My thumb grazes her nipple back and forth until it becomes rigid beneath my touch.

She's allowing me quite a bit more freedom tonight so maybe I won't be waiting until Thursday after all. "Let me take you home with me." I trail my lips over her jawline until my mouth reaches her earlobe. I suck it between my teeth, tugging gently, and her body bends to me. "There's really no need to wait three days to experience pleasure when we can start tonight."

I move my hand between her thighs, rubbing up and down. "I

swear I'll make it all about you. The only thing I need is a chance." She grasps my wrist. At first, I think she's going to push it away but then I realize she's moving it to a more pleasurable spot. "I don't think you want to wait, either."

I'm waiting for her reply when my phone vibrates in my pocket.

Dammit. I'm not a man with the luxury of avoiding calls. If someone's calling this late, it's important.

I take my hands off Bleu so I can retrieve my phone. It's Dad. Something is going on. "I'm sorry. I have to take this."

"Aye, Dad?"

"William Calhoun's been arrested. Rodrick is already on his way but you need to be down there with him."

This is how my life will be very soon—getting calls at all hours of the night to handle whatever legal messes the brothers have gotten into. "Now?"

"I need you there thirty minutes ago. I don't trust Calhoun. He has a problem with keeping his mouth shut. The bastard better hope they don't talk him into saying anything he'll regret later."

Well, my fun with Bleu is over—at least for tonight. "I'm in Old Town but I'm leaving now. I'll let you know how things go."

I need to touch her again before I go so I glide my hands over her arse and pull her against me. I suck her bottom lip into my mouth and then release it. "I really don't want to leave you."

"Then don't."

This is painful. "I have to."

"Will I see you tomorrow?"

"Maybe." I'm already behind on the case I was assigned and I'm sure this new mess isn't going to help. "Probably not. I'm already really behind with work. I shouldn't have come tonight but I couldn't stay away. I was going crazy."

"Don't act as though you've been bewitched." She laughs. "You came because you were hoping to get laid."

"A guy can hope." I grin and shrug. "Were you going to say yes?" I really think I was about to get a shag.

"Doesn't matter now. You're getting a kiss goodnight instead."

That's a yes. Dammit, I was so close to banging her. I may get William Calhoun out of the slammer just so I can beat the shit out of him.

"Three days." I kiss her lips one last time before I go. "Be ready."

CHAPTER NINE

BLEU MACALLISTER

Tonight's the night. I've been preparing myself for this since I made the decision to use Sinclair as collateral damage. Getting off won't be enough. Anyone can do that for him. He has to experience the unexpected and like it enough to keep coming back for more. Could there be anything better than an untouched virgin in his bed?

I think not.

My hair is down with the ends loosely curled. Sin's never seen it that way. It goes perfectly with the tight, black dress I'm wearing. The hair, the outfit, the shoes ... they make me feel confident and sexy— like I could seduce a saint. I suppose it's all a bit much since Sin is certainly no saint and wouldn't resist my sexual advances, even if I were on fire.

Thank God he's a horny bastard. That makes him putty in my hands.

There's a knock at the door so I take one last look in the mirror and push my boobs up in my dress. "Stella Bleu, I hope your bullshit is exceptional tonight," I say to my reflection.

Sin's standing on the other side with a single white long-stemmed rose in hand. I'm taken aback by the gesture. "Awe ... Sin. Thank you." I take it and bring it to my nose for a smell.

"The florist told me a white rose conveys 'I'm worthy.'" I

understand the meaning and I'm touched he'd put effort into wooing me. He knows I'm a sure thing tonight, yet he chooses to romance me anyway. That's both unexpected and uncharacteristic for Sinclair Breckenridge.

"Do you give roses to all the girls?"

"You're the first." That's not a shock.

"I have a feeling there's going to be a lot of firsts for both of us tonight."

He's driving us to the restaurant and I go through my personal undercover rules in my head, just for a refresher.

Rule number one: lies are like boomerangs. You better throw them out as hard and as far as you can because they always return eventually. I have that covered. Nothing will come back to me before I'm out of here. Once I'm gone may be a different story since I'm not using an alias.

Rule number two: always know my boundaries and never allow the lines to become blurred. I have no limits to what I'm prepared to do or where I'm willing to go when it comes to Thane Breckenridge.

Rule number three: when undercover, you'd better have a map because there are a lot of ways to get lost. I know Thane, Sin, and The Fellowship inside and out. I'm good.

Rule number four: it's not a lie if you believe it. I am who I say I am and I have no motive. There is no evidence that will prove otherwise.

Rule number five: know and understand that Sin's a special kind of animal. He's perfectly fine with surprise and things going wrong. He's a dangerous man, but I'm prepared to kill him if the situation arises.

Rule number six: be headstrong but vulnerable, confident yet cautious. I'm the one in control tonight, yet I'm giving myself to this monster. I will do it with confidence but understand his reaction could be a volatile one. Again, I will kill him if I have to.

Rule number seven: know and understand that I'm straddling two worlds—his and mine. I laugh about this one since I'll soon be straddling him.

Rule number eight: conceal any personal feelings I have. He can never see how much giving my body to him disgusts me.

Rule number nine: say or do whatever's necessary to sell it. I will say anything I think he wants to hear. I will perform any act to make him trust me enough to bring me into Thane's circle.

Rule number ten: it's all about the right move at the right time—pacing and patience. I'll read his emotions and body language to know what needs to come next.

A necessary sin. That's what tonight is.

"You're quiet. Are you nervous for later?"

I shake my head. "Eager would be a better description for what I'm feeling." That much is true. I'm nervous but ready to get this behind me.

"I like the word eager much better than nervous."

He holds the door for me when we enter The Witchery. He places his hand on my lower back when I walk past. A shiver travels down my spine, causing my body to quiver and chills to rise to the surface of my skin.

We're seated at a table in a dark, quiet corner. I'm not surprised. I think he likes having me to himself, away from the other patrons. "We're off to ourselves."

"So we are."

"Is this the proposal table?"

"It could be." He laughs.

"You aren't going to propose, are you?"

"No." He's grinning, amused by my question. I like that I'm able to tease him.

"Good, 'cause I'd have to decline."

He brings his fist to his chest and pretends to remove something. "Your refusal would be a dagger to my heart."

"Then let me put your mind at ease. I'm going to let you do what you want with my body but I'll never give you my heart."

"Because you can't or won't?"

"I guess that's a matter for a shrink."

"I don't need someone's analysis of why you can't or won't give away your heart. I get it. I understand. I'm not sure you know it yet but we're very much alike."

He's wrong. I share no similarities with him. He's the spawn of a monster. "Perhaps. I suppose only time will tell."

Dinner is served and I'm hardly able to eat a bite. My stomach is in knots. I order dessert but not because I'm craving chocolate raspberry cheesecake. It's a ploy to procrastinate.

A strange feeling has settled in my stomach. I've had weeks to think about this night, yet I'm not nearly as prepared as I thought. "Want a bite?"

"Aye." He leans forward and takes the bite I'm offering. "Mmm … delicious but not the sweetness I'm in the mood for."

He's eager so I need to be as well. "Are you ready?"

"Very much so. You?"

I nod because I'm afraid I won't be convincing. "I need to visit the ladies' room."

"Sure."

He stands as I leave the table. I scurry in the direction of the restrooms. They're located next to the entrance and I seriously consider bolting out the front door. There would be no shame in forgetting the whole thing and going home. Except I can't. I want to push forward.

I sprint into the ladies' room and go inside a stall to experience the panic attack I feel approaching. It's the same as always. I'm short of breath. My heart is racing. My chest hurts. I'd believe I was dying if I didn't understand what was happening.

I work to slow my breathing. "You're fine, Bleu."

A hot flash begins and I use my hands to frantically fan myself. "Calm down. Breathe."

It lasts several minutes before subsiding. I'm lucky this time. My attacks are often debilitating, lasting at least twenty minutes.

When it's over, I leave the stall and dab my neck with cool, wet cloths. I feel like my old self so I reapply lipstick and return to Sin. "I'm ready if you are."

I've previously familiarized myself with Sin's residence, as well as my escape plan should things go awry. Instead of using the drive to get my bearings, I spend the time psyching myself up.

I realize I'm repetitively popping my knuckles when Sin places his hand on top of mine. "Relax."

I'm afraid he'll see the fear behind my eyes or hear it in my voice, so I smile but say nothing.

Sterling pulls through the gated entrance and parks the car in front of a series of weathered stone buildings. Each structure is three levels high. The windows are gorgeous, surrounded by ornate designs, but I can't appreciate their beauty. I'm too nervous.

"That'll be all for now, Sterling."

We enter and Sin barely shuts the door before pulling me into his arms. He's silent as he searches my face.

"What are you looking at?"

He pushes my hair over my shoulder. "I do believe you're the most beautiful woman I've ever seen."

More romance. That's unexpected. "You say pretty things like this to all the girls?"

"Never. Just like I've never brought a woman to my house, yet here you are, waiting for me to make love to you in my bed—two more things I've never done."

I've procrastinated long enough. It's show time.

I glide my finger down his tie. "Take me to your bed. We've waited long enough."

He clasps my hand in his and kisses my knuckles before leading me through his flat. "You'll get the full tour tomorrow."

Oh. That means I'm staying the night. I sort of expected to be taken back to my flat when this was over, maybe even hoped. "I didn't bring an overnight bag."

"Don't need one for what we're doing."

He takes me into his bedroom. No matter how many times I enter one of Edinburgh's beautiful, old buildings, I'm always surprised by its modern décor.

His room is masculine with hard lines. There's nothing soft or romantic about it. Not that I'm into that kind of thing or would expect him to be.

We stand in the middle of the room. I think he's giving me time to survey my surroundings and maybe even waiting for me to say something. So I do. "This is nice."

"Nice?"

I shrug. What does he want me to say? "Pretty doesn't seem like the right word."

"Nice works."

He places his hand on the back of my neck and pulls me close. "This way is new to me, Bleu. I've never been with a woman for any other reason than to please myself, so you may have to guide me. Tell me what you like and want."

What the hell? I'm in no position to guide anyone.

I only nod in agreement.

He brushes his lips over mine softly and slowly. It's the kiss of two people preparing to make love. I think.

It's nice. His slow pace is helping me relax.

He pulls downward on the zipper at the back of my dress and chills erupt all over my body. I tense when he grasps the top and tugs it from my shoulders. His mouth moves down my neck and he kisses the bare skin there. "Is this good for you?"

His question sparks a thought I've not considered. He's fucked numerous women but this is his first time to make love as well. He's as uncertain and lost as I am.

"Yes. Quite."

He pushes my dress down until it falls to the floor and then steps away to look at me. I feel self-conscious. I've never stood in front of a man wearing only my panties and bra. It's nothing like wearing a bikini and my instinct is to cover myself with my hands. "You're fucking gorgeous."

I'm surprised at how pleased I am to know he finds me attractive. "I'm happy you think so."

He puts his finger under the strap of my bra and glides it down. "I've been imagining black lace beneath that black dress all night but I'm really enjoying the sight of you in white. It makes you look innocent."

It's fitting for a virgin to wear white. "There are more surprises to come."

He grins and his dimples make an appearance. Those are a sign of happiness, right?

I pull the knot of his tie until it's free and drop it to the floor. I unbutton his shirt until it's completely open and push it away as I glide my hands up his shoulders and chest.

I step away so I can admire him fully. His body is flawless, contoured in all the right places down to that perfect V at his waist.

My eyes pause at the underside of his bicep when I find an intricate inked Celtic pattern. The artwork is breathtaking with a design composed of complex mazes, knots, and labyrinths. "My God, this is beautiful."

"My body or my tattoo?" He laughs.

"Both."

The reaction he's getting from me is genuine because this is unexpected. Nothing in his file mentioned ink but I guess it wouldn't since none is visible when he's in a suit. "I had no idea you had this."

"I wouldn't expect you to." He grasps my shoulders and turns me around so I'm facing the bed. "Stand here. There's something you have to see before we go any further."

He's acting weird. "O … kay."

He unbuttons his pants and lowers the zipper before pushing them to his knees. He sits on the edge of the bed. "There's a reason I prefer a quick fuck instead of bringing women home to my bed."

I'm not experienced at this but even I know this isn't normal.

"I choose to keep this a secret because a rival—or even my own brothers—could see it as a weakness. No one knows, with the exception of five people: my father, Abram, Jamie, Leith, and my brother, Mitch. I live as though this never happened because I won't allow it to hinder the way I experience life."

He pushes his trousers to the floor and watches my face. "Another thing you can't see unless I'm out of my clothes."

My God, he's an amputee. His left leg is missing below the knee, replaced by a prosthesis. How could I miss something so important during my surveillance?

"I was shot six years ago and they couldn't save my leg. This is why I don't bring women into my bed. There's no way to hide this."

But Sin isn't hiding from me. He's making himself vulnerable.

"No one can know."

This is good. Sin believes I won't reveal this secret. "I understand."

He watches me come to him. "I need to know what you're thinking."

I hold his face in my palms. "I think you should make love to me."

I look down. "Doesn't your prosthesis need to come off first?"

His smile is back, as are his dimples. "Probably."

He removes and props the leg against the bed railing before grabbing me around the waist to pull me closer. He reaches around to unfasten my bra and then buries his face between my breasts. He cups them with his hands on the underside, pushing them together. "I love these. They're absolutely perfect." He's accustomed to quickies that only please him, so I'm betting this isn't something he's done often.

He moves his mouth to my nipple, sucking it in. He circles it with his tongue until it pebbles and then tugs gently with his teeth. A shiver spreads throughout my body and chills erupt over my skin. I look up at the ceiling because I can't watch what he's doing. I'm afraid I'll like what I'm seeing.

He places his palms on my hips and pushes them under my panties. He grasps my hips hard and pulls me against his groin. He's still wearing boxer briefs but I feel his hard cock rubbing against the front of my panties.

They don't get to stay on for long because he pushes them down my legs. When they fall to my ankles, I step out, leaving them in the growing pile of clothes on the floor.

His palms glide up and down the sides of my body as he studies every inch. "I knew you'd be perfect."

I'm self-conscious again, even more so now that I'm stark naked. I shake my head. "I'm in no way perfect."

He grasps my nape and brings me closer to kiss the side of my neck. "You are to me, Bonny Bleu."

He moves his hands to my waist and tugs while scooting backward on the bed. "Come up here and join me."

We lie on our sides facing one another and he hikes my leg over his thigh before possessing my mouth again. It must be instinct taking over because without any thought at all, I wrap my leg around Sin's waist and begin moving in a rocking motion. He grasps my cheeks in his hands and pulls my body hard against him. "I acted an arse when we met but I've wanted you since the first moment I saw you at Duncan's."

Rule number nine: say or do whatever's necessary to sell it. "I've wanted you since I realized you took the photograph of me from my flat."

He stops kissing my throat and looks at my eyes. "How long have you known?"

"I noticed it missing right after your first visit inside my flat."

He's smiling so he must like my answer. "Then that means you've wanted me for a while."

"What did you do with it?" I ask.

"It's on my desk in my office." Liar. I don't believe that for a second, but I'm not calling him out on it. Things are going too well.

"Good." I entwine my fingers in his hair and pull his face closer so our lips brush.

He sucks my bottom lip into his mouth and lightly tugs before releasing it. "I don't kiss."

That's not true. I recall several times he's kissed me.

I skim my fingertips over his lips. "I beg to differ."

He shakes his head. "What I mean is that I don't kiss other women. This compromise is only for you."

"Never?"

"No, never."

Hmm … He's quite good at it. "Why am I the exception?"

"You asked me to make love to you. I can't imagine doing that without kissing." Good answer.

"Whatever the reason, it pleases me."

"I haven't even begun to please you." He moves his hand around and down to touch me between my thighs. I involuntarily jerk because my body is hypersensitive. "Someone's jumpy."

"I'm feeling a little extra responsive right now." God, did that sound stupid? Yes. I think it did.

"I like responsive, but your body is too tense. Relax and breathe. I want you to enjoy this."

I do as he says. I inhale deeply through my nose and then blow it out slowly through my mouth.

"Keep breathing in deeply and then out slowly. In and then out," he says as he slips his fingers inside me. I tense again but he reminds me, "Don't forget to relax and breathe." He moves his fingers in and out in a torturously slow motion.

I grind against his hand because it's not enough. I want more of what he's doing. As though he reads my mind, he moves his fingers faster but this time adding another one—his thumb, rubbing my clit.

I've never had penetrative intercourse with a man but I'm not ignorant to the act or how one achieves an orgasm. I've simply never had anyone else do it for me.

But he's about to, and soon.

My eyes are squeezed shut, my mouth open and panting as I grind against his hand. "Look at me. I want to see your eyes when you orgasm."

I open and look at him. "Why?"

"Watching you come apart is my reward for making it happen." He smiles.

My panting increases. "Omigod." Here it is. "Ohhh … "

It feels like rhythmic contraction squeezing low in my pelvis. Warm bliss spreads throughout my body and pulsates through my limbs down to the tips of my fingers and toes.

"Fire, meet gasoline." He kisses me quickly. "You have a beautiful come face."

He rolls away and reaches into the nightstand drawer to take out a condom. He tears it open and I watch him roll it on because I've never seen a man do that … at least not in real life and certainly not so he could use it on me. It's enthralling. And stimulating in a way I never imagined.

Sin rolls on top of me, his body nestling between my legs.

I've known real-life monsters existed since I was seven years old so I thought nothing in this world had the power to ever scare me again. That clearly isn't true because I'm terrified.

I'm giving my body—and a piece of myself—to this man. We are about to join and become one. This is far beyond the physical act I expected. I'm handing over a part of … my soul. I didn't know being with him would feel like this.

I can't recall ever wanting anything so much in all my life, but I'm simultaneously fighting an urge to push him off so I can run.

I don't have long to fear the unknown because he enters me in one fluid motion and I feel a ripping pain when he pushes through my virginity. He has no idea I've never done this, so his first thrust isn't gentle. The tearing is sudden and sharp and unexpected. I grasp the sheet beneath me and twist it violently.

I thought I'd be able to hold my response inside but I can't. My gasp is loud. I turn my head to the side and cover my face with the fisted sheet so he can't see the pain there.

He goes completely still. "Did you feel that?"

Umm … hell yeah, I felt my hymen being shredded into pieces. "Yeah."

"What is it?"

This is it—the part where I either instill a desire for him to want to keep me to himself … or he freaks the fuck out. "My virginity."

"Virginity? What the hell are you talking about?"

I look at him quizzically. "I don't want to talk right now." I reach for the back of his neck and pull him down for a kiss. "I'd much rather finish what you started."

He pulls away so he can see my face. "A virgin?"

"Yes."

He's shaking his head, as if to make sense of the whole thing. "What was all that bullshit about demanding I pleasure you?"

"It's not bullshit. It all stands, and right now I demand that you properly fuck me." The pain has subsided while he's been busy trying to carry on a conversation, so I rock my hips against him. I'm ready for this now. "Don't tell me you don't like the way this feels because I know I do."

He growls when he pushes my legs back and starts rocking back and forth inside me. "Oh, fuck, you're so wee. And wet."

I can't lie. I like hearing him say those things. I want to be the best he's ever had. It ensures he'll keep me around longer. "Am I worth the work and the wait?"

"Hell." He thrusts between words. "Yes."

"I told you when it's good, it's very good."

"It's pure magic," he groans. "The best ever."

I smile against his neck. That's exactly what I wanted to hear.

Giving him my virginity hasn't been for nothing. Everything is going according to plan.

CHAPTER TEN

SINCLAIR BRECKENRIDGE

I'VE GOTTEN OFF PLENTY OVER THE LAST SIX YEARS BUT I'VE MISSED SHARING A bed with a woman. Having Bleu here with her bare, sweaty body pressed to mine while I move inside her feels amazing. I've been robbing this luxury of the recognition it deserves. It's incredible and Bleu is the only woman I'm willing to risk this with. She has no ties to anyone in The Fellowship—or rival cartel. She'll keep this to herself because she has nothing to gain and everything to lose by opening her mouth.

I can't believe how good she feels. I move slower. I want to make this last as long as possible but decreasing my pace doesn't help. The tight grip of her body around mine is going to push me over the edge soon.

I tense and clench my teeth as the bliss approaches. I thrust into her deeply with the onset of the rhythmic spasms. I know I should—and I always do—but I cannot pull out. I'm greedy. I don't want to give up a second of this pleasure.

I'm completely spent and empty when I crumple over Bleu. Our bodies are wet and sticking to one another. She probably prefers me anywhere but the place I am—on top with my weight pressing against her—but I don't roll away. I love the sensation of her soft skin touching mine.

She's gone lax beneath me, her limbs outstretched on the bed. My mouth is pressed to her throat and I can feel the pulsation in her neck against my lips. Her heart races.

She brings both hands to my back and the tips of her fingernails graze my skin as she drags them up and down. Chills erupt all over my body. "I hope it was good for you."

Good? Is she kiddin' me?

I lift my head and look at her face. "Seriously … it was the best ever."

She blushes as her mouth curls into a large grin. "Really?"

"Unquestionably." I kiss her quickly before rolling onto my back to lie next to her.

"Is this a one-time thing?"

I don't think I can bear it if this only happens once. "You're asking, so does that mean you're open to a second time?" And a third. And so on …

"I think I am."

"Good. I'm very open to it again." Do I dare to do this? Start a relationship, even if it's only sexual? I've never been in any kind of an arrangement like this with a woman. "You should probably be aware of something. I might not know how to treat you. It's something I've never learned." She should understand my ways early on so there are no surprises later. "I only know how to use fear and violence to make people behave the way I want them to."

"You should probably understand now that I won't allow you to control me with threats."

"Then we should be an interesting couple." I laugh. This is going to be fun.

"We're going to be volatile. We should prepare now for this to end badly." She couldn't be more right.

"We're damned from the start," I say. "The odds of us working out even for a short time are unfavorable."

"You shouldn't expect much from me."

"I'm going to put your worries to rest right now. I expect nothing from you." That's good. I doubt I'll give her anything more than a good heartache.

I reach to remove the condom and see the blown-out tip. "Aww …

fuck!"

"What's wrong?"

"Your virginity shredded the condom." She lifts her head and stares at the busted rubber on my cock. "Please tell me you're taking birth control."

"We probably should've discussed this before you came inside me through a broken rubber." That's a no.

She was a virgin until five minutes ago, so that means she has no reason to be on any kind of birth control. "When is your next period due?"

"My body doesn't work like that."

"What does that mean?"

"I don't have periods like normal women. There's no need to go into details about something you care nothing about. Just know that you'll never have to worry about a baby with me."

She can't get pregnant. Bleu's pro list is growing. I wonder what's going on with that. She's made it clear she doesn't want to talk about it, so I'll respect that boundary for now.

"A pregnancy isn't a possibility, but I still have to worry about infected penises giving me diseases. When's the last time you were tested and how many women have you been with since?"

I just had a quarterly check. "I was tested last week. Everything came back clean. I haven't been with anyone since. Except you."

"Good. Make sure you keep it that way."

I was fifteen years old when my father told me to never fall asleep next to a woman, especially one I'd just fucked. He said I couldn't trust her to not kill me in my sleep. I figured Dad knew what he was talking about, so I've never taken the chance. Although I once brought women into my bed, I never allowed any of them to spend the night—until now.

Bleu promised it would be a night of firsts, and it certainly has been.

I watched her sleep for a while before I turned off the lamp. It had nothing to do with worry or fear she'd kill me while I was sleeping. I simply wanted to enjoy seeing her in my bed.

I think she had nightmares. She was restless and often mumbled incoherently. Her sleep became so fitful at one point, she screamed. She looked like a frightened animal ready to sprint when I woke her. I encouraged her to tell me what it was about, but she wouldn't. Instead of talking, we made love again.

I'm lying on my side with my elbow pressed into the bed and my head propped in my hand when Bleu wakes and looks at me. She smiles and rolls onto her side to face me. "Good mornin'."

I grab the bed sheet and give it a yank so I get a peep show of her tits. "Good morning to ye, girls."

She playfully slaps my shoulder and pulls the linen up to cover herself. "You live up to your name very well."

"Aye, as I should. My sins are very well practiced."

"They were very well practiced last night." She's grinning, her cheeks blushing.

I move to get on top of her so I can practice some more, but she puts her hand to my chest, stopping me. "Are you sore?"

"Not terribly."

"Then I didn't do my job well enough."

"You did a fine job." She crinkles her nose. "But I think my virginity has ruined your linens."

I kiss the top of her hand. "I genuinely enjoyed ruining them."

"I'll put them in the wash when we get up. Maybe they're salvageable."

"You don't have to do that. Agnes will take care of them."

"Who's Agnes?"

"My neighbor. She comes in a couple times a week to straighten up and do laundry. She's disabled—has a bad knee from a fall. She's unable to work so it helps her out with a little extra cash."

She's making that face, the one generally followed by an "aww." "That's really generous."

"Not really. She gets the funds she needs for her bills and I get a clean place to live. It's a good partnership." As this one will be as well.

She sits up and crisscrosses her legs. She still has the sheet tucked under her arms and I'd like to give it another yank. "Will you be taking me home on your way to the firm?"

I forgot to tell her. "I worked late the past two nights so I could have today off. I was hoping you'd want to spend it with me."

She's all smiles. "I'd like that very much, but I need a change of clothes." She crinkles her nose again. "And a toothbrush."

The toothbrush is an easy fix but everything else could be a problem. "We'll go by your place and pick up an overnight bag."

"An overnight bag as in the one I should have had for last night, or one for tonight?"

"Both."

I wait on the sofa while Bleu gathers her things. "Do I need an outfit for going out tonight?" she calls from the bedroom.

It's the third time she's yelled to ask me a question so I get up and go to her bedroom. "Do you want me to take you out?"

She jerks around and yelps. "Shit! I thought you were still in the living room."

I laugh. "Do you want to go out?"

"Maybe." She shrugs. "Dinner and dancing?"

"Sure, if it's what you want."

She takes out a black dress and holds the hanger at her shoulders to display how it might look on her. "Do you like this one?"

It looks really short. "Aye. I bet you look great in it."

She tosses it on the bed next to her bag and packs a pair of tall, red heels to go with it.

"Where do you keep your bras and knickers?"

Her brow lifts and she points toward a small chest. "Top one."

I open the drawer and go through her intimates, choosing the ones I like best. I hold up a red lace G-string with matching bra. "You have some exceptionally sexy garments for someone not having sex."

"I like the way they make me feel. Would you prefer I wear granny panties?"

"I don't know what granny panties are."

"Never mind." She laughs. "You don't want to know."

I hold up a satin bra I don't particularly care for. "I'd like to take you shopping so I can choose sexy things for you to wear."

"Do you have any idea how overbearing that sounds?"

I don't care. "I want you to have pretty things."

"I have plenty of pretty things."

"You do." But she deserves quality pieces. These items were bought on a photographer's budget. "I think we can do better. And it'll be fun."

She's frowning. "I'll feel like I owe you."

"You won't owe me." I move toward her and push her back against the wall. I encage her within my hold, pressing my hands against the wall on each side of her head. "If you belonged to me, it would be my job to give you everything you need. And want. I'd very much like to claim you."

"What does that mean? To claim me?"

"It's me saying you're mine and no one else's. I take responsibility for you and your well-being. Physically—I'll keep you safe. Financially—I'll take care of everything you need and want. You won't work because I'll see to all your expenses." She gave me her virginity. I'm the only man to ever have her. I plan to keep it that way. "Sexually, we've already worked that one out. I'm the only man you'll give yourself to and vice versa. I won't be with other women."

"It sounds like a formal arrangement. Is this a well-known practice observed by The Fellowship?"

"Yes, but ours would be a little different. You're an outsider so you wouldn't be an acceptable consort for me to claim. We'd be forced to keep it a secret from the brothers, except for Jamie and Leith."

"I'm feeling very discriminated against right now."

"It's a rule put in place to prohibit us from going outside the conglomerate to find romantic relationships. It's necessary to enforce, but I know your intentions. The Fellowship need not fear you."

"I suppose I'm not very threatening." She laughs.

"Not so much."

"You said you'd protect me? Is there a reason I need protection?"

"I recall you having an issue with grabby hands and I resolved that for you."

"We solved that problem together."

"Okay, I'll give you that one."

"Financially. I might have a problem with that one. I don't like feeling like I'm not making my own way."

"Then you can do some freelance photography if you like."

"You mentioned taking care of me sexually. It's part of claiming?"

"I enjoy having you in my bed. I'd like you to be in it every night."

"That sounds like you're asking me to move in."

She catches on quickly. "I am."

"We've spent one night together."

"I don't care. I want you there."

She's silent.

"Say yes."

"I don't know. What if I snore or do things that irritate you?"

"You won't." I kiss the side of her face. "Say. Yes. Bonny Bleu."

"I love hearing you call me that."

"If you move in, I'll call you bonny every night."

"I may only be here a few more weeks if things are wrapped up with Aunt Edy's estate."

"Then spend those remaining days with me."

She bites her lip and squeezes her eyes. "You're being very persuasive." She begins nodding. "I guess we can give it a try. Maybe we won't kill one another."

"Perfect. Pack what you need for tonight and I'll send Sterling for the rest of your things tomorrow."

"You never told me what we were doing today."

"We're meeting Leith and Jamie at the gym."

She puts her hands on her hips. "You want to take me to work out?"

Bleu has an incredibly fit body. "Definitely not. The three of us box, been doing it since we were lads. I thought you might enjoy watching."

"Nice. I wouldn't mind seeing a little friendly battle of swinging fists. I might even join in."

I hope she's kidding. "No way I'm letting you in the ring with those dickheads."

She's grinning. "You think I'll get hurt?"

I think Jamie and Leith would be too damn scared to touch a hair on her head. "No, it's not fitting to put a woman in the ring with a man."

She looks offended. "Really?"

"There's no match. You're at least sixty pounds lighter than any one of us."

"I can throw a pretty fast punch. My opponent never sees it coming." She sounds as though it's something she does on a regular basis.

"Today, you observe." I say it as though I might let her get into the ring at some point in the future, but that'll never happen while she's with me.

She grins as she folds a blouse and stuffs it into her bag. "We'll see."

Jamie and Leith are already in the ring when we arrive. They stop midfight to ogle us. This should be fun.

Jamie and Leith know there are things going on between Bleu and me, but I expect both to be completely shocked when I tell them I've claimed her.

"Hello, boys," Bleu calls out as we walk past. She grins up at me and whispers, "You haven't told them we've been spending time together, have you?"

"No."

"Then this shouldn't be at all awkward." She looks at Leith and then back to me. "Are you planning to tell Leith about us while you're in the ring together?"

Ah. I think she at least suspects he's into her. "Aye, and I'm telling him I've claimed you as well."

"Why would you do it like this?"

"Leith has a thing for you. If I tell him while we're wearing the gloves, he can get pissed off and vent so we can get back to good. It's how we work."

"You're going to let him punch you because you won me?"

"Hell, no. He'll have to earn a hit on his own, but by getting in the ring together, I'm giving him the opportunity. He wouldn't come by it otherwise."

She nods. "I get it."

"You'd be the first woman."

She smiles. "Have you yet to understand that I'm not like other females?"

"I figured that out the day we met."

Bleu sits on the bench as I approach the ring. "You didn't mention you were bringing anyone," Jamie says.

I climb into the enclosure. No need to discuss who my opponent will be—Leith steps into the role without a word. He slams his gloves on top of mine. "Let's do this."

Jamie moves to the corner. "Something going on that I don't know about?" He's confused. That means Leith hasn't confided in Jamie about Bleu.

"No. Sin's fucked me over again," Leith says. "But that's nothing new."

Completely untrue. "I didn't fuck you over."

"Says the mate who's with the girl I wanted."

"She isn't interested."

"She didn't have a chance to be. You made sure of that."

"Bleu met you before me. She'd be with you if she wanted to be."

"Hello? Right here, guys," Bleu calls out. "I can hear everything you're saying."

I stop foot working and bobbing. "Hit me, Leith. You'll feel better so just do it and get it over with."

"Not with a sucker punch. I'm going to beat you fair and square."

"We've never done anything fair and square in our lives." I resume the defensive stance.

"Come on, mates," Jamie says. "You're both being arses."

"No, Jamie," I call out. I'm pissed off now. "My best pal wants a real fight so that's what he's getting."

I bob, dodging Leith's signature right jab. "When you goin' to learn that punch is predictable coming from you?"

Leith's an out-boxer fighter. That means he stays out of my reach because he knows when I hit, it's a potential knockout. He steps in and makes the identical punch again, landing it against my right cheek. I roll my shoulder upward and rub it against my face. Motherfucker, that hurt.

"I don't guess it's too predictable since you didn't see that one coming," he says, laughing.

He's slipping, a maneuver to evade my coming punch, but it's not enough to avoid the left uppercut I land against his jaw. "Just like you didn't see that one comin', pal."

I'm a brawler. I don't have the finesse or the footwork I had before my amputation but my strength is in the power of my punch. I win with knockouts. Hard ones.

He stumbles backward and shakes his head before stepping in too soon and taking a hook. He closes his eyes and I suspect it's because he's seeing stars. "Had enough yet, mate?"

He growls and charges, attempting to trap me in the clinch so I can't throw a straight punch, but it's me who pins his arms instead. The clinch isn't a strong defense position for me because of my amputation. He knows this so he's using it against me. He means to take me down in front of Bleu.

He uses his foot to sweep my prosthesis off balance. I go down hard and fast before he straddles me and begins punching. "Why do you always have to take everything I want? Every. Fucking. Time." I have no idea what he's talking about.

I have to defend myself so I flip him onto his back and land punch after punch against his face before Jamie grabs me beneath my arms and drags me away. "Stop!" he yells.

I stand and adjust my prosthesis so I can regain my balance. Bleu rushes to get between Leith and me, holding me at bay while looking at my nose. "That escalated quickly."

I feel warmth oozing down my face. I put my glove under my shirt and wipe it away. It's blood, as I suspected. "This is what we do when we have a problem." I lean around Bleu and look at Leith. "Except for the part where my best mate uses my prosthesis as a way to drop me in front of a lass." I wipe at the blood continuing to stream from my nose.

"She knows?" Jamie asks.

"If she didn't, she would after that cheap shot." I take my gloves off and pull my shirt over my head so I can use it to stop the bleeding. "By the way, Leith. Bleu won't be back to work for you at the bar."

"Why?" He looks at her. "Is he paying you to be his whore?"

Bleu spins around and the peacekeeper becomes the assailant. "Me and you. Gloves off."

"Don't be ridiculous. I'm not fighting you," Leith says, laughing.

"You don't mind insulting a woman but you're too much of a gentleman to hit one?" I recognize the stance Bleu takes and laugh inwardly. Leith is in deep shit. He has no idea he needs to take the defensive against Bleu, but he'll get no warning from me.

"Come on. You just saw what I'm capable of doing."

"I wasn't impressed." Bleu delivers a short-straight punch to Leith's chin, a hit he clearly wasn't expecting based on his reaction. "You want to know why I chose Muay Thai over the other forms of martial arts and kickboxing?"

Leith rubs his chin. "Damn, Bleu."

"Knee and elbow strikes are permitted." Bleu darts to Leith's side and spins before delivering a well-placed elbow strike to his ribs, sending him to his knees. "Just so you know … he isn't paying me to be his whore. He's claimed me."

CHAPTER ELEVEN

BLEU MACALLISTER

ONE NIGHT TOGETHER AND HE ASKS ME TO MOVE IN? I SUPPOSE MY VIRGINITY was a bigger asset than I anticipated. Who knew it would be so easy? But I won't mistake confidence for trust. Sinclair Breckenridge shared his secret because he would have no qualms about killing me if I even thought of talking.

I feel bad about what I did to Leith. But in my defense, he called me a whore. He shouldn't have done that. I'm certain it's a mistake he won't be making again. All ended well between us, though. He apologized, and I accepted. Water under the bridge as far as I'm concerned.

Sin looks at me frequently during the drive to his house. Sometimes it's my face but mostly my body. He has a hungry look in his eyes. It's the same one I've seen each time my tenacious side has made an appearance. A strong woman turns him on. That means I know what we'll be doing when we get back.

We barely make it through the front door before he pulls me into his arms. His mouth crashes into mine and it isn't gentle. He's made love to the virgin and now he wants to fuck the fighter.

I move my mouth down his neck and taste the salt. "God, you're sweaty."

"I was last night as well but I don't recall you minding."

He's shirtless, his saturated with red, and he has small traces of blood still around his nose and upper lip. "And you're bloody."

"So were you last night but I don't recall me holding it against you." He snickers.

"That was crude … and true."

He urges me to the sofa, forcing me to fall on it when he pushes me backward. "Who are you and where did you come from?" He's wearing a seductive grin so I know I'm safe. "I have a hard time believing a typical small-town girl from Tennessee would be a grand master in Muay Thai."

Rule number one: lies are like boomerangs. You better throw them out as hard and far as you can because they always eventually come back. "My uncle is an instructor."

He lowers himself to the sofa so he's lying on top of me. His mouth immediately goes for my neck. "He taught you well. You delivered that elbow strike with extraordinary precision. I was very proud." He's hard. I feel it pressed against my stomach.

"And very turned on."

"You can tell, aye?" He hovers above me and moves his mouth down my cheek. He puts his hand between my legs and rubs my crotch through my yoga pants.

I want to do it again but I haven't emotionally dealt with the actuality of what I've done with Sinclair. I loved every touch and sensation my body experienced last night—and then again early this morning after my nightmare.

When I awoke to him comforting me, I'd been dreaming of that night. He held me and stroked my hair, whispering in my ear, "I have you, Bonny. You're safe. It was just a bad dream."

He makes me feel feminine and desired. No other man has ever done that so I couldn't help myself. I had to have him again, so I was the one to initiate sex. And it was magnificent.

This is messed up. Sinclair isn't just any petty criminal; he's a killer. And a monster. He didn't kill my mother but he's the spawn of the man who did. I'm supposed to be sickened by his touch, so why am I desperate to have more of it?

Something must be terribly wrong with me.

We hear the sound of a shutting car door and look at one another.

"Seems you have a visitor." We rise to a sitting position as a knock sounds on the door.

"Aye, and whoever it is decided to come at a very inconvenient time," he groans. He goes to the window and draws the drape for a look. "This can't be good."

"Who is it?"

"My father."

Holy shit. I'm about to come face to face with Thane Breckenridge. "I can't be introduced to your dad looking like this." I won't meet him wearing yoga pants and a ponytail. I grab my bag from the floor and run toward the stairs. "I just need ten minutes."

He calls out my name but I don't acknowledge it. I'm afraid he'll tell me I can't meet Thane. "Okay. Make that fifteen."

I burst into Sin's bedroom and look at what I have in my bag. Not much. I could put on the dress I brought for tonight. That would catch his attention but it's not what I'm looking to do. I need Thane to look at me and see my mother. I want him to be reminded of what he did to Amanda Lawrence.

It won't be difficult to jog his memory. I have my mother's … everything. Thick chestnut hair, identical shade of steel-blue eyes. I got nothing from my biological father. I'm sure everyone would comment on how similar we look if she were still living. But she isn't. Thane made her an angel in the ground.

I completely expect him to be confused when he looks at me and sees my mother's face. He'll try to work it out in his head—how a young woman can look so much like a person he killed. Even if he suspected I was her daughter, Stella Lawrence is dead according to the forged death certificate.

The world wasn't so technologically advanced eighteen years ago. It was pretty easy to have me declared dead on paper since Harry knew all the right people to make it happen. He took extreme measures for my protection, going as far as having a headstone placed next to my mother's, so her killer would never return for me.

I'm still rummaging through my bag for something to wear when Sin comes into his bedroom. "Bonny, you can't meet my father."

"Why not?"

"I told you that The Fellowship won't approve of us being

involved with one another because you aren't one of us."

"Oh." I shrug and fold the blouse I was considering and return it to my bag. "I didn't think of that."

"I don't know how long I'll be. Perhaps you'd like to read in the study while I'm tied up. It's well stocked."

"I guess I can do that." I could, but I won't. I'll be formulating a plan to get to Thane. There's no way I'm going to be in the same house as my target and miss being introduced to him.

"Are you always so agreeable?" He embraces me and places a featherlight kiss on my temple.

"Never. I guess you just have a way with me." I return his embrace, my arms around his middle squeezing tightly. "I'll be here waiting when you're finished."

"We might have to take a rain check on spending the rest of the day together. It depends on what we decide to do about our problem."

Perfect. I know exactly how this will play out. "Do what you must."

I wait forty minutes and decide to put my plan into action. I place my bag on my shoulder and make my way toward Sin's office. I knock softly, waiting for him to tell me to enter, but he doesn't. Instead, he opens the door and stares at me. I did this knowing I was risking his wrath. Well, I think I have it. He looks furious.

"I'm sorry to be interrupting but I can see that you're very busy," I whisper. "I'm gonna go. We can do this another day when you aren't tied up with business."

"I don't want you to go," he murmurs. "I need another thirty minutes. Maybe forty-five."

His large frame is blocking my view of Thane but I hear him. "Sin, you didn't tell me you had a visitor. I'd like to meet your guest, son." His voice makes the hair stand up on the back of my neck.

Sin says nothing and opens the door the rest of the way so I may enter. Thane rises and turns to greet me. The shocked expression he's wearing sends chills down my spine.

He holds out his hand and I place mine inside his. I'm touching the finger that pulled the trigger of the gun that killed my mother. This hand is one of two that held a pillow over my face until I could no longer breathe. "I'm Thane Breckenridge."

I see where Sin gets his good looks. Father and son are very similar. I didn't realize that until now. I can imagine a younger Thane looking very much the way his son does today. For the first time ever, I can consider the reason my mother might have been having a relationship with this man. Despite the gray hair at his temples and crow's-feet around his eyes, he's very handsome. "It's a pleasure, Mr. Breckenridge. I'm Bleu MacAllister."

"Bleu," he whispers while studying my face. "You're American."

"Yes. I'm in Edinburgh to settle my late aunt's estate and final arrangements." He's blatantly staring at me. It's unnerving. "Is something wrong, Mr. Breckenridge?"

"You remind me of someone I once knew. The resemblance is uncanny." Perfect. He's seeing me just as I hoped he would.

"You know what they say—everyone has a twin somewhere."

"True, but it's more than your appearance. Your voice sounds just like hers. The accent is a dead ringer."

"She must have been southern." I laugh. "I hope I've spurred happy memories."

"Aye. I loved her very much." He could've said anything but that. He didn't love my mother. If he did, he wouldn't have killed her.

"It's good to know I don't bring up bad recollections for you." I adjust my bag on my shoulder. "My apologies, again. I didn't mean to interrupt your meeting." I look at Sin. "We'll try this again at a more convenient time."

I've planted the seed in Thane's mind. His head must be spinning about who I am and where I came from.

"Stay, Miss MacAllister." There's no request in the tone of Thane's voice. It's a demand. "Go change into something suitable for dining out. I'm taking you to lunch. I want to get to know the young lady in my son's life."

I look to Sin, as if to ask permission. He nods, not really able to go against his father's request. "I'd like that very much."

I turn to leave but stop because a picture frame captures my attention. It's the photo of me, the one he took from my apartment. It's sitting on the corner of his desk facing his chair—staring right at him while he works. He was telling the truth.

I've finished showering and I'm applying makeup when Sin comes into the bathroom and stands behind me. I line my eyes and smudge it, not looking up. "I'm not at all pleased with you. I specifically said you couldn't meet my father. I explained why and you ignored what I said."

I knew this was coming. I've made a huge problem for myself and now I must fix it. "I'm really sorry. I was going to quietly slip away but I was afraid you'd get angry if you found me gone without a goodbye."

"I need you to understand that there are boundaries you don't cross with The Fellowship. I'm pissing all over one of the most important ones by being with you."

"Do you want me to leave?" I try to look pouty since it seems to have struck his soft spot when I did it before.

"Of course not, but I need you to listen and do as I ask."

"You should know now I'm not very good at that."

"Then become good at it."

"I can do that for you." I turn and wrap my arms around his shoulders. I kiss him hard so he'll forget our quarrel.

He nips my bottom lip and pulls back just enough to look at my face. "I think I've figured out what you are."

I watch his eyes for any sign of my cover being blown. "And what have you decided?"

He's grinning so I relax. "A sorceress. You must be because you've enchanted my father."

I couldn't ask for better news. "How did I manage that? You were there and heard our conversation. I said nothing of consequence."

"Despite what you said, or didn't say, he's quite taken with you—as am I." He laughs. "If he wasn't waiting for us, I'd take you back to bed right now." He smiles before placing a kiss on the top of my head. "But he is."

I lift a brow, giving him a seductive look. "He won't be later."

"I'll remember that when we get home."

"I'm in the mood for a romantic tale. Tell me more about your

American." My elbow is propped on top of the table. My chin is resting on my palm and I attempt to appear dreamy-eyed.

He's grinning, as though his head is filled with fond memories. "Oh ... it was many years ago."

I'm not letting it go that easily. I want to hear what he has to say about my mother. "Let me guess. Your American girl came to Edinburgh as a tourist and you had a whirlwind romance before she returned home."

"No, it was nothing like that." He shakes his head. "I met her in the US while I was on business."

"Was your first meeting a romantic one?"

"It was anything but. She was my blackjack dealer. The pretty lass took me for twenty thousand dollars during a span of thirty minutes."

That can't be the reason he killed her. If so, she wouldn't have been having him over at our apartment on her nights off. "Wow, I bet that stung."

"It was the opposite. She mesmerized me. No other dealer had ever been capable of taking that amount of money from me. I wanted her to come to work for me."

"But she didn't?"

"No. She had a daughter she didn't want to uproot. A beautiful little girl named Stella." Until the day you yanked me from beneath my bed and pressed a pillow into my face.

"Where do they live? I should look her up when I get home."

"I wish you could. Amanda and her daughter were murdered eighteen years ago. It's still an unsolved case."

I gasp in horror. "That's terrible."

I hope Thane loses sleep tonight remembering my mother. I curse him to go mad working out how I can look so much like his lost love. And just when he thinks he has it all sorted, I'll be there holding the barrel of my gun to his temple. He's going to die the same way my mother did. It's only fitting.

CHAPTER TWELVE

SINCLAIR BRECKENRIDGE

Dad drops us at home after lunch and I feel I owe Bleu an explanation for my father's bizarre behavior—except I don't have one. I only know he's completely taken with her. And this is good. It means he isn't concentrating on her being an outsider, which triggers a thought in my mind. Dad was having an affair with a woman not within the circle of The Fellowship. Did the brothers know or did he keep it secret as I'm doing now?

"I feel like I should apologize for the way my father conducted himself today. I'm not sure why he felt compelled to continually talk of his lover and her daughter. I'm sorry if it made you ill-at-ease."

"I probably encouraged him with my questions. I shouldn't have pried, but I truly had no idea there was such a tragedy behind his love affair."

I remember how Dad would be in a pleasant mood when he came back from his trips to the US. I always assumed it was because business had gone well. Now that I know about this woman he loved, I'm guessing she was the reason. "I remember him grieving for her, the American."

"How so?"

"He returned from one of his trips and went MIA for days. No one knew where he was—not even Abram. I remember the brothers going crazy. They thought an opposing adversary got to him so he was assumed dead. There was lots of talk but I didn't know what to believe. I've never been so scared in all my life."

"Where did he go?"

"I never knew. But he was different when he came back. His drive was gone."

"How old were you when that happened?"

"Nine? Maybe ten?"

Thane was a married man when he was seeing my mom. I don't like the thought but I have to wonder if she knew he had a wife and children. "You don't seem upset for your mother."

"They've never cared for each other. She wouldn't be hurt by his relationship with another woman so why should I be?"

"I guess I thought maybe deep down, she loved him. Women can be that way."

She's never met Isobel Breckenridge. "Not my mother. Loving my father would require emotion I don't think she possesses."

"Those are strong words to say about one's parent."

My mother can be very harsh. It was difficult growing up with her as a mum. "She's indifferent to all of us—Dad, me, my brother, Mitch. The only person she ever cared for was my sister, Cara."

"You haven't mentioned a sister."

"She's gone."

"Oh. I'm sorry to hear that."

I still nearly become sick every time I think of what happened to my baby sister. "She was five years old when someone came into her room and smothered her. To this day, we don't know who." They used her favorite stuffed animal, a leopard-print cat, a gift for her birthday. She loved that thing so much.

Bleu suddenly becomes pale and fidgety. She seems heavily affected by hearing of Cara's death. "Is child killing a common practice in your world?"

I can't believe she would even think that. "Never! No one in The Fellowship condones the killing of a child. We aren't monsters, Bonny. None of us would harm a child. There's no place for that in my brotherhood."

"What does The Fellowship value most? Do they hold anything

dear?" I don't care for her tone. It implies she believes we have no feelings or emotions.

"Nothing means more to us than family and loyalty. We have codes concerning both that we don't break." Some believe our devotion is misguided because of the things we do and find acceptable, but I don't question the trust I have in my brotherhood.

"What would you do if you found out a comrade had harmed a child?"

"I'd kill him." No second thoughts.

"You'd do that even if it was someone you loved dearly?"

She has misjudged me. "We should become clear about one thing. I love no one dearly. But back to your question … I wouldn't hesitate if the circumstances warranted. It's my place to carry out swift justice."

"How many people have you killed?"

She should know she can't ask that. She'll need to learn she isn't privy to Fellowship information. "I'm not discussing that with you."

"Why not?"

Is it not obvious? "Because you aren't Fellowship."

"But you've told me other things."

"I've told you nothing of consequence. Admitting to murder is something entirely different. Don't forget I'm a lawyer. I'm intelligent enough to avoid incriminating myself."

"I don't ask because I'm going to run to the authorities. I know you'd kill me if I did."

"Aye. I would."

Bleu understands how I operate, yet she's still here. She isn't afraid of what might happen. I choose to believe that's because she isn't planning to be anything but trustworthy.

If I were capable of having feelings for a woman, I think I'd have them for Bleu. It's really too bad she'll be leaving sooner rather than later. I think I could see this thing between us going somewhere if she stayed.

This conversation needs a new direction. "Did you enjoy lunch?"

"I did. Your father was very charming toward me considering I'm forbidden fruit."

Of course there's the issue of The Fellowship but it felt like my father was understanding of my liaison with Bleu. I guess he would be since he's been there. "I feel good about Dad's reaction. He seemed encouraging. That's never happened with any woman."

"Why would he not urge you to have a relationship? I would think he'd want you to eventually marry and have children."

"I'm guessing they haven't been pushing for it because I'm still in my traineeship. Once I'm finished, I expect them to press for a marriage. They'll expect me to produce a son." That doesn't bring pleasant thoughts to mind.

"Then you may only have a few months of bachelorhood left. Do you have your eyes set on a lucky lady?"

"Not a one."

"Will your father choose a wife for you if you won't?"

"He might try, but I'd prefer to not marry at all if I have to live the way my parents did." I lace my fingers through Bleu's and squeeze. "I'm not attracted to weak women willing to give their bodies to men to get what they want. Most of The Fellowship women have been passed around by my brothers. I don't want to wonder how many of them have fucked my wife."

"I can see where that might be a turnoff."

"Aye, a huge one. But I have a new favorite turn-on—a woman who's only had me inside her."

"I'm happy you're pleased." She gets up from the couch and tugs on my hands. "Come to the bedroom with me. We'll see if I can please you again."

The shifting of the bed wakes Bleu when I move to the edge to put on my prosthesis. I don't usually apply it for a visit to the toilet but I'm not doing the naked hop in front of her.

She slides over and kisses my bare back. "Where do you think you're going? It's too early to get out of bed. "

"The toilet."

"Will you be coming back?"

It's already later than I usually sleep—but it's Saturday, so I don't have work today. "Do you want me back in bed with you?"

"I do but you probably shouldn't get any ideas about a morning shag. I fear my body is protesting your exploitation of it last night. I'm not feeling my best down there."

I wasn't rough with her at all since I suspected she could be sore. I'm surprised she's having discomfort. "The condoms may be irritating you. They do that sometimes." I turn on the lamp. "Let me have a peek."

I push her onto her back and she clamps her thighs closed. "No way. You can forget that."

"You may be having an allergic reaction."

"I don't need you to look at my stuff for me to be sure this kind of swelling isn't normal." Her face is pained as she wiggles. "What would you say if I told you I didn't want to use condoms anymore?"

I'm clean. She's clean, and infertile, so I guess it would be all right. We've sort of already been together without one anyway, if you count the first time when the rubber busted. "I guess it's okay if you're one hundred percent positive you won't get pregnant."

"I've been evaluated by more than one doctor and they all agree a pregnancy won't happen without extensive—and expensive—medical intervention."

I want to know what's wrong with her.

I guess wrong probably isn't the best term to choose. I wouldn't want her to say something wasn't right with me because I have an amputation. Infertility is a medical condition. It doesn't define her, just as this steel blade attached below my knee doesn't define me.

"I'm up for doing it bare if that's what you want."

"You've claimed me so I guess that negates the conversation about sexual monogamy." She quickly looks up at me. "That is absolutely nonnegotiable. Understand?"

I can't think of a lass I'd want after having her. "I told you I wouldn't be with another woman."

"I know that's what you said, but this is serious—like catching a disease kind of serious—so I feel like I need to stress the importance. Can you solemnly promise me there'll be no one else?"

I twist around so I can face her. I stroke my hand down her cheek before kissing her quickly. "Aye, I swear you'll be the only one."

I return from the toilet and remove my blade, the one I wear around the house, before getting back into bed. Bleu moves over to rest her head on my chest. She touches the inked pattern on the inside of my upper arm using her fingertips. "I love this pattern. What does it mean?"

"It's a Celtic shield knot. It's symbolic of protection."

"I thought it might be some kind of love knot you got for a girl," she giggles.

I'm pondering Bleu's romantic notion when my phone rings. I reach for it on the nightstand but feel compelled to clear her notions about my tattoo. "I assure you it wasn't inspired by romantic ideas such as that."

It's Abram. He never calls on the weekend so I'm guessing something has happened. Dammit. Whatever it is will tear me away from spending the day with Bleu. Another day is hijacked. "Aye."

"Your father tells me you have a lass, an American."

I should have known Dad would tell him. "Aye."

"I should meet the woman in the life of The Fellowship's future superior. Bring her to my house for dinner tonight at seven."

I wish I could refuse. "Of course."

"We've been invited to dinner at my uncle's."

"Your father's brother?"

"Aye, Abram."

"I heard his name a lot at the bar. Is he ahead of you in line to take over?"

He wishes. "Abram can never be in the head leadership role. He was adopted and only a blood Breckenridge can become sovereign."

"Was he adopted as a baby?"

"His parents were Fellowship but they were killed in a car accident. My granda always favored his father so he took Abram. I think he was around five."

"Does he have children?"

"He's Jamie's father. He also has two daughters, Westlyn and Evanna."

"Oh. Then y'all are cousins and best friends?"

"We are—known each other our entire lives."

"I haven't spent much time with Jamie. He doesn't come into Duncan's often."

"He used to but he's in the middle of his trainee rotation in trauma surgery. He stays busy with that and his studies."

I see the surprise on her face. "I didn't know Jamie was in medical school. Is he leaving The Fellowship?"

She doesn't understand the dynamics of our brotherhood. No one leaves The Fellowship, not alive at least. "No. Trustworthy physicians are few and far between. There's always an issue when a brother has an injury the infirmary is required to report to the authorities. You can see how that's a problem. The Fellowship decided to send one of our own for medical training and Jamie volunteered. When he finishes his traineeship, he'll come to work for us as a private physician. He'll never work a day for the public."

"You're being trained to criminally defend the brotherhood, Jamie will treat them medically when things go awry, and Leith will get them drunk. I do believe the three of you are the perfect trifecta."

Trifecta. That's the perfect word to describe us.

CHAPTER THIRTEEN

BLEU MACALLISTER

"YOU SHOULD PROBABLY EXPECT TO BE UNDER A MICROSCOPE." THIS IS MY warning to be prepared for a lot of probing.

"I understand why and I don't mind. I have nothing to hide." This is completely expected. "But you should know now that I'm not consenting to a body cavity search." Sterling stares ahead but I hear him cackle beneath his breath. I look forward and can see the reflection of his grin in the rearview mirror. "Do you blame me, Sterling?"

He's a man of few words. Or maybe no words. I don't believe I've ever heard him utter a single one, at least not to me. And he doesn't this time, either.

I'm a little concerned that Abram has such a say in Sin's life. "Your dad is leader. Shouldn't Abram accept me without further evaluation if Thane approves?"

"Ideally, yes. But Abram is a controlling bastard. He likes things done his way. It often creates a power struggle between him and Dad. In the end, my father is always in command and wins—but not until after being forced to flex his muscle."

Thane likes me very much. I hope it's enough for him to do some flexing.

Abram's home can easily be called a castle. The main house's exterior is weathered stone, much like most of the buildings you see in Edinburgh. I'm no real estate expert but it has all the classic architecture of a home built hundreds of years ago.

It's surrounded by lush green pasture. The air smells of freshly cut grass. And cleanliness. It's very different from what I'm accustomed to in Memphis.

We go into Abram's home and his expression is telling. He looks as though he's seen a ghost. That convinces me he at least knows what my mother looked like. I'd not given that much thought but it's likely he knew her as well.

Sin introduces me to Abram first. "My God. Thane was right. Your resemblance to Amanda Lawrence is uncanny."

"You've heard the old saying, 'like father, like son'? It often rings true." I'm guessing this woman looking me over is Thane's wife.

"This is my mother, Isobel," Sin says.

She's a very attractive woman with short, bright red hair styled in a pixie cut. Her eyes are vivid blue. I'm instantly reminded of Sharon Osbourne. At first glance, I see no part of her in Sin but then I notice something around her eyes that reminds me of him.

"It's lovely to meet you, Mrs. Breckenridge." I'm expecting her to be a hard one to win over.

"The pleasure is all mine, dear." She seems very pleased by my presence, maybe even exceedingly so. I didn't expect a warm welcome considering the things Sin has told me about her.

I'm introduced to Abram's wife and then the six of us go into the formal dining room. Despite the age of their home, the interior is modern and filled with exquisite furnishings. My surroundings could pass for those belonging to royalty. It makes me sick to think of the people who have suffered or been killed so they can live in this manner.

Abram pulls out the chair next to the head of the table. "Please do me the honor of sitting next to me, Miss MacAllister."

I look to Sin, unsure if it's what he'd have me do. He nods his approval so I take the seat. I have two of the most notorious criminals in Scotland sitting to my right and directly across the table. I'll be questioned and ogled by them both. That shouldn't be at all stressful.

Abram allows the first course to be served before he begins his cross-examination. "How old are you, Miss MacAllister?"

Sin sighs loudly, displaying his annoyance. "Not this again."

I put my hand on his knee beneath the table. "It's okay. I don't mind." I look at Abram. "Twenty-five."

"The same age as Amanda's daughter would have been. That's a very unlikely coincidence. Wouldn't you agree?"

"I wouldn't know." I shrug and return to my soup.

"Allow me to address all the concerns and questions you might have, Uncle," Sin says. "I understand Bleu has an uncanny resemblance to Amanda Lawrence but she didn't know her or her daughter. She would have been a young child when they were killed, so please stop harassing her about something she knows nothing about." Sin's drawn a line in the sand by expressing his loyalty to me. It'll be interesting to see the shit this stirs.

Isobel clears her voice. "My son is right. And I'm sure Miss MacAllister is nervous enough without you performing an inquisition, Abram. Leave her be."

Sin looks at his mother as though he has no idea who she is.

I wait until Thane and Abram aren't looking to mouth "thank you" at Isobel. She gives me a kind smile followed by a single nod.

I don't think she's the woman Sin claims her to be. I believe I could find an ally in her. It's definitely worth a try since she may very well hate Thane as much as I do.

It's after two in the morning when Sin's phone comes to life on the nightstand. "Aye ... okay ... I'll be there in twenty."

The bed moves when he rolls toward me. "Bonny Bleu." He spoons me from behind and kisses my neck. "I have to go out for a while."

"Mmm ... hmm."

He nuzzles my neck with his facial hair. It tickles. "Did you hear me, Bonny? I have to leave."

"I heard you." My voice is slow and lazy.

"I probably won't be back before morning."

"'Kay."

The mattress shifts. I hear rustling in his closet, followed by water running. I don't think he's even trying to keep the noise to a minimum. But I'll forgive him. He isn't accustomed to having a woman in his bed.

I get up and slip my robe on over its matching gown. I stand in the doorway with squinted eyes watching Sin slip into his shoulder harness.

Some women love a man in a uniform. I have a fondness for ones who pack heat—especially in gun harnesses. It's even hotter when he's exacting justice for a crime that would otherwise go unpunished. I can't help it. It's my thing.

"What's happened?"

"The daughter of a Fellowship member was taken from her bedroom tonight. The lass was beaten and raped. She's in surgery right now to fix what they did to her."

That's sickening. "Oh God. Who would do such a thing?"

"One of our rivals has claimed responsibility. It was an act of retaliation." For what?

"What are you going to do about it?"

He stands straight and tightens his harness. "They harmed one of mine. It's worse because she's a child. The doctors can fix her physical injuries but she's probably emotionally ruined forever. It's my place to avenge the wrong."

His words strike a chord with me as my heart goes out to a child I don't know. "A revenge kill is over too quickly and yields far too little satisfaction. They need to suffer before they die."

"I strongly suspect you may have a vengeful side that rivals my own. You're host to a very dark companion inside your head." He comes to me and pushes my hair from my face. He cups my cheeks in his palms and stares at me. "You've never said so but I know something bad has happened to you. I'd like it very much if one day you'd lift the veil and allow me to know what has made you the way you are."

What kind of person does he believe I am?

He passes his thumb over my bottom lip. "What do you find a suitable torture for men who would do this?"

He's putting me on the spot. "I'm not sure the means, but it would involve the loss of a highly valued appendage."

"And you could do this?"

"For child rapists, yes."

"Aye. I believe you would." He smiles and kisses my forehead. "This isn't the right time but there's potential for you joining me another night."

He pulls me close and squeezes.

"Come back to me safely." I sound like a wife sending her husband off to war. At least I think I sound pretty damn convincing.

"I shall." He slaps my ass cheek. "Back to bed with you, bonny one. Sleep in if I haven't returned by morning. I want you ready and waiting for me when I get home."

"I'm still not back to normal."

A mischievous grin spreads. "You don't have to be for what I have in mind."

He kisses me one last time as he's leaving. I lock the door behind him before returning to an empty bed. I turn onto my side and grab his pillow, hugging it. Sleep doesn't find me because I'm worried about his safety.

I shouldn't care if he lives or dies? But I do.

I lie in bed tossing and turning for at least two hours before I hear Sin return. That was much faster than I anticipated. I didn't think he'd be back until the sun was up.

I don't want him to know I've been lying in his bed worrying about him, so I pretend to be asleep. I listen to his footsteps coming nearer as he approaches me from behind. Perhaps he means to slip into bed without waking me since it's still the middle of the night. But something isn't right. I've come to know his gait. He's nearly mastered a perfect one without a limp—almost. The stride I'm hearing now doesn't belong to him.

So I wait. This predator is unaware he's about to become the prey.

His footsteps stop. My gut tells me this is my one and only chance to strike before my brain gets bedazzled with a shiny lead slug. I spin around and sweep my arm through the air, knocking what I assume is a handgun from his grasp.

The shadow in the dark pushes me to the bed and grabs at my throat. He's going for my air supply but he's unaware no one will ever suffocate me again.

I'm calm and collected when I place my soles against his chest and shove. I get to my feet and stand on the bed, waiting for him to advance again. I listen carefully and deliver a straight foot thrust into his throat, causing a temporary spasm in his trachea. The convulsion will clench his throat closed and he won't be able to breathe. He'll feel as though he's suffocating and I'll have less than thirty seconds before it functions normally again.

I tuck his head beneath my armpit. I clamp my arm around his neck so my forearm is pressed against his spasming throat and I squeeze. I wrap my leg around his midsection with body scissors and arch backward, pulling his head forward, stretching his torso and neck. "Who sent you?"

No answer. But of course, I do have him in a chokehold while his throat is contracted. "Can't answer, huh?"

I let up lightly. "The good news is that your throat is going to open again in about ten seconds. The bad news is that I'm cutting off your air supply and you won't be able to breathe even when your trachea stops spasming."

He's fighting against me but I have a death grip on him. "I'm going to ask one more time. Who sent you?"

He bucks backward and hits his skull against my cheek. He isn't talking and if I let him up, he's going to kill me. It's kill or be killed. Of that, I have no doubt so I squeeze until he stops fighting.

I'm physically spent and shaking so badly I can't get up from the floor. I manage to reach over to feel for a pulse and confirm there's nothing. I lie there motionless for a moment because my muscles are too weak to carry me anywhere.

Shit. The room is in a shambles and there's a dead body lying in Sin's bedroom. I'm not really sure what he's going to say when he returns from his kill and finds that I've done the same thing—inside his home.

I sit and wait because there's nothing else to be done.

As promised, it's morning before Sin returns. I'm sitting in the chair when he comes into the bedroom. He sees the body on the floor and looks more like a frightened animal than the untouchable organized crime boss he's destined to become. "I was lying in bed when he attacked me from behind. Sorry about the room."

He strides across and pulls me from the chair. He holds me in his arms and squeezes tightly. "Are you hurt?"

"You can't hurt a steel magnolia."

He embraces me for a while before taking his phone from his pocket to make a call. "There's been an incident at my flat. I need a cleanup immediately."

I guess this is how they do it. No authority. No crime scene investigation. No evidence.

"I want you to take your things into the guest room and have a long, hot shower. Clear your thoughts and when you've finished, go into my office and wait for me. I'll come to you after this is taken care of."

He's protecting me. He doesn't want anyone to know I'm here or that I did this. "Okay."

I take my time in the shower because I know that mess won't be clear anytime soon. I stand under the falling water and wish the memories of the night would wash away, but it isn't possible.

I've killed before. It too wasn't by choice. I know all too well that the feelings to follow won't go away with the snap of a finger—or a shower.

I go into Sin's office after my shower per his instruction. His music library is open on his computer, so I scroll through his tunes and find a song titled "A Little Death" by The Neighbourhood. It seems a fitting song for the situation. It's slow and seductive, nothing as I expected. I like it.

I'm sitting on Sin's desk with my back to the door when I hear it close. I turn and watch him come toward me. I recognize that hungry look again. He stops, standing between my parted knees. He puts his hands on the outer sides of my bare thighs beneath my simple cotton dress and glides his palms upward.

He's showered. His hair is wet and he smells of cologne. I wonder if his cleansing cleared his mind of the things he did last night. Mine certainly didn't.

His eyes trail down my neck and he lowers his mouth to place a kiss there. "These bruises will disappear with time and it will be as though it never happened. I've taken care of everything. This will never come back to you."

He's made the night's unfortunate events disappear. I'm not certain if his motive is to protect me or himself, but I'm inclined to think all of this is directly related to the feelings he's developing for me.

"I like the way this feels—you shielding me from harm."

"I promised you I would protect you." He strokes his thumb over my cheekbone, the one my attacker hit when he slammed his head against my face. There was a large purple bruise developing beneath the skin when I examined myself earlier.

I'm surprised by how arousing it is for him to take care of me. "I'd like to withdraw a pledge I made. I once said I would never allow anyone to fuck me across a desk, but I think this is a very different kind of circumstance. I'd like it very much if you'd have me right here and now."

He grasps my hips and slides me closer to the edge of the desk. He presses his body into mine and I feel how hard he already is. "Ask and you shall receive."

I glide my hands up his arms as his mouth meets mine. He holds the backs of my knees and bends them, bringing my legs to wrap around his waist. He presses his groin against me, hard.

His mouth abandons mine to move down my neck as he palms one of my breasts in a circular motion. My nipples grow hard.

I really want to be out of this dress. It's in the way so I grab the bottom and drag it over my head, throwing it onto Sin's office chair. He echoes my motion by removing his shirt. I slide my panties down as he pushes his trousers to the floor. I unfasten my bra while he gets out of his pants. It's perfect timing on both of our parts.

He pats the desk. "I want you right here."

I scoot back onto my assigned seating, legs dangling. He sits in his chair and rolls toward me. "This is my office and I'm a busy man, Miss MacAllister. I have a lot of work to do." He puts his hand between my breasts and drags it down my chest and stomach until his fingers threaten to touch me, but don't.

Does he want me to ask him to touch me? Because I will.

"Lie back, bonny one."

I'm lowering my upper body onto the desk when he grasps my feet and pushes my legs back and apart. I tremble with an impatient desire to be touched. I anticipate his fingers entering me at any second. But they don't. I'm considering begging when he moves my legs so they're draped over his shoulders, his head between my legs. My mind hardly has time to register what he's about to do when I feel the flutter of his tongue. I jolt, just as I did the first time he touched me there.

I could have never guessed it would feel like this. Just as I grow accustomed to one motion and rhythm, he stops and changes to a completely different speed and direction. It's a guessing game as to what he'll do next and how it will feel. I only know he's going to bring me to orgasm very soon.

Sin inserts his fingers and slides them in and out while he uses his mouth to form a suction over my clit. I instinctively lift my hips from the desk in a rhythmic, rocking motion. My back arches and I tense when the quivering begins in my pelvis. He sucks harder and it's almost more than I can stand. "Ohh … uhh."

My body shudders around his fingers, squeezing them. My womb flutters rhythmically for several seconds before it's finished and a pulsating warmth spreads through my body. I tingle in my face, hands, and feet.

Sin comes up to hover above me so he can see my face. "I hope that was good for you."

"The best ever." I repeat the words he said to me the night he took my virginity.

"Good. I want it to always be the best." He grins and grabs my hands to help me to a sitting position. "Can I kiss you?" I nod—not understanding why he thinks he'd need to ask. But then I understand his meaning when he brings his mouth to mine. Hmm … I'm not sure I'm crazy about that, but I suppose it's tolerable considering the orgasm he gave me.

The song ends and another begins. This one I recognize. "You like Pearl Jam?"

"Aye."

"Me too." The song emanates an entirely different feeling.

"Sirens" plays as Sin's hands glide up my thighs and bring them around his waist again. He's moving back and forth, his erection rubbing against me. "The last thing you told me was no more condoms."

"Mmm … hmm."

"Is that still what you want?"

I grab his face and bring it to mine so we're eye to eye. "That's exactly how I want you."

"I'll never deny you of the things you want." He situates himself at my entrance. "I've claimed you. That means it's my job to give you everything you want." He pulls my hips against him as he enters me. I put my arms up over his shoulders and press my body to his while moving with him.

Skin on skin. I'm not experienced but even I recognize the difference. It's a more pleasurable feeling but it's so much more than that. I feel a kind of connection I didn't experience the other times. I gave a part of myself to Sinclair Breckenridge before. Now, he's taking all of me.

He moves his fingers to where we become one and massages the sensitive spot above our connection. I press my forehead to his, holding on for dear life.

"Look at me, Bonny Bleu." He slows his pace and our eyes are locked. "Into me … you see. Say it with me."

"Into me … you see," we repeat together. I have no idea what it means but I like the way it makes me feel to say it with him.

"I'm going to come." His entire body tenses when he thrusts one last time. He's deep inside me when I feel his body shudder. "Ohh … "

When he's finished, he presses his forehead to mine. We're both grinning. "I hope that was good for you."

"The best ever," he says, laughing. He pulls out and sits in his chair, patting his leg. "Sit in my lap."

I sit and put my arm over his shoulder. His hand is on my back, rubbing small circles into the muscle. "What was that?"

"A magnificent orgasm."

"I mean the into me … you see thing."

He leans his head back against the chair and caresses my cheek as he looks at me. "Intimacy means into me … you see."

Oh, I see the association now.

"It's the private and intimate part of the claiming. You say it during moments you feel closest to your partner."

"Only during sex?"

"Doesn't have to be. You can say it whenever you're feeling especially connected."

Saying those words together was profound. It felt comparable to allowing him into my heart. He breeched the walls of the fortress surrounding it, the one I built to keep everyone in my life at a safe distance.

But I don't feel distance between us. It's as though it never existed.

That isn't part of the plan.

CHAPTER FOURTEEN

SINCLAIR BRECKENRIDGE

I BARGE INTO THE CONFERENCE ROOM AND FIND DAD AND ABRAM ALREADY waiting for me. I don't greet either because I'm not in the mood for pleasantries. I'm mad as hell. "Which one of you did it?"

I see the puzzled expression on my father's face and know immediately who the culprit is.

"It was me," Abram admits.

"What did you do?" Dad asks.

I'm not at all surprised to discover last night was Abram's doing. I'm glad to learn my father wasn't party to this. I'm not sure how I might have handled a stab in the back like that from him.

"Abram sent me out on Fellowship business last night. While I was away, he ordered Malcolm to come into my home and go after something that belongs to me."

"Tell me my son's mistaken."

Abram ignores my father, as he often does. "Since when does the American belong to you?"

He is asking if I've claimed her but I purposely do not respond. "What you did can be considered a betrayal."

"You should select your words very carefully, Sinclair." He's pointing his finger at me. "Betrayal is a strong accusation."

"What would you have me call it?"

"Investigation. But since you're the one bringing up disloyalty, what about your involvement with her? She's an outsider. You don't consider that a form of treachery to your brotherhood?"

I don't acknowledge his allegation against me. "You sent Malcolm after Bleu. How can you call that investigation?"

Abram gets up from his chair. I know his tactics well. This is a maneuver intended to intimidate. It places him above me so he may talk down—but it won't work. I will not concede. "A girl from who knows where inserts herself into our world. She sways her arse and you go completely stupid. Have you not considered that she's been planted among us by our enemy?"

"Of course I have. I'm not a fool. I did my own private investigation the moment I knew she'd been hired by Leith. We ran her prints and found nothing. I did a sweep of her place and a web search. Everything pans out. She's clean. I've looked from every angle."

"What about the matter of her looking like Amanda Lawrence? That's no coincidence."

"Are you never going to be able to move beyond Bleu's resemblance to her? Amanda Lawrence is DEAD! Her daughter is DEAD! You have to get over this fixation you have with them!" It's madness.

"I'm telling you this is no coincidence. Someone handpicked her and she's here to destroy us."

"Bleu is one person, not an army or coalition. She doesn't have the power to destroy us. If you'd stop for one damn second and think rationally about this, you'd realize you're wrong about her."

"I'm not mistaken."

"Then we must agree to disagree. Unless concrete evidence proves I'm wrong, I won't allow you to send anyone else to execute her." And what was he thinking doing that in my home?

"I didn't send Malcolm to kill her. His assignment was to scare the lass into admitting who she is and why she's here." I'm not sure I believe him.

"You should've been clearer with your instructions because that isn't what happened. He attacked her while she was sleeping." I can't tell him Bleu killed Malcolm. It will only arouse more suspicion. "I came home and found them struggling. It was dark so I had no idea it was a brother."

"What did you do?"

"He's dead."

"And so it begins," Abram sneers. "Don't you see? We've lost a good brother because of her."

"We lost Malcolm because you sent him into my home behind my back. This one is on you."

"Mark my words. That girl's lying in wait. She's the devil in his most beautiful form and she's here to sabotage us."

"I'm warning you, Abram." Now it's my finger pointing at him. "Don't send anyone else after her."

"Or what, Sinclair? You'll kill me? You'll choose a stranger over your own family?"

"Enough!" my father growls. "No one in this family is killing another member."

"I saw the way you looked at her, Thane. You have a soft spot for that lass because she reminds you of Amanda."

Abram's obsessed with Bleu's likeness to Amanda Lawrence. I'm afraid he won't be over it soon.

"Bleu reminds me of a happy time in my life but it doesn't blind me to the risk she poses. And my son isn't a fool. He'll take the proper action if needed."

Abram must understand he doesn't get to deliver the verdict on Bleu. "You come to me if you have any further concerns about her and I'll be the one to take care of them. Not you."

"Do tell, Sinclair … what will you do if you find she's not who she claims to be?"

There's only one way to deal with a betrayal such as that. "Then it'll be my place to kill her."

He looks pleased. "When the time comes—and it will—The Fellowship and I will hold you to that."

"If she's working for the enemy, I won't hesitate."

"It's good to know she hasn't completely impaired your judgment."

I'm not telling Bleu that Abram sent a brother after her. It's better she believes Malcolm was an intruder coming for me. There's also no need for her to know my uncle suspects she's an informant.

I want to keep things exactly as they are. I've secretly claimed Bleu so she's my responsibility. If her presence becomes a problem, I'll be the one to deal with it.

It's peculiar how quickly one can become accustomed to the presence of another in their home. I enjoy having Bleu here—but she won't stay forever. I'm slightly regretful about ending her employment at the bar. She's free to spend her days tending to her aunt's final arrangements while I'm working. That means she'll return home sooner than I'd like. I'm not pleased about that prospect. I've become attached to her in a short time. I didn't think it was possible.

I'm sitting in the living room sipping a whisky and listening to Violin Sonata no. 9 when Bleu arrives home. She comes through the door carrying two armfuls of bags and I recall her telling me she'd be going by the market. I'd forgotten about her cooking dinner for me tonight—something southern.

I move to get up. "I'll get those for you."

"No, I'm good. Nice song choice."

She stops by for a quick kiss on her way to the kitchen. "Hi."

"Hi." She giggles and looks at the drink in my hand. "Rough day?"

"Aye, my leg was giving me a little trouble but it's much better now."

"Would it help if I rubbed it for you?"

"I'm good but I might take you up on that offer another time."

I follow her into the kitchen. I've missed my Bonny Bleu today. "Were you able to find everything you need?"

"It was a struggle." She sighs. "I'm used to huge stores where they sell everything plus a kitchen sink. There's only small markets in this area, which I guess is okay since I can't carry a shit ton of groceries home anyway."

"Sterling can drive you to a bigger supermarket."

"I bought enough for a few days. Maybe he can take me toward the end of the week if we run low."

She's unloading the bags so I help. "I was thinking about

something today. Would you consider staying in Edinburgh once you've settled your aunt's estate?"

"Hmm … let me think about this one. I don't work. I get to do what I want all day and then have great sex every night. Living the life of a claimed woman is tough stuff." She laughs. She closes the cabinet and looks at me. "Oh. You're not kidding."

"I'm very serious."

She leans against the countertop and crosses her arms. "I don't know. It's not something I've considered."

"What if I told you I want you to stay?" I ask.

"I'd be taken by surprise."

"But you wouldn't say no?"

"It's something I'd have to think about. I have a family to consider. And a business with a lot of financial responsibility tied up in it."

I go to her and hold her face in my hands. "Think about it. For me." I kiss the top of her head. "I'll take care of you. That includes any debt you've incurred in your business." She opens her mouth to speak. I suspect she's going to argue so I place my finger over her lips. "Nothing would change. You'd still do as you please each day. And I'd do as I please each night." She grins at the last part. "But babies and brides need to be photographed in Edinburgh as well. Bleu Mac's Photography would fit in quite well if you wanted to work."

"I'll think about it."

"Perfect. Are you getting closer to finalizing the estate?" I could've assisted her and had the proper paperwork done a week ago, but I didn't want to speed the process.

"Yes. Maybe another week."

"Then you don't have long to sort out what you want to do."

"No, seven days isn't long when you're considering a decision like this. But even if I decide to stay, I can only visit a total of six months on a passport and visa."

"I want as many days as possible with you." I sweep a stray hair from her face. "I can think of nothing worse than having an ocean between us," I say.

"The last few weeks have been the best of my life." She presses her palm to my face. "Is this that thing people call happiness?"

"I think it could be." But if it's not, I believe this is the closest I'll ever get.

I leave Bleu in bed every morning when I get up for work but today is different. She's up and I'm surprised when she comes into the shower with me. "Why are you awake so early?"

"I have something to do today." I don't recall her mentioning plans. I guess something with the estate fell through. Good. I want to keep her here as long as possible. It's a reminder her days with me could be winding down.

Unless there's a problem with selling the flat, she'll no longer have it to deal with after next Friday. That's when she'll have a decision to make—pack her remaining things to bring here or ship them to the US.

"Did something go wrong with the flat's buyer?"

"No. Everything is fine with the sale," she says. "I'm meeting your mother in an hour. We're going shopping together."

Surely, I didn't understand her correctly. "You're doing what with whom?"

"You heard me."

"How did this come about?"

"I decided I should make an effort to bond with her since I'm going to be living with her son for an indefinite amount of time."

"That's a clever way to tell me you've decided to stay."

"I thought so."

"You hadn't mentioned it since I asked, so I was expecting you to leave next week."

"I get this ache in my chest every time I think about leaving. The closer next week comes, the worse the pain gets."

"You don't know how happy you've made me, Bonny Bleu." I don't have the words to tell her. But I can show her.

CHAPTER FIFTEEN

BLEU MACALLISTER

My reason for shopping with Isobel today is twofold. I want to know more about what makes Sin tick, but I'd also like to get close to her. If she's my friend and confidante, I'll be invited into her home—the one she shares with Thane. That is where I plan to kill him and make it look as though an adversary is responsible.

I'm not stupid. I know I'm being surveyed and analyzed but it's because I'm a suspected informant. They have no idea I am the actual adversary. Even after Thane is dead, they still won't know. That's why I've had no qualms about using my real name. They're idiots, giving too little credit to women and their capabilities, so I'll never be suspected as a skilled assassin.

"What about this one?" I run my hand over the soft pewter comforter. "It's not a feminine color but the detail and embellishments on the throws make up for that. I think it would be beautiful against the wall color."

"What color 'tis that?"

"Soft blue." I see a comforter almost identical to his walls so I point it out. "Very similar to this except a wee more on the steel-blue side."

"I agree. The platinum set would be lovely."

"I think so too." I catch the attention of the sales clerk. "I'll take this one in a king. I want it just as it's displayed with all the throws." I remember the sheets ruined on the first night I spent with Sin. "And add an extra set of linens."

Isobel and I stroll through the home department while we wait for the sales associate to return with my purchase. "Has Sin told you how I came to be married to Thane?"

Isobel's accent is much stronger than Sin's. I'm not sure why. I sometimes have difficulty making out some of her words.

"He said his grandfathers arranged your marriage for a stronger Fellowship."

"Tis true. I was born into this role. I didn't have a choice, but you are free to choose any man in the world."

I'm not sure where she's going with this. I say nothing.

"My son is cut from the same cloth as his father. Thane took him from me when he was a bairn, so I was unable to have a say in molding him into the man he is today. I wasn't kiddin' when I said like father, like son. They're both monsters."

She's right about one of them. "Sin is not a monster." I'm angry so I begin walking away but stop and turn back to look at her. Without thinking, I point my finger at her. "Never say that to me again."

She smiles, as though she likes my reaction. Was she testing me? "Ye already have feelings for him. Are ye in love?"

"I think I could find it very easy to be." It grows easier every day.

"Do ye think he's in love with ye?"

I'm not sure Sin is capable of such things. "I don't think so."

"He will be. But there's something ye should know about being with a Fellowship leader. Being in love is a double-edged sword for my son. Whoever hears him say 'I love ye' is condemned. Loving ye will make him vulnerable and he'll come to despise ye for that reason."

Is that what happened between my mother and Thane? He loved her but she became his weakness so he killed her? I don't believe that's it. He could've walked away so much easier.

I finish my purchase and we're returning to Isobel's car. "I like ye, Bleu. That's why I feel prompted tae warn ye. I wasn't trying tae be cruel or vindictive toward ma son. I love him verra much." Sin doesn't know that.

"I think you'd be surprised to learn how much he's told me."

"Fallin' in love with Sin 'tis a mistake because ye don't understand about oor world. Once ye come tae know oor ways, it'll be too late tae get oot." She hesitates before getting into the car. "I'd really like us tae be friends—but I dinnae think we can be if I bring this up again—so I won't. I'll keep ma gob shut. Does that sound fair?"

"Yes, thank you. I'd appreciate that."

I enjoyed my day with Isobel. She turned out to be a fun lady when she wasn't trying to convince me I shouldn't be with Sin. Her heart was in the right place, so I have to give her props for looking out for my best interests. And I think the impasse means she won't lecture me anymore.

I beat Sin home so I go into the master bedroom to change the bedding. I want him to be surprised when he sees how inviting it is. I'm almost positive he'll like it. Regardless, I'm certain he'll enjoy breaking it in. As will I.

We may not be in love but we are most certainly in lust. Sometimes it feels like we can't get enough of one another. Being with him is crazy good. I never imagined I could want someone so much. I wonder if it's like this for everyone. It can't be. People would never leave their houses if it was.

Playing the part of Sin's lover isn't a bad way to bide my time until I'm able to get close enough to kill Thane. But I must never forget the mission. I may need a reminder from time to time so I don't lose focus.

Sin texted earlier and said he'd be home by ten, so I shower and shave my legs twice. I apply my favorite body lotion and then put on the new black silk nightgown and matching robe I purchased today.

It's nine forty-five when I stretch across our new bedding to wait for him. Ten comes and no Sin. By eleven, I'm annoyed. By midnight, I'm worried, so I text. No response. I consider calling but I'm sure he's tending to Fellowship business. I don't wish to irritate him or look like the bothersome girlfriend.

I bet Lorna knows if something is going on. You hear a lot working in a bar full of Fellowship members.

I dial her number. One ring goes through before I hear the front door open and close, so I end the call before she can answer. I rush over to the bed and resume my seductive pose.

A moment later I hear voices—what sounds like several of them—coming up the hallway toward the bedroom. I go into panic mode. I slide across the bed toward the nightstand drawer where Sin keeps his handgun when the door bursts open. Two men carry Sin to the bed. His shirt is saturated with blood, concentrated on his right shoulder. "My God! What happened?"

I move off the bed just in time for Sin to plop on it and fall backward. "I've gone and got myself shot again."

"Then why are you here and not at the hospital?"

He unbuttons his shirt and slides it off. "Not bad enough to take the risk of being reported to the authorities."

This is crazy. "You are aware people get infections and die from untreated gunshot wounds?"

"It won't go untreated. Jamie is on his way. I'll be stitched up, good as new. I'm sure he'll give me antibiotics so it doesn't get infected. All will be fine, Bonny." He nods at the two men standing in the bedroom. "Go wait in the living room. Feel free to help yourselves to whatever you'd like from the liquor cabinet."

They leave and I'm alone with an injured, bleeding Sin. I take a moment to gather my thoughts on what I've been taught in the immediate care of a gunshot wound. "I need to apply pressure."

"No, Bonny. You don't have to do that."

"I can't stand here and do nothing."

"Would you like to run down the street and pick up a needle and thread so you can suture it?" He isn't hurting too much to be a smart-ass.

"I'm not too handy with sewing so you'd probably prefer I leave it to Jamie." I sit on the bed next to him. "Are you in pain?"

"Aye, like a son of a bitch. I'm not ashamed to say I wouldn't mind having a little nip of something strong."

"I can do that much for you."

I return with the whisky and help him to a sitting position. "Will Jamie give you something for the pain?"

He grimaces when he sits up to toss back the entire tumbler of

Johnnie Walker. "Aye, and I'll gladly take it."

"Another?"

"Aye." I'm through the door when I hear him call out, "Bring the bottle."

I'm shaken by my concern for him. I shouldn't care if he lives or dies—but I do.

I return to his side and he strokes his hand over the soft, silky fabric of my nightgown. "You look lovely."

"Thank you."

He puts his hand on my thigh and rubs it up and down. He's lying on the bed with a gunshot wound and is still making the moves on me. Horny bastard. "You should know I'm not happy about my men seeing you in this. This sight should be for my eyes only."

"That was the plan."

"And the bedding is new." I'm surprised he's noticed. "I like it."

"I liked it too, until you bled all over it." I grin because I know the crude remark he could make. "Don't go there, Breck."

He laughs. "You've come to know me well in a short amount of time."

I slide off the bed and kneel on the floor so we're face to face. I grasp his hand in mine and hold it tightly. "Tell me what happened tonight."

"Sometimes I have to be a handler. When a brother commits a transgression, I'm the one who delivers them to the person who will carry out their punishment. They don't always come willingly … but I make sure they come."

"Does that mean if I'm bad and need punishing, you'll have another man do it for you?"

"Absolutely not. I'm the only one who touches you." He rubs his thumb over the top of my hand. "I was really looking forward to touching you when I got home. I thought about it all day."

"I know. Me too."

Jamie comes into the bedroom and stands over Sin. "What have you gone and gotten yourself into this time, brother?"

"That fucking Neil Allaway piece of no-count shit has been dodging me for weeks. I found him tonight and he shot me when I went after him."

"Did you at least catch the bastard?"

"Hell yeah, I got him. He's in Sangster's hands now." Uh-oh. I have no idea who Sangster is but it sounds as though Neil is in deep shit. Even I know that.

"Let me take a look."

I slide over so Jamie can move in for a better assessment. "It's still in there?"

"Aye."

"You told me it was only a flesh wound." The asshole lied to me.

Jamie reaches into his bag and takes out a portable light. "When I extract it, I'll need you to shine that on the wound so I can find it."

What is this? Medieval times? "Seriously? You're going to be digging into his flesh while I stand over him holding a flashlight?"

"It's how this is done, Bonny."

"Can you hold the light or do I need to fetch one of the goons to come in here instead?"

"My bonny one is tough." Sin squeezes my hand. "She's got this."

He wants me here with him. How can I say no? "I can do it."

I've been with fellow agents when they've taken a bullet but this is an entirely new experience. I don't want to watch what Jamie's doing. Each time I attempt to look away, the light moves and he scolds me, so I'm forced to keep my eyes on Sin's wound when he injects him with local using a long ass needle and again while stainless steel pliers dig into his shoulder. "Can you not give him something for pain?"

"I did. I injected him with lidocaine and gave him a shot of morphine. He'll be fine."

"He doesn't look fine." He's clenching my hand so tight it hurts. "You need another drink?"

"I won't turn it down."

I fill his tumbler and he downs it in one gulp. "Thanks."

He sighs as he lies back on the bed. "Let's get this done."

"Have one of those men come in and hold the light so I can talk to him." I'm sure I won't be able to distract him from all the pain but maybe I can help take his mind off it a little.

The skinny one comes in after Jamie calls for him. I take Sin's hand and Jamie returns to his previous task. "I had to have a few IVs when I was a kid and this is what my dad did. He'd kneel at my bedside, hold my hand, and talk. His voice didn't take away all the pain but it soothed me. There's something special about hearing a father's voice tell you everything is going to be okay. You can't not believe he's telling the truth," I say.

"I got pneumonia when I was a child and had to go into the hospital. They gave me an IV for the antibiotics and I cried because it was painful. My father told me to suck it up and stop being a baby. I think I was five."

Sin grimaces; I look over at Jamie. He's digging deep.

"Breathe in slow … and deep." He does and his chest expands. "Now, blow it out slowly. Close your eyes and concentrate on breathing. Push the pain out of your mind. You can do this."

We repeat the process through four cycles—me talking him through—and Jamie finally announces, "Got it."

Thank God!

"That fucker was in deep." He holds the lead slug up to the light in his gloved hand. "I'm sorry, mate. I know that hurt like a son of a bitch. I didn't have a needle long enough to get the local in that far. That's why it hurt more than usual."

He still needs to suture him so I pour another whisky. He takes it without hesitation. "This part won't be bad since the skin is numb. The deep digging is what was killing me."

I see a huge difference in his posture. It's more relaxed.

He continues holding my hand, stroking his thumb back and forth across my palm on the underside where it's hidden from Jamie. "How did shopping with my mum go today?"

Jamie stops and looks at us but doesn't say a word before returning to his suture job.

"Surprisingly well. She helped me choose this bedding." I want to tell him he's wrong about her but now isn't the time.

"The bedding that I've now ruined."

"It can be replaced. You're okay. That's all that matters."

He picks up one of the pillows next to his head. "I want you to buy this same set again, ruffled pillows and all."

"You like it that much?"

"You like it so I like it."

Jamie leaves after he's finished caring for Sin and it's the two of us.

"We should get you out of these trousers."

"Now, you're talking." He lifts his hips when I pull downward. "I believe you, Miss MacAllister, are trying to take advantage of a man while he's on the poppy."

"You wish."

"Aye. That is an incredibly accurate statement."

I wrestle his pants off and decide to leave him in his boxer briefs. The morphine is kicking in. I don't feel like dressing a giant toddler.

His breathing becomes heavy and steady. He's asleep.

I can't believe I've come so far with Sin in such a short period. It was my plan to make it happen as quickly as possible. I wanted to get the job done and return home but I never dreamed it would occur in this short time. At this rate, I'll be inside Thane's home very soon. And my work here will be done.

I push Sin's hair from his forehead. "I'm going to miss you when I'm gone. I truly will."

CHAPTER SIXTEEN

SINCLAIR BRECKENRIDGE

BLEU HASN'T BEEN HAPPY WITH ME IN DAYS. SHE THINKS I SHOULD HAVE STAYED home to recuperate longer. I think differently.

We're alike in so many ways but this isn't one of them. I don't know how to make her understand that this wound is nothing. It was a simple gunshot to my shoulder. I've been through so much worse.

"Mr. Breckenridge." I look up to see my secretary standing at my desk. "Are you feeling all right ?"

"Of course."

She looks puzzled. "I called your name three times before you responded."

"I'm sorry. I didn't hear you."

"You were looking right at me, sir." I don't think so. I'd remember looking straight at her while she said my name. "You don't look like your usual self, Mr. Breckenridge. You're pale."

The truth is I don't feel well. "I could be coming down with something. I think I'll take the rest of the afternoon off."

"Take it easy over the weekend," Heather says. "You'll be back to a hundred percent by Monday."

Rest. That's what I need. "I'll do that. See you next week."

I get into my car but the next coherent moment I have is when I realize Sterling is waiting for me to get out of the car. I can't remember the drive home from work. "Are you all right, sir?" No. I'm not. Something isn't right.

"I'm fine. That will be all."

I go into the house and call out for Bleu. I've come to know better than to startle her by coming home unannounced. She'd probably throat punch me before I knew what hit me. "Bonny, I'm home early."

She comes into the living room from the back of the house and I can tell she's recently come home from her daily run. "Hey. This is a nice surprise. I wasn't expecting you for a few more hours."

She's going to enjoy hearing me admit this. "I fear you were right, Dr. MacAllister. I believe the shooting has finally caught up with me."

"See? Do you believe that I know what I'm talking about now? You. Need. Rest."

No way I'm arguing with her. "I think I'll lie on the couch for a while. Maybe watch some TV."

"Can I get you anything?"

I shake my head no.

"Then I'm going to get a shower. I'm stinky." I usually love catching her hot and sweaty so I can help her out of her clothes and into the shower. But not today.

I fall onto the sofa.

"After my shower, I want to show you the pictures I took today." Her voice fades as she walks toward the bedroom. "They're magnificent. I think I could sell them to a travel magazine or something like that." Or maybe she's fading because I'm drifting.

I wake to Bleu calling my name. "Breck! You're burning up with fever."

"Hmm … ?" Again, I'm confused.

Hands are touching my face, moving from my cheeks to my forehead and back again. "You're on fire."

No, I'm not. I'm shivering because I'm so cold. "I need a blanket. I'm freezing."

"I'm going to help you up so I can take you to the emergency room."

I'm not confused about that. "Hell no, you're not."

"You're sick. Bad."

"I may be but I'm not going to the hospital." My voice is stern. I'm not in the mood to discuss it.

"Something's not right about this."

I curl into a ball so I can get warm. "Call Jamie."

"Excuse me if I don't have a lot of faith in his medical care right now."

I feel dizzy so I cover my eyes using my hand. "Just call Jamie."

She huffs but takes my phone from my jacket pocket. "It's Bleu. You need to come see Sin now. He has a really high fever and isn't feeling well at all."

She sits on the couch at my feet and rubs my leg. "He's on his way. How long have you had fever?"

"I have no idea. I was busy today trying to finish up research for a case going to court on Monday. I haven't had time to think about it." It suddenly seems important to tell her about my confusion. "I've had a couple of incidents today. I guess you could call them memory lapses."

Her hand stops moving. "What kind of memory lapses?"

"My secretary—she had trouble getting my attention."

"You said you were busy with an important case. Maybe you were preoccupied."

"She was standing right in front of me. I apparently stared blankly while she called my name three times. I have no recollection of it."

"Oh."

"And I don't remember the drive home."

"Infection wouldn't be unusual after a gunshot wound so I understand the fever and chills but your mental status shouldn't be affected. That concerns me."

She isn't the only one. "Tell no one except Jamie."

"Not even your parents?"

"Especially my parents." I don't want my father to tell Abram I'm not well. He could see it as a perfect opportunity to act out against Bleu a second time. "I mean it. I have important reasons for them not knowing. Not a word."

"I won't."

I lie on the couch waiting for Jamie. I didn't think it was possible but I feel worse by the time he arrives. "Your temp is 103. How long have you been running a fever?"

"No idea."

He listens to my chest. "Your respirations and heart rate are faster than they should be. Something's definitely going on." He pushes up my pant leg and squeezes my ankle. "You been pissing normally?"

"What constitutes normal?"

"Has the color or amount changed?"

I hadn't considered that until now. "It's darker and I'm not going as often."

"In the very least, you need an IV and antibiotics."

"Then let's do it."

He sits in the chair across from me. "I'd be treating you blindly. You need blood cultures to make sure this isn't something worse than a simple infection. I don't have a lab so you'll need to go to the hospital."

"Come on, Jamie. You know I can't go into a hospital." I haven't stepped foot in one since the day I was discharged six years ago. I'm not sure I can do it.

"I wouldn't advise you to go if I thought I could treat you here. I'm sorry but we need to rule out an inflammatory response to infection. I don't have the things I need for that."

"Inflammatory response? What does that mean?" Bleu asks.

"It's a way the body sometimes responds to infection."

I think this could be something serious but he's not telling me. "Don't dance around, bullshitting me with medical jargon. What do you think is happening?"

"Have you experienced any confusion?"

This isn't good. "I've had two incidents."

I'm not going to like this answer. "I think you're becoming septic. That means you can't wait. You must go now so a culture can be done immediately. The results will identify the antibiotic that will best treat your infection."

This isn't what I want to hear. I can't protect Bleu from Abram if I'm lying in a hospital bed. But I guess I can't if I'm dead, either.

I'm certain my condition has worsened by the time we arrive at the hospital. Jamie does all the talking when I'm being assessed, which is a good thing since I'm becoming increasingly confused.

I'm admitted and treatment is started as soon as I'm diagnosed with sepsis. The whole thing happens quickly and I'm concerned about who will watch after Bleu while I'm unable.

"Thane needs to know you're here and what's happening."

Jamie's right. I can't keep this from him. "Aye. When you call, will you ask my mum to come to the hospital? I need to talk to her." I need my mother for the first time in twenty years.

"Aye, I will."

Jamie leaves and Bleu comes in to sit with me. Neither she nor Jamie mentions it but I know my status is declining rapidly. I recognize it in my inability to concentrate clearly. "I have things to say to you before I'm unable to string two thoughts together."

She wraps her hand around mine and leans closer. "Okay."

"If I don't make it, you need to leave Edinburgh on the first plane out of Scotland and never look back."

"No!" She sits up, back stiffening, and stares at me. "What are you talking about? You're not going to die."

I don't want to use the last of my coherent time arguing. "Promise me you'll get out as soon as possible if I meet death."

She brings my hand to her lips and kisses it. "Yes. I will leave but you're not dying on me."

"Bonny, I'm nothing if not realistic. People die from sepsis all the time. I've seen it happen to brothers after gunshot wounds."

"No." She brings my hand to her face, rubbing against her cheek. "I just found happiness for the first time in my life. There's no way I'm letting it go."

"You never lifted the veil."

"Then I guess you better stick around if you want to learn my secrets."

"I want to know everything about Bonny Bleu." She kisses my knuckles and closes her eyes tightly. A single tear slips down her cheek. "I'm not choosing to let go. I'm going to fight but it's out of my hands."

She opens her eyes as she laces her fingers through mine and squeezes. "Into me … you see," she whispers.

I nod and bring our hands up so I can kiss hers. "Into me … you see."

I hear the sound of someone clearing their voice and discover my parents standing in the doorway. "We can come back after you're finished talking."

"No. Please, come in."

More tears spill from Bleu's eyes. She cares for me. "I need a moment with my mum and father."

She wipes the drops away. "Of course." She stands and leans forward to kiss my forehead. "I'll just be right outside if you need me."

I grab the back of her neck and pull her in for a kiss—a real one—since it could be the last time. "I want you to come back in as soon as I'm finished talking."

"Absolutely."

My mum sits at my side while Dad stands. "James tells us ye aren't doing well." She's always called him that.

"He's the doctor," I say, smiling weakly.

"He says you can make a full recovery," my father says.

"Or I might die. Flip of a coin."

"You're a Breckenridge. You'll survive this." I don't think sepsis cares what my surname is.

I cut straight to why I called them in. "Dad knows about my recent quarrel with Abram but I want you to know as well. He believes Bleu is an informant. He sent Malcolm into my house while I was away—supposedly to scare her into admitting who she's working for." I stop for a moment to catch my breath. "I'm not sure I believe that was his true intention but it turned deadly. I led him to believe I killed Malcolm by accident because it was dark and I didn't recognize him. But that isn't what happened." I stop again because my head is dizzy. "He attacked Bleu and she defended herself. She's the one who killed him."

"This isn't good." Dad sighs. "But Abram doesn't need to find out differently. It will only add fuel to the fire."

"That poor lass," my mum says. "She must've been petrified." I somehow doubt that since she put Malcolm in a chokehold and strangled him.

"I don't trust him with Bleu."

"With good reason, it seems," Mum says.

"Dad, I promised Bleu I would protect her and I can't do that from this bed. You're the only one who can if Abram decides to strike while I'm here."

"I will take care of her for you, son."

"Mum, I haven't asked anything of you since I was a child but I am now because I need you. Dad can't be with her at all times. Please take her into your care. He won't touch her as long as she's under your roof."

"I too will ensure her safety."

"Thank you." I feel a burden lifted.

"You care for this lass." It isn't a question. "I see it happening before my eyes."

I'm not sure I could admit the truth if I weren't straddling life and death. "I do, very much."

"I never thought I'd see you care for anyone." I'm aware of the wretched person my mother believes I am.

"It's unexpected." I never saw myself caring for any woman.

"She told me it would be very easy to fall in love with ye. I believe she has." Mum is all smiles. "Do ye love her?"

"Being loved by me will make her a huge target." Abram won't be her only threat. "I don't want to—but I can't help myself."

My parents look at one another and then back at me. "We heard what you said to one another. You've claimed her?" my dad says.

"I have. And I don't regret it. I would do it again."

"Yer wise tae keep it secret. It won't serve ye well if the brotherhood finds out."

"I've already told her she has to leave immediately if I die. She'll need you to help her get out safely."

"Dinnae lie here worrying aboot her well-being. She's in good hands. Rest and concentrate on recovering."

It's strange. I've connected with my mum for the first time in my adult life and it's a direct result of Bleu's presence in our lives. Another first because of her.

"Please ask Bleu to come back. I need to give her an explanation for why she'll be staying with you."

"Ye won't warn her about Abram?" Mum asks.

"I don't want to give her a reason to be paranoid around him. That will only make him more suspicious of her."

My mum comes to me and does something she hasn't done since I was a child. She hugs me. "I love ye, Sinclair."

"I love you too." I can't recall the last time I heard or said those words.

My mum leaves and she sends Bleu back. "I know you do a damn fine job of protecting yourself but I don't want you staying alone. I've spoken to my parents and you're going to their house until I'm out of here."

"I will if it'll make you feel better."

No argument? She's making this very easy. "It's what I want."

Good. I've ensured her safety. Now, all I have to do is survive.

CHAPTER SEVENTEEN

BLEU MACALLISTER

I'M NOT PREPARED FOR HOW QUICKLY SIN'S CONDITION DECLINES. WITHIN AN hour, he's dependent upon a ventilator to breathe for him because his body can no longer do it on its own. I'm terrified he isn't going to survive the night.

Oh my God. When did I start to care so much for this son of a bitch? How's it possible? If I disregard the part about who he is, the reality is that we haven't known one another long enough for me to be this attached.

I'm able to answer my own question before the thought is fully developed. He isn't a stranger to me. I've studied Liam Sinclair Breckenridge for years. He's been a part of my life for a long time. I came here knowing everything about him. Almost.

He's a thief who stole something much more precious than ever before—my heart. I never dreamed in a million years I could fall in love with the son of my mother's killer. How sick is that? I'm certain there's no psychological diagnosis to fit how morbid this is.

For so long I've wanted to feel what other people feel. Now that I do, I just want it to stop. I would give anything to go back to feeling nothing again.

I'm holding his hand when his critical care nurse comes into the room. "You haven't left his side in two days. You need rest as well."

I can't leave him. What if he wakes up for two minutes and looks for me but I'm not here? "I've been sleeping a little here and there."

"What you've been doing can't be classified as sleep."

I stroke his hair away from his face. He needs a haircut and his facial scruff could use a trim.

"Have you been together long?"

"Only five weeks but it feels like much longer, as if we've known one another forever." That's not the whole truth. I've been acquainted with him for years. He's only just met me.

"Have you been talking to him?" she asks.

"No." That sounds like something a nurturing person would do. That's not me.

"You should. They can hear you."

"I don't know what I'd say."

"It isn't about the words. He only needs to hear your voice to know you're by his side. It can be very reassuring if he's confused or scared but most importantly, it's healing."

I very much doubt the sound of my voice will help to heal him, but it won't hurt anything, either. "I can try."

I look at Sin once the nurse is gone and wonder what in the world to say to him. This kind of thing isn't me. But I'm determined to try if it might help. "Breck. It's Bleu. I'm here with you. You're not alone." I squeeze his hand. "Do you feel that?" I get no response. No grip of his hand or flutter of his eyes.

I move from the chair to his bed and slip in next to him, careful to not tug on any of his tubes or lines. If hearing my voice is good for him, then feeling my touch must be better.

I stroke my knuckles down his unshaven face. "Sinclair Breckenridge. You come back to me right now. Please. I'm here, waiting for you."

I move my hand to his chest and feel the beat of his heart beneath it. "I want you to listen for my voice through the darkness. Let it bleed through so you can hear me." I move my fingers to his inked Celtic shield of protection. "I'm not letting go of you. It's not time for our story to end."

Nothing.

"I need you to see into me."

Sin dances on the brink of death a few times before finally making a turn for the better. It hasn't been easy but he's almost fully recovered. He's well enough to be discharged from the hospital tomorrow, so that means I won't be sleeping under his parents' roof after tonight. I have no choice. It's time to kill Thane.

I've familiarized myself with all things within the Breckenridge compound–surveillance camera locations, Thane's schedule, the guards at the exterior entrances along with the times of their rotation. Lucky for me, they haven't considered the notion of the enemy being welcomed inside with open arms.

I'm struggling with my decision. Not because I care anything about Thane. My conflict is spurred by my feelings for Sin. I hate the thought of destroying his world, especially so soon after his brush with death. But I'm forced to choose who comes first–him or Harry.

I can't continue to stay. Time is my other enemy. I must do this and get home so I can be with my dying father. I've already lost more time than I intended.

I need to hear Harry's reassuring voice one last time before I go through with this. I use my burner phone to place the call and he answers on the first ring. "Hey, girlie."

"I'm calling about the status of my account." I spout off a phony number.

Harry and I have our own language no one else is privy to. Each line has been carefully chosen to signify something distinct. We do this because my voice could be heard through a planted bug. "I'm withdrawing the entire balance so I'll be closing the account today."

"You're inside Thane's?"

"Yes."

"You're proceeding tonight?" I have to. I'm not sure when I'll have another opportunity.

"That's right."

"Be careful, girlie. You're a lamb in the lion's den. There's no room for error." He's right. One false move and I'm dead. Game over.

"Of course."

"In devoting your life to making this right, it would be a shame to get it wrong. Take your time. Don't rush the kill." I've vested my entire existence around this moment. I've lived and breathed for it. I won't ruin it now.

"Everything appears to be correct."

"I expect a follow-up call as soon as you're able," Harry reminds me.

"I'll phone back to confirm everything was in order."

"I love you." We didn't cipher anything for this one.

"Thank you." I want to tell him how much I love him but this will have to do.

I return the untraceable burner phone to its hidden compartment within my bag. I walk the guest room floor as I go over my plan in my head one last time. Thane's working late in his office. He drinks bourbon, at least three, every night so his reflexes and mental status are sluggish. I'm going to knock and enter. He'll be on low alert, not expecting me to have any motive other than a request to talk. I'm going to tell him who I am before I kill him. I'll recount all the details about that night—how I heard the fired shots while I was hiding beneath my bed, the devastation of watching him kill my beloved dog, and how frightened I was as he held a pillow over my face. When I finish, I'm going to order him to his knees. I hope he begs me to not kill him when I place the barrel of my gun to his temple.

Time to do this.

I walk the hall and do just as I've strategized. I knock and listen for him to tell me to enter.

It's while I'm standing there waiting for Thane to respond that I realize I've traded my life and all I love for this moment. My entire existence has been dedicated to this execution and I'm suddenly overcome by emotions I don't understand. My purpose in life is ending. What will I possibly do once this is over? This is the close of a lifelong mission—the death of my dream. I should be happy, or at least satisfied, but I'm not.

There's no reply from within so I knock again, still without an answer. I open the door and go inside to find a sleeping Thane on his sofa. Correction: a passed-out Thane since he reeks of bourbon.

He's making his extermination too easy for me. But this isn't the way I want it. Killing an incoherent Thane will be less than satisfying. I need him to be looking into the eyes of the little girl he wronged as he dies. It's how I've envisioned it my entire life and I don't think anything less will fulfill me.

"Wake up, Thane." I nudge his shoulder but he doesn't budge. "Wake up. I want to see fear in your eyes when I put a bullet in your head."

He stirs and a photograph falls from his hand face down onto the floor. I pick it up—what does a man like him hold dear? What does he clench to his heart while drinking until he passes out?

It's him with my mother. They're embracing, smiling, in front of the entrance to a casino. They look … happy. In love.

Why is he clutching this photograph? Perhaps his actions have plagued him for the last eighteen years. I hope so.

I place the barrel of my gun against his temple, just the way I've planned all these years. I hesitate, something I didn't anticipate, and it has everything to do with Sinclair.

If I kill Thane, the mission is over and there'll be no reason to stay. My time with Sin will be over—the last grain of sand will fall through our hourglass. I'm suddenly aware of how unprepared I am to walk away from him.

I can't do this—not yet. I haven't had all the time I want with Sin.

"Dammit to hell!" I take my gun away from Thane's head. "This is your lucky day." Only because I love your son.

I'm standing over Thane, gun in hand, when the door opens.

"What are you doing in here, lass?" Isobel asks. Her eyes move to the gun in my hand. "Where did you get that?"

I do the only thing I can. Lie. "I couldn't sleep. I was on my way to the kitchen for a tea when I saw the light. I let myself in. I shouldn't have but I'm glad I did. Thane was holding this. I was afraid of his intentions so I took it from him."

"Blootered dunderheid." She takes the gun from me, shaking her head. "I'll see to this. Go to the living room and let's have a whisky together. It'll help you to sleep better than tea."

"Please don't mention this to Thane. I don't want him to know I saw him like this."

She goes to his desk and puts the gun in the top drawer. I'll need to come back in and retrieve it before Thane finds it. "I won't. It'll be our little secret."

I have a nightcap with Isobel and curse myself as I return to my room. I can't believe I got my gun taken away. I hope Thane had lots of bourbon since I'll be going back in after Isobel is in bed.

Once inside, I phone Harry. "Hey, Dad. I have great news. Sinclair is being discharged from the hospital tomorrow." This isn't a conversation we've rehearsed so I'm winging it.

"Is it done?"

"I'm afraid not." I hope Harry isn't disappointed in me.

"Nothing went wrong?" I'm glad we aren't having a real conversation. I'm not sure how I'd tell him there was a problem—but it was my heart.

"All is well but his recovery is going to take a little longer than expected."

"I shouldn't worry?" he asks.

"Not at all."

"Okay. When you're in the clear, call me ASAP so we can make revisions."

"Absolutely. I'll give Sin your best."

I dread making that call. I don't want to lie to Harry but there's no way I can tell him I couldn't go through with killing Thane because I'm in love with his son. He'd never understand that.

Sinclair is simultaneously all I could want in a man while I despise everything that makes him the person he is. I'm straddling two worlds. Love versus hate—and I'm not sure which is stronger.

Despite his dirty deeds, I think Sin is it for me—the one and only love of my life. My heart tells me so every time I look at him. The feelings I experience when we're together are everything I've always imagined when I pictured myself in love, minus the part where my beloved will be the next leader of an organized crime empire.

I did not see this perfect storm coming.

CHAPTER EIGHTEEN

SINCLAIR BRECKENRIDGE

"Would you like to lie on the couch or go to the bed?" Oh no. My mum didn't play the coddling game and Bleu isn't, either.

"Those are the only two choices I get?"

"Yes. The doctor says you need plenty of rest. I'm inclined to believe he knows what he's talking about." I guess she's right since it's possible he performed a miracle by bringing me back from the condition I was in a week ago.

"Will you come with me if I choose the bed?"

She tilts her head. "I will, but not for the reason you have in mind."

That's not what I was implying. I don't have the stamina for sex right now—and it's a damn shan. I've missed being with my Bonny Bleu. "Give me a few more days and then we'll make up for lost time."

She comes closer and hooks her hands behind my waist. "I look forward to that."

"No more than me." I kiss her mouth. "Mmm … I've missed that."

"Me too." She squeezes my midsection. "I'm happy we're home."

"How did you make out at my parents'? I mean, the times you weren't holed up with me."

A look I can't identify crosses her face. "Your parents were very good to me—exceedingly so. As a guest, I've never been treated so well. That's saying a lot since I'm from the South." She laughs. "We're very hospitable people."

"I'll need to thank them later." I think I should probably tell her about them overhearing us at the hospital. "They know about me claiming you."

She's clearly surprised. "And?"

"They're okay with it but both agree it's a good idea to keep it to ourselves." Especially from Abram.

She laughs and shrugs. "I don't have anyone to tell."

"Do you miss the friends you made at the bar?"

"Lorna was the only girl I'd consider a friend and that's a maybe. I don't think she cared for me much."

She better not have mistreated my lass. "Why is that?"

"She's in love with Leith." Lorna has shagged Leith plenty of times but I can't believe she has romantic feelings for him.

"Aah … and he was making moves for you."

"Then you see the problem that made for our friendship."

Makes total sense. "Clearly."

"I can't be friends with anyone within The Fellowship because they believe I'm an outsider and I can't tell them about the one thing that designates me an insider."

That makes for a problem in the friend department. "I see your dilemma. I'm sorry."

"But I've grown close to your mother. That's a good thing." I like Bleu and my mum being friends.

"She taught me her version of shepherd pie and now I have a crazy craving for open roast beef sandwiches with gravy. Maybe with potatoes and carrots?"

"That sounds really good."

"I was thinking of cooking tonight. I'm tired of hospital food and I'm guessing you are too."

"I'll never turn down your food." Everything Bleu cooks is fantastic.

"You like my southern cuisine?"

"Very much."

"To the couch with you."

My flat has an open floor plan so I can easily lie on the couch and watch Bleu.

She's a tough lass. Scraps as well as any man I know, probably better, yet knows how to cook a delicious meal. "Is there anything you're not good at?"

"I can't knit worth than a damn. My grandmother tried to teach me once. I got so frustrated I wanted to stab someone in the eye with the needle." Why am I not surprised by this?

"Remind me to never ask you to knit me a sweater."

She laughs and makes a stabbing motion with the fork in her hand. "Good thinking."

We finish dinner and then watch TV until bedtime. We're side by side doing our nightly routines, preparing for bed. It feels domestic—and comfortable.

It's odd the things a man will think of when he believes he's toeing the line between life and death. I was terrified to surrender to my body's exhaustion; I believed if I closed my eyes for even a second, I'd never wake again. It was in those last moments before everything went black that I looked at Bleu and recalled the simple things— holding her after one of her nightmares, kissing the top of her head as I leave for work, listening to her breathe in the dark. Of all my fleeting thoughts, this one was my favorite—standing side by side getting ready for bed, me wearing my sleep pants and her in one of her soft, flowing nightgowns.

Bleu notices me watching her reflection. She goes still and looks at me, her toothbrush hanging from her mouth like a stogie. "What?" Her mouthful of toothpaste foams and spatters on her lips when she speaks. She spits and rinses.

"I missed this." My eyes roam over the simple, satin nightgown clinging to her body. "Especially when you're wearing something like that."

She closes her robe, tying the belt at the waist. "You should probably stop looking because there will be none of that. Your body has been through hell. It needs time to heal."

I know what will cure me. "I don't want to stop looking."

"This is the least sexy gown I have, but I can change into a T-shirt and yoga pants if this is going to be a problem."

"Never." I move over to hug her from behind, slipping my arms around her waist. "Absolutely not. I've missed seeing you in your pretty bedtime things."

I kiss the side of her neck and she shudders as she leans into me. She moves her hand down my forearm and laces her fingers through mine. "I was so afraid. I thought I was going to lose you."

"I know." A confused look comes over her face. I decide to let that one sink in for a minute so I kiss the back of her head and leave the bathroom.

She comes out a moment later massaging in her lotion and crawls into bed next to me. She turns onto her side and looks at me. "How did you know I was afraid of losing you?"

I place my hand on her thigh, rubbing it in a circular motion. "I heard the things you said to me."

She scrunches her brow. "What do you think I said?"

"You told me you weren't letting go, that it wasn't time for our story to end. 'Let me be the reason you stay.'"

She neither denies nor confirms my account, but I don't need her validation. I know everything she said.

She rises to a sitting position and entwines her fingers in mine. "How do you feel about the things you heard?" I think that's an admission.

"I want to know the rest of the story."

She rises and moves one leg over my pelvis so she's straddling me. She leans forward, her elbows pressed into the pillow on each side of my head, and kisses my mouth. I place my hands on her thighs and move them upward until they reach her bare cheeks. "Miss MacAllister, I believe you have forgotten your knickers."

A mischievous grin spreads. "It seems I have."

She moves to kneeling between my legs. She hooks her fingers into my waistband and tugs. I lift my hips and she drags my sleep pants downward.

She lowers her body to mine, bringing us close enough to touch, but she isn't pressing her weight against me. Her nightgown is slick when she climbs upward to straddle me again. She arches back and my erection presses against her warm entrance.

I place my hands on her stomach and glide them up her silky gown. I palm her breasts, her hands covering mine, and her nipples become erect beneath my touch. Her hands move up her chest, to her shoulders, and then to the back of her neck. She lifts her long hair and holds it in a messy pile as she rotates her hips, grinding her groin against mine.

I slip my hands under her gown and she releases her hair to reach for the bottom. She pulls it over her head and discards it.

She is, without doubt, the most beautiful woman I've ever seen. Everything about her is perfect to me.

She holds the tip of my cock and positions it at her warm, slick entrance. She sinks down until I'm completely buried inside her. She leans back, placing her hands on my thighs for leverage, and begins moving up and down in a slow, deliberate rhythm.

I rotate my hand, palm side up, and use my fingers to find her clit. I know I've hit the perfect spot when a moan escapes her mouth. I start with a slow, spiraling motion and increase the speed as she moves faster. "Ohh … right there, Sin."

It isn't long before I realize I could be doing this too well. She may beat me to the finish line. "Are you already close?"

"Yesss!"

I won't ask her to slow down so I begin thrusting with her. A moment later, I'm there with her when my orgasm approaches.

She sinks deep and groans, "Ohh … ohh."

Mine comes right in behind hers. It's going to be a big one since it's been a while. I rise and grab her hips, bringing her down hard as I thrust deep. I hold her in place as I spasm, completely emptying myself.

When it's over, I move my hands to her waist and press my head to her chest. "I missed you terribly, lass."

"I missed you too. I'm very happy to have you back." She places her hands on my face and forces me to look at her. "Never do that to me again. Ever."

"I'll do my best, Bonny." But I'm Fellowship. She knows this. I can make no promises.

She's still holding my face. "Say it with me."

I know what she's talking about. Together we say the words. "Into me ... you see."

She sighs and puts her arms around my shoulders. I wince when she forgets about my injury and squeezes too hard. "Oh, I'm sorry. You should lie back down."

She's avoiding my shoulder. "I will if you'll swap sides with me. You're distancing yourself because of my injury." I crave her nearness. We've been too far apart this week.

She lies with her head on my uninjured shoulder while I rub her upper arm. We stay like that for a while, quiet, simply enjoying the gift of being together.

With silence comes thought, and my mind wanders back to the first night we were together. Bleu has never explained her infertility issues. She only said it was something I'd care nothing about. I didn't at the time. I was too busy being happy about it to question her, but things are different now.

Anyone knows healthy young women aren't routinely checked by their doctors for infertility unless they've tried to conceive and couldn't. Bleu came to me a virgin, so that clearly isn't the case. "How do you know you can't get pregnant?"

She doesn't answer right away. "I never said I couldn't get pregnant."

I sit up abruptly because I want her to look me in the face when she explains this one. "You told me you couldn't get pregnant."

"That may be what you heard, but that's not what I said."

"Then please, clarify."

"I said you shouldn't worry about getting me pregnant. There's a difference."

"We've been having unprotected sex because I believed you were infertile."

"I've had severe polycystic ovarian syndrome since I was seventeen. I lost an ovary when I was twenty and the remaining one is nonfunctional. My doctors tell me I'll likely lose it within the next couple of years, so in vitro is the only chance I have at becoming pregnant."

I'm no reproductive specialist but I understand the basics. "If you don't have ovaries, how can they do in vitro?"

"I did a retrieval procedure two years ago in case I ever wanted to have babies. My eggs are frozen until I choose to use them."

She wouldn't have done that if she didn't want children. "You want babies." I don't know why I'm surprised by this revelation.

"I do, very much, but only if the circumstances are right. Don't you?"

"I've never allowed myself to think of what I might want because I've always known what was expected—enter into a Fellowship-approved marriage and breed the next leader. That is what has been drilled into me for as long as I can remember."

"That's a bleak plight." She couldn't be more right.

"If my wife doesn't hate me from the start, she'll grow to once I take our son from her and rear him to lead The Fellowship." That's what happened between my mum and father.

"What would happen if you didn't choose a wife from within your circle?" she asks.

"The Fellowship would never accept that."

"Would they rally against you, their future leader?"

"They'd see my wife as a loose end. That's something they wouldn't tolerate."

"Would they kill her? Or you for choosing to bring her in?"

"The Fellowship has a strict code for dealing with acts against the brotherhood. It's called penance."

"Which includes …?"

"Bleu. You're highly accepting of this life, although you aren't from this world. I love that about you, but I don't really want to discuss penance. It isn't a pleasant thing."

"I want to know."

She's already up to her eyeballs in The Fellowship. "We have a secret location called a black site. Only a few brothers know its location. It's where many things take place—penance, initiation, the occasional torture or … It's not a place you want to be taken. If you find yourself there, you need to get out fast."

"Is that where you took those men you killed the night I was attacked?"

"We aren't going to talk about that."

"You never told me what you did to them." I'm not sure Bleu

could ever look at me the same if she knew.

"And I won't now, either."

"Why not?"

"Once you learn certain things, there's an invisible line you cross where there's no return. There are dark things that will keep your heart from ever seeing the light again. I don't want that for you." And that's why I'll never allow her to be tainted by the ways of The Fellowship.

CHAPTER NINETEEN

BLEU MACALLISTER

THE DRAPES ARE CLOSED BUT SUNLIGHT PEEKS INTO THE ROOM THROUGH A TINY gap in the fabric. I've been in Scotland for months and I'm still not accustomed to the long daylight hours. My mind and body remain confused by the short nights.

I reach for Sin but he isn't by my side. I'm sure he's in his office working. That's all he's done the past two weeks since discharge from the hospital—playing catch-up.

Against doctor's orders, Sin only took a few days off before returning to his duties at the firm. I'm not at all surprised. He has little to no concern for his health since he thinks he's invincible. His worry always lies with the well-being of The Fellowship. And me.

I'm certain Sin has come to care for me very much. Our relationship won't sit well with the brotherhood. It's possible it won't be tolerated. That could mean big trouble for me. The rational side of my brain tells me I'm being foolish by playing with a fire I can't extinguish. If I were smart, I would end this, kill Thane, and get out before I'm discovered.

But I'm not smart. I'm in love.

I move to sit on the edge of the bed and stretch. I plant my feet on the floor and hear a sound I could never mistake—the music of a violin. I fetch my robe from the chair and slip it on as I go toward

Sin's office to discover who the musician is.

I stop in the doorway to admire Sin's playing. It's as though he's making love to the instrument while playing Canon in D Major. I watch him drag the bow and I'm almost jealous of the loving manner in which he regards his instrument.

How could I not know he was a violinist? I love learning new things about him but this is another blunder on my part. I should have at least noticed calluses on his fingers.

His playing ceases when he catches sight of me and I'm left with wanting to hear more. "Please … don't stop. You play beautifully."

I move to sit on his desk and he grins before resuming the tune. I close my eyes, savoring every beautiful note until he reaches the end. When he finishes, he leans forward and places a soft kiss against my temple. "Did I wake you?"

"No. I was already awake when I heard you."

"I haven't played in a long time. I'm not really sure why I decided to just now." Okay. Maybe that's why it never popped up in my research. And he wouldn't have calluses if he hasn't played in a while.

I lift my brows and hold out my hands. "May I?"

He shrugs. "Sure."

He comes to stand behind me and places the lower bout over my collarbone. "Put your jaw here, against the chin rest." He takes my hand and wraps it around the neck. "Comfortable?"

I allow him to position the violin as though I've never held one. "Yes."

"Keep your wrist rounded. Don't rest it on the neck," he instructs.

"Okay."

He places my fingers where he wants them and then holds the bow for me to take. "Want to try?"

"Sure."

He steps away and I move my fingers to the place I prefer and stroke the bow across the strings. He leans against his desk and watches as I play the intro to my favorite song. "My choice in music is a little different from yours."

"I see that." He's surprised I play—perhaps even a little impressed. "I don't know the song but I can see you play quite well."

"It's called "Black Orchid" by Blue October." This is a song I've played no less than a thousand times, mostly when I've been in a dark place I couldn't escape. The lyrics are about deep depression but oddly, it brings me comfort.

I've allowed myself few things in life that had nothing to do with my plan to end Thane, but my love for catching still images through photography and the joy of playing my violin take the top two spots. Each has allowed me to decompress and express my feelings in ways no one could possibly understand.

I shrug when I finish and curtsy.

"You're full of trickery, Bonny Bleu."

"You should probably know it won't be the last time." Total truth.

Sin takes the violin and bow from me, placing both on his desk. He glides his hands down the satin gown over my hips and rests them at my lower back. "I've never had so much in common with a woman, or with anyone for that matter. Not even Leith or Jamie." He's holding me close and looks as though he wants to kiss me but doesn't. Instead, he studies my face, beginning at my eyes. "I'm not sure what to make of it." He strokes the back of his fingers down my cheek and rubs his thumb over my bottom lip. "You're the strongest woman I've ever known. You don't need me to protect you, and while I love that about you, I hate it as well. I sometimes find myself wishing you needed me, maybe just a little."

I emasculate Sin, just like every other man I encounter. It's my curse. My durability is going to cause me to blow this if I'm not careful. "I can be your china doll."

"That's not what I'm asking for, Bleu. I don't need to break you to feel like a man."

Then what does he want from me? "I don't understand."

"I want to be your protector. I'm asking you to let me do that if the time comes." I think there's something he isn't telling me.

I've never had a man, other than Harry, who wanted to protect me. The turmoil I'm experiencing is bewildering. He's asking me to submit to him. While that's everything I've never wanted, it's all I yearn to do when I look into his eyes.

"I'm yours to keep safe." My submission to Sin feels like a literal door swinging open to a world I've never known while the one behind me slams shut.

"It doesn't escape me that your agreement to this is a concession." He brushes his lips across mine. "This isn't just about protection. I want to take care of you in every way possible."

"You already do."

He pulls me close and squeezes my bottom while tugging my lower lip with his teeth. "Go get yourself ready. I'm taking you out today."

"Where are we going?"

"Breakfast first, and then I'm giving you a proper tour of the city. Wear comfortable shoes."

"Good. I can put my camera to use. It's been collecting too much dust."

We're sitting at a booth table at the Royal McGregor looking at the menu. "What will you be having?"

My options are limited, as always. I'm not a huge fan of Scottish cuisine. "I think I'll go with the French toast."

He peers over his menu at me. "I brought you out today to show you authentic Edinburgh and you're going to start the day with French toast and Canadian maple syrup? I don't think I have to tell you that's not the least bit Scottish. You should be having the traditional breakfast."

I look at what it includes. "Your sausage isn't like what I eat at home. It's … ugh. And your bacon isn't bacon. It's ham from a weird part of the pig. And you can forget me touching black pudding or haggis. I'm not eating anything that includes blood or intestines. I don't do that at home and I'm not doing it here. French toast and coffee are safe, so that's what I'm going with."

He places his menu on the table. "You can try mine."

He's wrong if he thinks I'll be budging an inch. "Oh … no, sir. That won't be happening."

He smirks, appearing confident he'll have his way. "We'll see."

We're halfway through our meal when he makes his first offer of haggis. I don't as much as glance in his direction. "Try it. You'll love it."

"No, thank you."

"Come on, Bonny."

"I said no." He places a small portion on my plate and my stomach immediately churns. "Get that off my plate. It's going to make me sick."

He smirks at me. "You're being childish."

The churning is worsening. "This isn't taking care of me." I bring my napkin to my mouth hoping the nausea will pass.

"What's wrong with you?"

I point in the general direction of my plate. "That! It's grossing me out." I toss my napkin over my plate because now I have an aversion to everything on it. "Excuse me."

I get up from the table and go to the restroom. I pat my face with a cool, wet paper towel and breathe in deeply and slowly.

I must've been in the restroom for a while when I hear a knock at the door. "Bonny? Are you all right ?"

"I'm fine. Give me another minute and I'll be out."

Of course, he hasn't returned to his seat when I open the door. He's standing there waiting for me.

I'm pissed off so I walk past him but he grabs my arm. I yank it from his grasp. "You're a total ass for doing that. I told you that stuff made me sick."

He cups his palm around my cheek. "Are you going to be okay?"

I've always had a strange aversion to some types of meats and the medication I take for my insulin resistance with the polycystic ovarian syndrome isn't helping. "It's debatable, thanks to you."

"I'm sorry. I thought we were having fun. I had no idea it would make you feel ill." He puts his curled finger under my chin and lifts, forcing me to look at him. "How can I make it better?"

"I'd like some water with more than five ice cubes." No way I can look at that stuff again. "And have those plates taken away from the table."

"They're already gone." He loops his arm through mine and leads me back to the table. "She needs water over a full glass of ice, please."

I feel somewhat better after a few sips. "I think I'm okay now."

He cups his hand over mine. "We can tour the city together another day if you don't feel well."

"I'm really fine. It's passed."

"I promised you not even two hours ago I was going to take care of you and now you're ill as a result of something I did. I feel bad about that." He shakes his head as he looks down at his hand covering mine. "That doesn't instill huge confidence about my ability to care for you."

"It was a piece of haggis—not the end of the world. And I take medicine for the ovarian stuff. It's a diabetic medication for insulin resistance. It often nauseates me so it's likely that contributed as well." I lean forward and grasp the back of his neck, pulling him close for a kiss, not giving a damn who's watching. I press my forehead to his. "Not another word about it," I whisper. "Got it?"

He nods, causing my head to move with his. "Got it."

We leave Royal McGregor's, walking hand in hand up the steep incline of the Royal Mile. We go into several shops along the way but most are full of souvenirs and things you buy when you know you're leaving soon. I can't bring myself to purchase anything because it feels symbolic of my approaching departure.

"MacAllister is Scottish. Have you ever studied your genealogy?"

Harry has done some research into his family tree but I'm not a MacAllister by blood, so none of what he has learned applies to me. "No."

"You should. I bet you'd find some interesting facts."

"I should. I have lots of free time on my hands, being a claimed woman and all." I feel a few scattered raindrops against my face. I look to the sky. It's suddenly dreary, the complete opposite of the way it looked only fifteen minutes ago. I've learned that's typical weather for these parts. "Looks as though we're going to get wet."

"It rarely lasts for long. If it becomes heavy, we'll duck into a store or covered alley until it clears."

The raindrops fall faster as we trudge up the hill. "I'm glad I didn't work on my hair and makeup for an hour."

"You're beautiful without all the fuss." He gives me a crooked grin. "Come on. I know a place we can go."

He leads me into a dark, cool alley with seats burrowed into the stone. "We'll wait here until it stops." He fidgets with my hand, running his thumb back and forth across the top.

"Will you tell me about losing your leg?" The records I have about Sin's shooting are obviously incorrect since none mention an amputation.

"What do you want to know about it?" Everything.

"What were the circumstances?"

"I was ambushed by a rival alliance called The Order. They had uzis. My leg was no match for that. It was barely hanging on when I arrived at the emergency room. There was no saving it." That sounds gruesome. And it's the kind of danger he faces on a regular basis.

"I don't understand how you've kept it secret."

"It wasn't difficult. Dad sent me to Lucerne for months. I was rehabilitated by the best doctors in Europe. I could walk almost flawlessly by the time they finished my physical therapy."

"It must have been awful." He never exhibits signs of PTSD. I wonder if he sees a therapist.

"It wasn't pleasant."

I never suspected before I knew. "I notice times when your gait changes. But it's only because I know."

"The stump bothers me from time to time."

"Thank you for sharing this with me."

He rubs his thumb over my hand again. "I was thinking we might go for drinks later."

"But not Duncan's?"

"I'm afraid not. We'll need to find a different drinking hole."

I look at the street. He's right. The rain didn't last long. "Looks like it's stopped."

I'm almost disappointed. I like hiding in this little cubby with Sin, away from the rest of the world. "I do believe you're right."

We leave the refuge of our hiding place. We resume our former path along High Street toward Edinburgh Castle and come up on a line of sidewalk vendors. There is a wide variety of goods and services but one in particular catches my eye: a psychic medium.

People claiming to be able to communicate with the dead and see the future have always interested me, mostly because I like observing how they read people. I don't believe in them for a second but I'd like to see how this one will take my words and reactions and use them to facilitate what she should say next. "I want the psychic to read me."

"Don't tell me you believe in fortunetellers."

"Of course not. It's for entertainment purposes only." He looks none too excited, so I grab his hand and give it a yank. "Come on. It'll be fun."

We go over to her table and the lady smiles. "Mornin' to you. Would you like a reading?"

"Yes." A real psychic would already know that. "How much?"

"Twenty pounds for one or thirty for the both of you."

"Both, please." I have faith Sin won't be easily manipulated, so I want to see how she'll pull this off.

"I agreed to come over with you, not participate."

"Sorry. I've already paid for you." I look at the psychic and smile. "He's going first."

"Take a seat." She gestures toward the stool opposite her.

Sin stares daggers at me but does as she asks. "I'll remember this later and so will you."

"I'm Mary."

"I'm …"

"No," she quickly interrupts. "Don't tell me anything." Hmm … that's unexpected. "Have you ever been to a medium or psychic before?"

"No," we answer in unison.

She positions a notepad and prepares to write. "I communicate with those on the other side using a sixth sense. It isn't always exact so a lot of times I must interpret the things I see, feel, and sense." Of course it isn't an exact science. If it were, it could be explained and therefore, she couldn't milk money out of people. "Any questions before we begin?"

"No," Sin replies. I shake my head.

She puts pen to paper and begins to write a series of numbers. "Do the numbers five, ten, and thirteen mean anything to you?"

He hesitates before answering. "Aye."

"The young girl I see—she was five when she died ten years ago on the thirteenth. Do you understand this?"

Sin looks up at me, clearly spooked, and then back to Mary. "Aye."

"Her name begins with a C. Something like … Clara."

"Cara."

"Oh, good." She sketches a heart dangling from a chain. "And she wore this?"

"That's her locket."

"Perfect. And this young girl was your sister?"

Sin brings his hand to his chin and rubs it, something I've noticed him do when he's uncomfortable. "Aye." He looks up at me and then to Mary. "Who gave you this information?"

"Cara."

"Cara's dead."

"Thus the reason I'm able to communicate with her." Mary returns her pen to the paper. "It's hard for me to catch my breath. This is my sign she died with something related to the lungs." She stops drawing. "A terrible thing was done to that child but she wants you to know she did not suffer."

"She was murdered—smothered. We've never found out who did it." Sin appears to be growing more anxious. "I need to know who it was."

"I see the shadow of a man in a dark room, her bedroom, I presume, but I can't make out his face."

"Can you tell me anything? Is he young? Old? Tattoos?" Oh my God. He's actually feeding into this. This woman is damn good.

"Your sister's moved on to a different image. That's my sign telling me she doesn't want you to dwell upon what happened to her."

"What are you seeing now?"

"You—and you're happy. She wants you to know you'll find joy in a family of your own. You'll have a wife and children, and soon, from the looks of what I'm seeing."

What bullshit!

Mary turns the page of her book. "Are you ready, my dear?"

I nod but say nothing as Sin stands to switch places with me. "Your mother has passed?"

Sin knows this but I must be careful about what I admit to so nothing contradicts what I've told him. "Yes."

"And a mother figure as well."

Hmm … if this were real, I'd think she was referring to Julia, my adoptive mom. But because this is a fraud, I can pretend she must be referring to my faux aunt I just lost if need be.

"Yes."

She writes a word and holds the pad for me to read. Bluebird. "Do you understand this?"

She spelled it wrong. It should be Bleubird, but how could she possibly know? "Yes."

"It's what your mother called you?" She couldn't possibly know that—except she does.

"Yes." I can see how easy it is to feed into this. I must be careful to give away nothing.

"This is your mother's way of validating her presence and my ability to communicate with her. She says you're cynical."

I'll give her that one. "That's very true."

She smiles, maybe as though she's accepting the challenge, and returns to scribbling in her notebook. She holds the pad up when she's finished. Chocolate chip cookies. "Do you understand this?"

"Yes." My voice breaks and my eyes flood with tears. I feel the supportive touch of Sin's hand on my shoulder.

I'm being reeled in because it's nearly impossible for a random stranger to guess such specific things. I don't want to believe in her, but I can't stop myself. "My mom's okay?"

"I couldn't communicate with her if she weren't." Mary reaches across the folding table and takes my hands. "Listen carefully, because this is very important. This thing you're planning to do isn't going to make you happy. If you go through with it, it'll eat at you and rob you of the joy you're supposed to have with your husband and children."

The fact that she just called me out on my plan to kill Thane briefly escapes me because I only hear two words. "Husband? Children?" I whisper.

"Nothing you do will change what happened." She pats my hand and my body shudders from the chill. "Your mother doesn't want you to put your future happiness in jeopardy by chasing an empty dream."

A single tear rolls down my cheek as I search through my purse for a tip. I'm glad my head is down. I don't want Sin to see me cry.

"Thank you, Mary."

We walk without talking for a while before Sin finally breaks the silence. "Could you stand that drink now instead of later?"

That's the best idea I've heard all day. "Quite honestly, I think I could stand a few."

CHAPTER TWENTY

SINCLAIR BRECKENRIDGE

I HOLD UP MY EMPTY GLASS SO THE BARTENDER MAY SEE OUR NEED FOR REFILLS. Two isn't going to cut it. Bleu nods in agreement and a couple of more Black Labels are sitting in front of us within minutes.

Neither of us has mentioned what happened with the medium, but I know we're both spooked.

I give up on Bleu being the first to broach the subject. "That wasn't real, right? It had to be a hoax."

"The logical side of my brain is trying to convince me it was a ruse but then I have this other side arguing against that. There's no explanation for how she knew my mother called me Bleubird unless she was for real. And the chocolate chip cookies … how could she know that was something special I did with my mother?"

"I have no idea."

Believing that she's the real deal means accepting I'll be married soon. Oddly, hearing that I'll be happy with a wife and children doesn't bring me joy—because that life doesn't include Bleu. My time with her will be over much quicker than I'd like and I'm not excited by that prospect. "I don't want to think about the things that woman said. All I want to do is drink a lot of whisky and then take you home to our bed."

Bleu holds up her glass for a toast. "Agreed." We toss our whiskies back.

I lift my empty glass for the bartender to see again. "We'll take the bottle."

A half-full bottle is placed in front of us. I fill our glasses to the rim. "Toast?"

"Yes."

Bleu and I look at one another and I suspect we're feeling the same. "Here's to the present."

Bleu smiles but it doesn't touch her eyes. She looks … sad. "To the here and now."

Bleu kisses me like crazy as I work to unlock the door. I blindly succeed and we fall through the entrance together. She's walking backward, pulling me toward the couch. "I want you right now."

She leans back against the arm of the couch, pulling me to stand between her parted thighs. Her hand is on the back of my neck and she pulls me down so my mouth meets hers. She's rougher than usual. I suppose I have the liquor to thank for that.

Her knees are bent and her legs are wrapped around my waist. I move my palms up her thighs until they're cupping her bottom. "I love your arse. It's perfect."

She squeezes her legs around me so my groin is pressed hard against hers. "Yours is perfection. I love digging my heels in when you're between my legs so you'll fuck me harder."

There's nothing I love more than Bleu urging me on.

I move my hands from her arse to the front of her shorts. I unfasten the button and tug them, and her knickers, down her legs. They drop to the floor and I kick them away as she reaches for her top, pulling it over her head.

I pull her forward so her lower back is against the couch arm, her bottom hanging over the edge. I drop to my knee and plant her feet on my shoulders. Her legs are sprawled wide. "You have a way of bringing men to their knees."

Her body shudders and a moan leaves her mouth when my tongue slowly drags upward through her center. "Ohh."

I sweep my tongue up and down before changing the motion to a circular movement over her clit. I push two of my fingers in with my hand turned palm side up, and use them to stroke her on the inside.

Turning Bleu on turns me on. This sometimes means I'm not always aware of how fast I'm moving. In this case, it's a good thing. "That feels … SO good, like a fluttering butterfly in just the right spot. Don't stop."

I wouldn't dare stop. I love licking Bleu until she comes. "I am so close." There's only one thing I love more than making my Bonny Bleu come—that's knowing I'm the only one to ever have done it.

I alternate the suction and release of her clit until she arches her back and cries out. "Oh God! Right there. Just like that." I feel her inner body spasm around my fingers and she calls out my name. "Ohhh, Sin!" Her legs tense, her toes digging into my shoulders.

Then all goes lax and I know my lass is in post-orgasm bliss. "Good?"

She's wiggled down so she's inverted with her head on the couch cushion. Her eyes are closed and they remain that way. "Mmm-hmm," she moans.

She isn't talking. That means it was very good for her. Perfect.

I pull my shirt over my head and toss it into the pile of clothes. I unfasten my trousers and push them away before wrapping my hands around her hips to hold her in place. "My turn now."

I enter her fast and hard. She always has the same reaction. Gasp. Tense. Relax. I'm quite fond of all three.

I grasp the soles of her feet and push her legs back and apart. I move in and out of her slowly because the position is so intense. I love the way it feels but I'm a little afraid of hurting her; it feels much deeper than ever before. "Does this feel good for you?"

She smiles up at me, biting her bottom lip. "Mmm-hmm. I like it."

That means I can keep going. "I'm glad because this way feels so good, I didn't want to stop."

I thrust faster and a minute later I feel the onset of an orgasm. I slow my speed in hopes of prolonging the pleasure but it's too late. Being this deep inside Bleu feels too damn good to not come quickly.

I don't know why I try. I'm never able to hold back with her.

I release her feet and grab her hips to hold her in place. "Ohh, I'm coming."

She wraps her legs around my waist and digs her heels into my arse, slamming our pelvises together. There is no beginning and no end. We are one. And then I erupt inside her.

When my orgasm is over, I notice Bleu grinning. "What are you smiling about?"

"You have a great come face." She laughs.

"I happen to like yours as well. I enjoy seeing it often."

"I have no objections to showing it to you on a regular basis."

I slap my hand over her arse cheek and squeeze. "Move up, Bonny. I want to lie with you."

Bleu slides up the couch and I stretch next to her. We're facing one another. She hitches her leg over mine and snuggles close. She traces the tip of her finger from my hairline down my forehead, the bridge of my nose, stopping at my lips. She moves her finger back and forth over my bottom one. "I love this mouth."

"This mouth has a confession."

A wrinkle appears across her brow. "Okay."

I think she's worried about what she's going to hear from me. She should be. I've had a lot of whisky and my tongue is loose.

"I'm a selfish bastard. I'm certain you've never met a bigger one. That means I don't want to share you with anyone. The thought of another having you this way … it sends me into hysteria. I think I might kill any man who dared touch you."

She says nothing but leans forward to kiss my mouth. Her hand strokes my leg, not at the top close to my cock. It's near my amputation.

My divulgence isn't over. "I may never let you go, Bonny Bleu."

"I doubt your Fellowship-approved wife will care for that." Oh. She's going to bring that up, huh?

"She'll like it about as much as your husband will." I know it's irrational to be angry about a future that has nothing to do with the present—and is likely a hoax—but the thought of Bleu one day having another man as her husband pisses me off. It feels like a betrayal she's yet to commit, but I know it's coming.

"Sin." She props her head in her hand. "You sound like you're mad at me."

Do I dare admit it?

Aye, I do. "Hell yeah, I'm angry. You're going to be with someone else."

She hits my uninjured shoulder with her fist. "Why are you getting pissed off at me? You're going to be with someone else too. And soon—with babies. You'll have everything I desperately want but will probably never have. Do you know how that makes me feel?"

She thinks this doesn't bother me as well? "No worries. You and your husband can thaw out your wee one whenever you decide you're ready to welcome him or her into the world."

"Frozen eggs are more susceptible to damage during the freezing process. I didn't have a highly successful retrieval. That means my chances for having babies aren't good."

I wouldn't have done the reading had I known it was going to cause a problem between us. "Psychics aren't real. None of that stuff she said is true."

"I didn't need a psychic to tell me you're going to be a stupid crime boss lording over a bunch of dumb-asses. Or that you're going to allow them to dictate who you can and can't be with." She sits up and spins around so her back is turned. She leans forward with her head in her hands. "I'm thinking about you being with somebody else and now I'm pissed off."

"Is it nuts to say it feels like a betrayal?" I ask.

"It totally does. I have an aching throb deep in my chest."

She doesn't have to describe it. I know the exact feeling.

I put my arm around Bleu's waist and pull her to lie next to me again. "We didn't need a fake or real psychic to tell us we won't last forever. That's a given, but we have this time together. Let's make the most of it."

I drape my arm over her body and pull her close. My cheek is pressed against her back and I feel her body shudder. She's crying. I rub my hand over the back of her hair. "Shh … please, don't."

Crying women have never fazed me but Bleu crying … that's something different. I don't take it lightly. This isn't a performance. She isn't shedding tears with an ulterior motive in mind. This is her coming to terms with the fact that we'll be over soon.

I don't know when it happened but I've fallen completely and madly in love with this woman. I could be out of my mind but I think she may love me too. It's an unexpected surprise considering what an unlovable bastard I am.

We're not over. I refuse to accept any future that doesn't include Bleu. I will not give up the best thing that's ever happened to me, not for anything or anyone. Now I must figure out a way to work this out with The Fellowship.

The woman sitting across the table gave birth to me, yet she's practically a stranger. We resided in the same house most of my life but I have very few memories of being parented by Isobel Breckenridge. I don't know her, yet she's the only person I want to talk to right now.

"I asked you to join me for breakfast because I need advice, and I feel you're the only one I can trust with this."

She's smiling, appearing pleased. "Yer talking aboot Bleu?"

I nod. "I've not spoken to Abram since our altercation but I'm certain he hasn't changed his mind. I don't see him letting this go."

"Ye knew that before ye chose tae start seeing her. I dinnae know why yer surprised."

"Abram reacted just as I expected." My own response is the one that surprises me. "I never intended for our relationship to mean anything. It was only about ..." She knows what my intentions were. I don't have to say the words.

"But then yer feelings evolved."

I won't insult my mum by denying what's happening between Bleu and me. "What do I do?"

"Expect complications—great large ones."

That's not helpful. I'm well aware of the problem I have on my hands. "Trouble is a given."

"I can think of one solution tae all of this madness." She grins while lifting a brow. "Recite rule number two of The Fellowship code."

"You must never violate the wife or children of another member." Is she suggesting what I think she is?

"Marry her. She would become part of the brotherhood and then no one could say a word aboot her not being one of us."

I've never heard of a member forcing the approval of an outsider by any means. "Has it ever been done?"

"Never."

"I don't think that would sway the brotherhood to accept her."

"Maybe not, but no one could harm her."

It's such an extreme measure. "We've only known each other for two months."

"I knew yer father for eighteen years. What did it get me?"

If I had to marry, Bleu would definitely be the only prospect—but I don't want to, and neither does she. It would ruin everything. "It would be like marrying so we could date."

"People have done it for less. At least ye love her. And it would keep her safe."

Am I that transparent? "I never claimed to be in love with her."

"I dinnae need tae hear ye say the words." She adds a sugar cube to her coffee and smirks. "Are ye going tae tell me yer too blind tae see that she loves ye too?"

Does she? I don't know; she's never said so. Whether she does is of little consequence. "Married or not, the brothers will never accept her."

Isobel Breckenridge pushes her shoulders back and sits straighter. Her expression clearly changes. "Ye will step intae yer father's role as The Fellowship's leader. That means ye never have tae request their permission and ye damn sure don't ask for their forgiveness." She points her finger at me and I see a fire in her eyes, one I've never noticed before. "Ye make the rules … because yer the ruler. Not the other way around."

I'm not their leader yet. "I'm afraid Abram will get to her."

"Ye should be afraid. He won't blink an eye at killing her. But he cannae touch a hair on her head if she's yer wife. It's a sovereign code among the brothers even he wouldn't dare break."

"Marriage is too extreme."

"If ye dinnae love the girl enough tae keep her safe, then tell her goodbye. And soon."

"I'm neither prepared to marry nor say goodbye to her."

"Ye brought Bleu into oor circle and put her in danger. It's yer responsibility tae protect her at any cost. The manner in which ye do it is up tae you, but heed ma warning. Don't allow Abram tae make the decision for ye. He has plans of his own and it won't end well for that lass."

If she knows something, she has to tell me. "What are his intentions?"

"He wants ye tae marry Westlyn."

What? "I can't marry her. She's my cousin." As if I really need to explain this.

"Not by blood."

I know Abram was adopted but he's out of his mind if he thinks I'd consider marrying his daughter, a lass I very much consider family. "Why does he think I'd want to do that? Being with her would feel like incest."

"He has no consideration for what ye or Westlyn want. He only considers himself. But just so ye know, she isn't opposed tae the union. In fact, she's very much in favor of it. He's groomed her for a long time, making her believe she'd be yer wife one day."

Abram will never have a chance at being leader. It's something that's always eaten at him and he thinks being my father-in-law will bring him another step closer to the leadership role. He wants to be my puppeteer. Too bad for him—I'm no one's minion.

I've loved Abram as an uncle my entire life. I couldn't see him for his true self when I was a child, but that isn't the case anymore. The rose-colored glasses are off.

I won't be forced into a marriage. When I decide to take a wife, it'll be because it's my decision. "I have a lot to consider."

"If ye don't listen tae anything else I say, hear this," my mum says. "Backing down tae Abram will be the biggest mistake ye'll ever make. It's yer responsibility tae stand up and put him in his place early. Show The Fellowship ye will not be manipulated. I fear for the structure of the brotherhood if ye dinnae."

CHAPTER TWENTY-ONE

BLEU MACALLISTER

Sɪɴ ʟᴇғᴛ ᴡɪᴛʜᴏᴜᴛ ᴀ ᴡᴏʀᴅ ᴛʜɪs ᴍᴏʀɴɪɴɢ. Oʀ ᴀ ᴋɪss. Oɴʟʏ ᴀ ʜᴀɴᴅᴡʀɪᴛᴛᴇɴ note in place of his warm body that should've been next to me. I suspect it has something to do with last night's incident. I could've been crying for any number of reasons, but I wasn't. And he knows. I don't want this relationship to come to an end. I'm certain that's why he didn't kiss me when he left this morning. He's disgusted by my display of vulnerability. He has to be; Sinclair Breckenridge isn't attracted to weakness.

It's very likely I've blown the facade—the one where I'm not attached to him. Or in love. A stupid woman. That's what I am. And it's all his fault for making me love him.

> *Good morning, Bonny Bleu. You were sleeping so peacefully, I couldn't bear to wake you, even for your morning kiss. I wonder what you could have possibly been dreaming about.*
>
> — S

"I was dreaming of you, Sin—always you."

I fall back onto the bed, the note against my chest. These aren't the words of a man preparing to tell me to leave. They are ... endearing.

And I'm relieved. That's the only word to describe what I'm feeling.

It's Monday. That means it's call day to Harry.

Since the intruder, Sin is always certain to lock the door when he leaves, but I follow procedure and inspect it anyway. The last thing I need is him slipping in unnoticed while I'm retrieving my phone or using it to talk to my dad.

It's clear, so I peel the tape away and free my burner phone from its hiding place beneath the bedside table. Although Harry understands, I hate calling at this time—it's the middle of the night for him. He needs all the rest he can get but this is my safest time of the day to talk.

Things would've gone much differently if Harry weren't sick. I would've gotten a couple more years of undercover experience beneath my belt but more importantly, he'd be here with me. That has always been the plan. Thane was always going to be my kill but Harry was coming to do this job with me. We were going to be a team.

Fuck cancer and the horse it rode in on.

Ellison answers Dad's burner and my heart plunges. I immediately know something is wrong. He'd never give it to her unless his health had taken a turn for the worse. "What's wrong?"

"Don't freak out. Everything's fine."

Bullshit. "Everything's not fine if you're answering this phone." I'm imagining the worst so I take a cleansing breath and blow it out slowly. "How bad is he?" She doesn't reply. "Elli! Answer me. Now."

"Hold on to your horses." I'm barely able to make out what she's saying because she's using her quiet voice. "I'm stepping into the hall so I can talk without waking him."

I'm right. Harry is in the hospital. "When did he go in?"

"Two days ago. He was originally diagnosed with pneumonia but they ruled that out yesterday. It's radiation pneumonitis."

My sister sometimes forgets that she's a nurse and I'm not. I don't speak medical language so I have no clue what radiation pneumo-whatever is. "Explanation, please. Dumb it down in terms I'm able to comprehend."

"It's an infection of the lungs caused by his radiation treatments."

But he hasn't had radiation in weeks … unless he's been lying to me. "When was his last treatment?"

"Six weeks ago." Okay. I feel remotely better knowing he hasn't been lying. "It's normal for there to be a delay in the onset of the infection."

I was afraid something like this would happen while I was away. "Is this serious? Do I need to come home?"

"He'll be okay. They're treating him with steroids to decrease the inflammation. I expect him to be released today or tomorrow, depending on what his white count looks like." That's a blood test indicating how infected he is. That much, I know.

"He's stable. I don't anticipate anything happening soon but we need a plan in case I'm the one who needs to reach out to you. I might not be able to wait on you to call home. Can you please give me your handler's information?"

She's aware of the risk that poses. "Ellison, you know that's not a good idea."

"But what if something emergent happens and I need you? You aren't checking in with him often. And if he declines, he isn't going to tell you. I don't want something bad to happen and then have to wait on your weekly call to tell you."

I already feel like shit without her reminding me what a terrible daughter I am.

"He says this assignment is the most important op of your career and we can't jeopardize that, but I need to tell you something, Bleu. I'm here alone with him and it's not fair. I'm scared." Her voice cracks. "I don't want to be by myself if things go wrong." I remember how bad it was with Mom. We had each other to lean on and it isn't fair for me to leave all this on her shoulders.

Now I'm crying. "I just need a little more time and then I can come home."

"Please, hurry. Get your job done and get here as soon as you can."

Elli doesn't understand what's going on; she's in the dark. She's unaware I no longer work for the Bureau or that I've gone freelance. "I'm going to give you a cell number, but no name. It's a safety measure." I call off the contact number for Debra. "A woman will answer. When she does, you'll tell her you're having a problem with your account: alpha three one four delta seven nine."

"Hang on. I'll never remember that if I don't write it down."

Amazing. She has all that medical shit floating around in her brain but she can't remember a series of numbers without writing it down for the wrong person to find. "Fine. Write it down on a single piece of paper using your palm to bear down on. No notepad where the impression can be seen. Once you memorize it, destroy the paper. No storing the number anywhere." She says nothing and it's because I know what she's planning. She'll put this in her phone in her notes. "I mean it, Elli. This is serious. Your head is the only place these numbers can be stored."

"I got it, Bleu." Smart-ass.

"Tell Dad I called and that I love him," I say. "I'll call again as soon as I'm able."

"Please try to as soon as possible. He'll be nuts because he didn't get to talk to you." She groans. "I dread telling him you called; he's going to be pissed I didn't wake him."

"Blame it on me. Tell him I told you not to because I want him to get his rest. I'll try tomorrow if I'm able to get away."

I end the call before I completely lose it. By saying that, I don't mean I just cry. I go nuts—cussing at the top of my lungs, kicking the couch, throwing myself onto the sofa and screaming into the cushion.

I feel strong arms circle me from behind and I'm pressed into the couch. "Stop fighting me." It's Sinclair's voice next to my ear. "It's okay, Bonny. It's me. I'm the only one here with you. No one else." My body relaxes, as does his.

He presses his lips to the bare skin of my back above my nightgown. "It's just us—only me and you."

"I'm sorry," I cry. "So sorry."

"It's okay." He gets up and I twist around. He sits on the sofa and pulls me onto his lap, looping his arm around my waist. "Tell me about it."

I shrug. "Tell you what?" I ask, aware that it isn't going to fly with him but it gives me a minute to think of a lie.

"What—or who—forces you to always be on the defensive, ready to fight without a moment's notice?"

"I don't know what you mean," I lie.

"Come on, Bleu. We're beyond this."

"Beyond what?"

"Lies." He rubs his hand up and down my arm before kissing my shoulder. "You can always tell me the truth. Don't you know that by now?"

I can't. The truth will get me killed.

Sin's left me no choice. He's asking for an explanation about my constant defensive behavior and I have to say something. "I was attacked by a man when I was younger. I fought him off but I've never been able to put it behind me. It triggered something inside. I've had an irrational fear of being held down, among other things, since it happened."

"Who did this to you? I'll hunt him to the ends of the earth and choke the life out of him." I almost believe he would, if it were anyone other than his own father.

"He was a neighbor," I lie. "He died years ago."

"Yet his aftermath lives on." He puts his arms around me and I rest my head on his shoulder. "I'm happy you feel comfortable enough to share this with me. Thank you."

I don't reply because I'm not sure what to say.

"What triggered the episode you were having when I came in?"

How do I explain my come-apart so I don't look like a total head case? Think. Think. Think. "I woke up and realized you were gone without saying goodbye. I tried to go back to sleep but couldn't so I came to lie on the sofa. I must've dozed off because I was in the middle of a horrid nightmare when I awoke to your voice with you lying on top of my back."

"Your peaceful sleep didn't last long … but then it rarely does." Just like that, he believes me. It seems a little too easy.

I extinguish one fire but another breaks out when I realize I don't know where the burner phone landed during my fit of rage.

I wiggle in Sin's lap so I can inconspicuously take a look around. It's on the floor next to our feet. Shit. How am I going to keep him from seeing it?

A distraction—sex. It's my only hope.

I run my nose up the length of his neck until my mouth is at his ear. "I'm peaceful when you're lying next to me." I lace my fingers through the hair at his nape. "And on top of me." I suck his lobe into my mouth. "So … maybe you should take me back to bed and make me feel … safe."

"Hmm." He moves his hand up my leg until it reaches the crotch of my panties. "Maybe I will."

I leave his lap and tug on his hands so he'll stand with me. "Please?" I loop my arms over his shoulders and pull him in for a kiss while finding the phone with my foot and slowly pushing it beneath the sofa.

"This isn't the reason I came home."

"Then consider it an added bonus."

I must be more careful. If Sin had come home two minutes earlier, he might have heard me on the phone with Ellison. That could've been disastrous.

"We need to talk about something." Good news never follows someone saying that.

"Ahh … hence your reason for coming back?" I ask.

"Aye." He pushes into a sitting position with his back against the headboard. "I met with my mother this morning."

"Oh." How odd. He rarely has anything to do with her. "How did that come about?"

"I asked her to join me. I needed to discuss something personal and she's the only person I felt I could confide in," he explains.

"I see." He chose to talk to a woman he hardly knows rather than me. That seems a setback for where I thought our relationship was.

He reaches out to stroke my hand and smiles. "It was about you, so I couldn't very well ask you to meet me to discuss you."

"What made me the topic of conversation?"

"I haven't been completely honest with you about something."

"That's no shocker." Laughter erupts from my mouth before I think to turn it off. "I'm sorry but you do remember that I'm aware of who and what you are?"

"The knowledge of you knowing more about me than anyone else in this world never escapes my thoughts," he says.

"So what have you felt you needed to lie to me about?" I ask.

"It's not a lie. But I may not have divulged all information about a particular situation. There's a difference."

"What is this about?" He looks so troubled. "I know you can't tell me everything. It's something I was resigned to when we began seeing one another. I won't be angry with you."

"That's debatable," he sighs. "There's something I didn't tell you about the man who attacked you a few weeks ago. He was one of ours —a brother of The Fellowship."

I've always heard the phrase, "I felt the blood drain from my face," but I never knew what that meant until this moment. "I killed a brother?"

"It wasn't your fault." He reaches for my hand. "You didn't know."

The realization of my actions sinks in. "I don't understand. It's been weeks and nothing has come of it—not a single word said. What does that mean?" Oh God. They're planning to come for me when I least expect it. That has to be it. They're going to kill me for retribution. "I have to get out of here."

Sin squeezes his hand around my wrist, his eyes locked with mine. "You're not leaving."

Oh God. It's Sin—he's the one who's going to kill me.

I can't think of a worse way to die: to be killed by the man I love.

"His name was Malcolm. Abram sent him. He wasn't there to kill you—only to coerce you into admitting who you're working for." I don't have to ask why.

"You should've told me I killed a Fellowship member." He may have signed my death sentence by keeping this to himself.

"And what would you have done if you'd known?" he asks.

"I'd have gotten out of here while I could."

"I took care of it. No one knows it was you except my parents. But there's a reason I'm telling you this now. Abram sent Malcolm because he believes you're an informant. He still isn't convinced you're not, so there's reason to be concerned for your safety."

I'm a sitting duck. "Is this your way of telling me I should leave?"

"No. This is me telling you to stay and allow me to protect you." He squeezes my hand. "Do you trust me to keep you safe?"

"I do. But I'm scared for both of us." I don't know what this means for him. "You'll be going up against the brotherhood for me. That's not something they'll take lightly."

"This will be me showing them what their next leader is made of. It's a good move for me and a good lesson for them."

His words hurt. His actions have nothing to do with his determination to be with me. They're about proving he won't bend to them or their rules. This is about changing the game to suit him.

I've been needing a good kick to bring me back to reality. Well, here it is, right square in the middle of my ass. Time to finish this mission and get the hell out.

"Of course it's a good move, but maybe you shouldn't rock the boat since I won't be around forever."

"What does that mean?"

"I'm just saying I won't always be here, and this is something your brothers won't easily forget. They may feel as though you betrayed them for a woman, so maybe you should choose your battles wisely."

"You're worth the fight."

Now I'm confused. I don't understand his motive. "Is this about you choosing to be with me or showing them you can be if you so choose?"

"Both." He cradles the side of my face and caresses his thumb down my cheek. "You silly lass. You don't see it, do you?"

"See what?"

"The extremes I will go to have you." There it is. The validation I so desperately need to hear. My God! It's ridiculous how much I love this man but the tragedy is that he'll never know.

The one person I hate most in this world brought me to the one I love most. Who could have possibly imagined that?

CHAPTER TWENTY-TWO

SINCLAIR BRECKENRIDGE

IT'S BEEN A WEEK SINCE BLEU AND I DISCUSSED HER PLACE IN MY LIFE. I CAN'T tell her I love her so I show her the only way I know how. I possess her—often. I've made her mine in every way possible, short of saying those three little words. But she seems content. For now.

She's in the kitchen making chocolate chip cookies. It's what she does when she's upset or worried. It somehow brings her comfort.

I sneak up behind her to place a kiss on her neck so I can swipe a piece of dough from the cookie sheet. She slaps at my hand but misses because I'm too fast. "Oh, you are a very naughty boy."

I pop the dough into my mouth. It's from scratch, not the store-bought kind, so it's extra buttery. "Does that mean I need a belting?"

"Maybe." I wrap my arms around Bleu's waist from behind and she leans into me as I swipe a second piece. "Make that definitely."

"Sweet Bonny," I say against her ear before kissing the side of her neck. "I have to go to my meeting."

She twists in my arms to face me. "Are you very worried? Because I am—enough for both of us."

I won't lie about this. It's too important. "I have some very serious concerns about what the outcome will be."

She looks as though she might cry. "You don't have to do this."

"Aye, I do." My mum is right. I must put Abram in his place now.

"It's necessary for more than one reason."

I pull her close and she squeezes me hard. "I'm scared for you."

I'm not incredibly confident myself. "I could be gone for a while depending on how this goes." I kiss the top of her head. "Don't fret if I'm not back by morning."

She pulls away to look at me. "Are you serious? You could be gone all night?"

"I don't know. Maybe." I shrug. "Sterling is coming for you in an hour. He's going to drive you to my parents' house. It may not be safe for you to be alone tonight so you're staying with my mum." Not a single Fellowship member would dare to seek her out at my parents', even if Abram ordered it. They all fear my father's wrath. My place is obviously a different story since he's already sent one brother in.

"Is that really necessary?"

I don't like to think so, but I'm not sure where Abram's head is right now. "I don't want to find out too late that I should have sent you away." I've told Bleu I would protect her and I plan to keep my word. When I can't actively do that, I will always make provisions for her safety. "You should probably take a bag since you could be staying the night."

"Why do I get the feeling this is far more serious than you've made out?" Because it is. She's come to know me well enough to predict the story within the book before opening it.

I press my forehead to hers and rub our noses in an Eskimo kiss. "No worries, my Bonny Bleu. Everything will be fine and well this time tomorrow night."

"Sin. I …"

I know what's coming, the words she's toying with in her mouth. I can see affection pooling in her eyes, threatening to spill down her face, so I put my fingertip to her lips and shake my head. "Shh … don't. Save it for a better occasion, a happier time."

She snickers and a tear drops onto her cheek. "I can do that."

"I must go."

She holds my face and kisses me hard. "Come back to me when you can."

"No fear. I'll return the moment it's possible."

My father has taken his place at the table's head in the conference room while Mitch and I sit opposite Abram and Jamie. If one didn't know the chain of command, he could easily guess it by our seating arrangement.

Abram will lose his footing at the top once I finish my traineeship. He has acted as second-in-command to my father for years. It's what he and my father agreed he would do until I was of age. That occurred a while ago, but I was needed elsewhere. I volunteered to become sole solicitor since my father still had years of leadership left in him. It made sense at the time but now I'm not sure about my decision. Abram enjoys exerting control and power far more than he should.

"As you're all aware, we're here to discuss my relationship with Bleu."

"You're fucking her," Abram groans. "That doesn't constitute a relationship."

This is going to start off on the wrong foot.

Abram—and everyone else as well—is completely in the dark when it comes to Bleu and me. "You know nothing about our relations so you don't get to have an opinion about its authenticity."

He slams his hand on the table. "There shouldn't be an interrelation at all. The Fellowship prohibits any pairing with someone outside the circle of the brotherhood. You know this, yet you've chosen to continue seeing her. What do you think they're going to say when they figure it out?"

"The brothers know," Jamie says. He looks at me. "Leith called me while I was on my way here. He says it was the only thing being discussed at Duncan's tonight."

How very convenient—the brotherhood finds out right before we hold a meeting to discuss a solution. I'm certain I have Abram to thank for that shitstorm.

"Do tell, son. What do our men think about their future leader consorting with an outsider?" Abram looks so satisfied with himself.

"They're not pleased."

"As one would expect," Abram says.

Jamie looks at me instead of his father. "Bleu is seen as a loose end. There's talk of eliminating her."

"She can be trusted. She's more like us than you could possibly imagine. If you knew her, you'd see this." She never stops amazing me. It's as though she was born to be a part of us.

"But we don't know her and there's a reason for that. She isn't one of us."

"I asked the council to meet so we might come together for a solution." I say.

"You're breaking one of the most vital rules we have. You want us to pat you on the head and say it's okay because you're Thane's son. We're expected to roll over and accept this American because you do, but let me ask you this: what's going to happen when one of the brothers wants us to bend a rule for him and we tell him no?"

I'm not sure how to respond to that. As much as I hate to admit it, Abram's right. We can't have the brothers believing they can break the rules.

"Son, being leader of The Fellowship is a double-edged sword." Finally someone besides Abram speaks up. "As a leader, you are entitled to choices the brothers aren't—yet you're accountable to them. A good leader must lead by good example," my father says.

I can't believe he's talking to me as though he didn't once experience the same issue. "You mean, the way you were a fine example when you were having an affair with the American blackjack dealer?" I need him to remember what it was like to love a woman who isn't a part of our circle.

"Amanda wasn't living with me in the middle of the brotherhood. She was in the US where she had no contact with any of them. I kept her secret, as you should have with Bleu. Too late for that now."

Mitch holds his open palms in the air. "Who are we talking about?"

"Dad's American lover," I answer.

"What? Does Mum know?"

"It was years ago, Mitch." Dad sighs. "Let us get back to the reason we're here. I think we can all see that Sinclair is choosing to continue his relationship with Miss MacAllister. The floor is open for suggestions."

"Sinclair's traineeship will be over very soon. I think it's critical for the vitality of the brotherhood that he end this affair with the

American now so he can marry from within The Fellowship. It's time for him to choose a wife."

Mum says Abram wants me to marry Westlyn. Let's see if my mother knows what she's talking about. "Do you have a suggestion on the woman I should choose?"

"I do. I believe Westlyn would make you a fine wife."

"Dad!" Jamie says, clearly outraged. "You can't be serious. They're cousins."

"Not by blood. His union with your sister would strengthen The Fellowship far more than the daughter of another brother."

He should know now there's no hope in this plan. "I can never marry Westlyn."

"Because of the American!"

"My decision has nothing to do with Bleu."

"If you spent time with her, I think you'd change your mind," Abram says.

I've spent my entire life around her. "I can never see Westlyn as anything but my younger cousin. I can't do it." I knew they'd begin pressuring me about a wife, but I thought I'd at least make it out of my traineeship first. "I'll choose a wife when the time comes but until then, I'm not giving up Bleu."

"Then I have a suggestion for how to make this work," Abram says. "Bleu must become one of us."

He isn't suggesting I marry her. That wouldn't suit his plan. "By what means?"

"Initiation."

"Women aren't initiates," Mitch argues. "It isn't done."

"It's never been done. There's a difference," Abram says. "We're living in a world of equal rights. Who says a woman can't be an initiate?"

I should have expected something like this from him.

He means for her to be beaten—to be put through endurance in the name of the brotherhood. He thinks she'd fail but I know better. No woman in this world is stronger than my Bonny Bleu. But I won't allow her to be hurt because it's what Abram wants. "No! No member of this brotherhood will ever strike her."

"Miss MacAllister will never be accepted as long as she remains an outsider. Initiation is the only way to make her one of us."

I could force them to accept Bleu by making her my wife, but marriage isn't something either of us wants. It's a permanent solution for a temporary problem.

Again, Abram is right. Initiation is the only way the brotherhood will accept her as one of our own. But there's no way I'll permit her to be put through the endurance. "Okay. She will become one of us through initiation with me standing in as her substitutionary atonement."

"No. It has to be her."

"Our men often stand in their wives' place for atonement," I argue. I have him on this one.

"He has a point, Abram," my father agrees. "It is an acceptable practice for a brother to take the place of his woman if he so chooses. This is no different."

I don't give him time to argue. "Then it's decided. Bleu will participate in a formal initiation ceremony and I'll stand in as her substitute for the endurance portion. When it's done, she'll be one of us and her loyalty will never be questioned again."

"Sin, are you sure you want to do that?" Jamie asks. "You know how many don't make it through to the end."

I've never been surer of anything in my life. "I might not be able to take it for me, but I can take it for her."

"This is so fucking stupid." Mitch slams his hand on the table. "Dad! Tell him he can't do this."

"I agree it's the only solution that will be accepted by the brothers. It sets a high standard for what is expected. They will respect him for such a sacrifice and it'll prove his genuine belief that Bleu will be a trustworthy member." I think I see pride in my father's eyes. "This is the decision of a true leader."

Abram is clearly pissed off. He's losing this battle—as well as his footing at the top—and we both know it. "Someone call Ferguson and tell him to meet us at the black site. We have a new initiate for him."

———

Alec Ferguson secures two metal chains around my wrists. "I don't want to do this to ye, boss."

I'm sure he doesn't. No one in their right mind would want to beat their future leader within an inch of his life.

The thing about your brothers is that you've known them your entire life, unless they're initiates. It makes it a little more difficult to inflict pain on someone you once played tag with. "It's fine, Alec. No worries. I'll not hold it against you."

The chain tightens when he uses a pulley to lift my arms over my head. "I shouldn't be doing this. It doesn't feel right."

"How is Shona? I've not seen her in a while."

"She's large," he says. "Our third is due in three weeks but I don't think she'll last till the end of the week. They tell us we're getting a girl this time. Shona's really excited about buying little pink dresses."

"Then congratulations are in order."

Alec married Shona several years ago but I can't recall the circumstances of their union. "Was your marriage arranged or did you pick your wife?"

"We chose one another. Her father didn't care for me much, though. He thought she could marry better—someone more like Jamie or Leith."

"Do you love her?" I ask.

"Verra much."

He pulls the chain until I'm on the tips of my toes—and prosthesis. I'm not sure how this is going work out. "What wouldn't you do to have Shona in your life?"

"There's nothin' I wouldn't do for her or oor babies."

He locks the chain in place so I'm dangling like a side of beef in a meat house. "Then you must understand why I'd voluntarily do this. I chose to take my lass's place, to endure the pain intended for her, so she doesn't have to suffer for a life she's yet to fully understand."

"I get it now, boss."

"I hope the brothers do as well."

"They've been a bit outraged by ye sneaking around with the American. They feel betrayed but what ye're doing now is going to change everything about the way they feel. No one in a leadership role has ever done something like this. Ye're choosing to lower yourself from a place of high regard to obtain their permission instead of forcing it on them. This is ye asking your people to approve of a lass ye trust. This will sit well with the brothers."

"I hadn't thought of it that way."

"Whether ye realized it at the time, this is a verra good decision for ye." He grins. "And it doesn't hurt that ye'll get your lass. She's a bonny one, that Miss Bleu."

"Yes, she's very bonny, indeed." I can tell he's preparing for the first blow. "No special treatment. This is being recorded as proof for the brotherhood. I don't want anyone to claim I had it easy. My only request is that you not hit my left leg below the knee. It still requires therapy."

"Of course. I trust ye're familiar with the process?" Alec asks.

"I am." It's been years since I've attended an endurance, but I remember how brutal they are. "Let's begin. I'm ready to get this over with."

The first blow is to my lower back, right over my left kidney. "Uhh … " It hurts so badly, I almost piss myself.

"Sorry, boss."

"No apologies every time you strike me or this could take all night. Keep going so we can get it over with quicker."

"As you say, sir."

The next blow is over my other kidney. I think it hurt worse than the first blow. "I should probably expect to piss blood for a while, wouldn't you think?"

"Probably."

I turn my face as I take a punch to my left eye. It's not as bad as the kidney jab. I guess boxing has made me immune to being hit in the face. Then he hits the opposite side. Warm ooze trickles down my face.

"Think about it this way, boss. When ye get yourself all healed up, your lass is going to be real good to ye for taking this for her."

I'll have her and she'll be mine. That's all I can think of right now —until Ferguson's fist lands in my gut. Then, all I can think of is that this is only the beginning.

CHAPTER TWENTY-THREE

BLEU MACALLISTER

"I don't understand why Sin's not back. He's been gone for over three hours." I make another visit to the front window to look for any sign of him. Nothing. "I know he said he could be gone all night but what could they possibly be discussing for so long?"

Isobel sits on the sofa reading the latest celebrity gossip magazine. "Who knows with Abram?"

"I take it you don't care for him much?"

"Not at all." She stops reading and places her magazine on the cushion next to her. "I believe he's a sociopath. He has no regard for anyone or anything. He doesnae feel any kind of remorse for his actions and often displays violent behavior." She's done her research.

After entering the Bureau, I found a place to study the criminal mind, particularly sociopaths and psychopaths, since I strongly suspected Thane was one or the other. I felt it necessary to learn the way his mind worked if I was to successfully blend into his world.

I believe most members of The Fellowship are at least borderline sociopathic because they are able to form an attachment to a group while having no regard for society or its rules. They aren't full-blown because they're able to hold jobs and stay in a single place on a long-term basis. Psychopaths are a different animal.

"Have you considered Abram to be a psychopath, rather than a sociopath?"

"I'm not sure I understand the difference."

"Psychopaths can't form emotional attachments or feel real empathy with anyone. They often have very charming personalities, are very manipulative, and easily gain trust. They pretend to have emotions, yet they don't feel them. Some are so good at manipulation that their families never suspect their true nature."

"My God! That's probably the best description I've ever heard for Abram. Ye just described him tae a tee. How do ye know all that?"

"I originally majored in psychology." Lie.

My phone vibrates and I hear my text tone. "Finally! I can't believe he's just now updating me."

This is what Sin's willing to do for you. For his sake, I hope you're worth it.

What does that mean? "He sent a video and a text message." I read it to Isobel.

"Someone else sent that." Isobel streaks to my side. "Play it."

I touch the triangle in the center of my phone and the video begins playing. It takes a moment before I realize what I'm looking at.

It's Sin. He's strung up from the ceiling, hanging lifelessly. A man I've never seen is punching him repeatedly and he barely reacts. "What the hell are they doing to him?" She turns away. "Isobel! Why is that man hitting him? The message says he's doing this for me. I don't understand."

"It's called endurance. It's a test one must go through tae prove his strength so he may be considered for membership if he's not been born and raised in The Fellowship."

This doesn't make sense. "But Sin was born and raised in the brotherhood."

"Yes, but ye weren't."

"I'm confused about what's happening."

"It's only a guess but I think he may have negotiated yer induction into The Fellowship."

"What?"

"Any person wishing to join from outside the circle must take and pass an endurance test to be accepted. I think he's volunteered as yer substitution."

"No! I don't want him to do that."

"Clearly it's too late, judging by that video."

The call came from Sin's phone so I immediately dial his number, knowing he won't be the one to answer. "I see you got my message, dear." I assume I'm talking to the psychopath himself.

"Please stop this madness, Abram. I don't want Sin to do this for me."

"Because you don't want him to suffer, or because you don't want to be part of The Fellowship?"

Neither. "I'll do my own endurance."

"We're almost finished, sweetheart. Sinclair isn't in much shape to object but I don't think he'd appreciate us stopping so we can start from the beginning on you." Has this been going on for three hours?

"Wait a minute, dear," Abram says. "He's trying to say something. What was that, Sinclair? I couldn't understand you ... Oh, I think that was a no. He's barely conscious so it's hard to make out what he's saying." I don't know what to do. I don't want him to suffer for me.

"Should Thane bring Sin home with him? Or would you prefer we drop him at his flat?"

I look at Sin's mother. "Thane is there." I can't believe a father would watch this happen to his son.

"Wait a minute," Abram says. "He's trying to say something else ... the best I could make out was 'home.'"

Yes, I'm sure he'll be more comfortable in his own bed. "Send him to the flat. I'll be there waiting."

"As you wish, sweetheart."

I'm numb when I end the call. I'm further convinced Abram is a psychopath. He sounded as though he was enjoying what was happening to Sin. "I have to go. I need to prepare everything for him. Can you call Sterling to drive me home?"

"We'll both go," Isobel says. "I'm not sure ye'll be able tae handle him by yerself."

"I should call Jamie." From the looks of Sin on that video, he's going to need some medical care as soon as possible.

Sin's best friend answers on the first ring. "I'm with him, Bleu."

My level of anger multiplies. What is wrong with these people? What kind of father and best friend sit back and watch that? "You're with him while they're beating the shit out of him? And you're not doing anything to help him?"

"He chose this for a very specific reason but he needs to be the one to explain why."

I feel absolutely horrid. "Do you have any idea how it makes me feel to know he's suffering in my place?"

"You should be very proud. It's an honorable thing he's doing for you."

These people are out of their minds. Why would I be proud or honored by his suffering? "Well, I'm not. It's killing me to know he's in excruciating pain and I'm the cause."

"It speaks multitudes about his feelings for you," Jamie says. "He basically took a beating to prove how much he loves and trusts you."

"He could've just said so instead. That would've been a lot easier."

"He's going to be fine, Bleu." Jamie laughs but I find nothing humorous. "I'll give him something for the pain as soon as they've finished. You should expect him to be out of it by the time he's home."

The last time he was out of it, he was in such bad shape I nearly lost him. "Promise me you'll take care of him, Jamie."

"I swear."

I'm looking out the front window of Sin's flat watching for headlights when Isobel catches me off guard. "Has ma son told ye he loves ye?"

"No."

"He doesnae have tae say the words for it tae be so." She hesitates a moment. "It might not be something ye'll ever hear from him."

"I tried to tell him I love him tonight, but he stopped me when he realized what I was about to say." I smile. "He put his finger to my mouth and told me to save it for a happier occasion."

"He wants it tae be special when ye say it for the first time. That's rather romantic."

"Yeah."

"Ye don't understand oor ways, so this must seem terribly barbaric tae ye. It isn't. This thing he's done for ye is an act of true love. Right now, ye can't recognize its beauty for the ugliness, but ye'll come tae understand how truly beautiful this is."

It's impossible for me to see the beauty of his body being battered to a pulp.

"Sinclair has zero experience with love. He had no examples to watch as he was growing up. Be patient with him."

"I think he's doing a pretty fantastic job." I come to attention when I see headlights on the street but they pass the building without stopping. "He wants to have a relationship with you."

"I know. And I have ye tae thank for that," Isobel says.

"I haven't done anything special."

"Ye've brought me and my eldest back together. I didn't know that was possible after all the years we spent apart. I thought Thane had made him hate me the way he does."

"Did you always hate one another?" I ask.

"No, Thane loved me when we were first married. I was the one in love with someone else and I blamed him for keeping us apart. Ma coldness eventually turned him into a different person—one nobody could love." That isn't true. I'm certain my mother loved Thane.

It's a peculiar thought—that she could've been in love with a monster—until I remember who I love. Am I not following in her footsteps? Is Sin not a younger version of his father?

"Would ye care for tea?"

It looks as though we'll be waiting a while longer. "I would."

I turn to leave the window and Isobel gets up from her seat. "No, lass. I'll take care of it. You keep watch."

A moment later she comes into the living room carrying a tray. "Ye take two cubes and a dash of milk?"

"Yes." She remembers from the few days I spent at her house while Sin was in the hospital.

I stir the hot tea, trying to cool it faster.

"Bleu, do ye ever wonder why ye've allowed yerself to get mixed up in this lunacy?"

"I'd be lying if I said no. But then I think of Sin and I know exactly why." I bring my tea to my lips to try a small sip but it's still too hot. "He'll be in bad shape, won't he?"

"Aye—and probably for a while. He's going tae need ye by his side."

"There's no way I'd leave him." I couldn't if I wanted to.

"Good." A smile spreads on her face. "He'll draw strength from having ye near."

Halfway through the cooling tea, the caffeine adds jitters to my already trembling hands. "It probably wasn't the best idea to drink this. I'm nervous enough as it is."

"It's going tae be a long day and ye've not slept. Ye'll need the fuel."

I hear the distant sound of a closing car door. I place my teacup on the edge of the cocktail table and rush to the window. "They're here."

I go to the door and stand in the entrance waiting for them. I want to scream in horror when Jamie and Mitch bring Sin into the flat.

He's bloody from head to toe. His face is swollen and distorted. I almost need convincing this is my Sinclair because this person looks nothing like him.

The only positive aspect is that he seems relaxed, not at all guarded. "You gave him something?"

"Aye. Morphine." Thank God. "Where are we going?"

"I have the bed ready for him." I knew he was going to be a bloody pulp so I removed our new bedding and replaced it with the old.

Sin drops like a rock onto the bed. I'm not sure if it's from exhaustion or the effects of the narcotic.

"He should sleep for several hours but you'll need to give him more pain medicine before the other wears off." Jamie takes a syringe from his bag and places it on the bedside table. "Give him this injection around eight so you can keep him ahead of the pain. It's difficult to get it under control if you wait too long to dose again."

What the hell? He's placing too much faith in my nursing abilities. "I don't know how to give him a shot."

"There's nothing to it." He places his hand on Sin's hip with his thumb and index finger spread into a wide V. "Hit it in the center. Pull back on the syringe. If there's no blood, you'll advance the plunger. Piece of cake."

I guess it might be for someone who's been trained to do it. "Piece of cake, my ass!"

"Do you want him to be in pain?"

He knows I don't. "Of course not."

"He took this beating for you, so you'll be the one to suck it up and give him the morphine shot." Well, that's one way to make me feel even worse.

"No worries. She'll do it," Isobel tells Jamie. "I'll help her through it." I have a feeling this isn't the first time Isobel has taken care of an injured member.

"It's been a long night, ladies, so I'm going to sleep in the guest room. If anything happens, don't hesitate to wake me."

Sin's filthy. I won't let him lie in dirty, bloody clothing. "He needs to be bathed. Will you help me get him out of his clothes?"

"It's probably easiest tae cut them off," Isobel suggests.

"Agreed." No way I'm attempting to launder anything on his body. I may even have a small bonfire out back.

Isobel returns with a pair of kitchen shears and holds them out for me. I start at the hem of his pant leg, working my way up. I hear her sharp intake of breath when I expose his prosthesis. "My God. His leg has been amputated."

I stop and look at her. Her hand is over her mouth.

"You didn't know?" I had no idea this would come as a surprise. She's his mother. How could she not be aware of such an important thing?

"No one told me." She walks to the bedside and strokes the top of his hair. "I had no idea anything like that had happened tae ma boy."

"He lost it when he was shot six years ago."

"I was told he was away having extensive physical therapy."

"He was, but it was because he'd lost his leg." She's crying—something I know Sin wouldn't want her to do. "It's okay. He's adjusted well. It's not an issue the way you might imagine. He's normal in every possible way."

"It's a secret they've kept well but he chose tae share it with you. That tells me how much he trusts ye."

"He knows I will never betray his secret."

I continue my work, slicing through the pants. I cover his groin with the sheet before moving on to the removal of his underwear. Once I'm finished cutting away his remaining clothing, I bathe every inch of his body.

He's in bad shape—countless cuts, bruises, and abrasions. He grimaces when I wash his side so I suspect he has broken ribs as well. One of his shoulders is disfigured so I'm guessing it's dislocated. "I don't think Jamie saw this. He's going to have to pop it back into place."

"Should I wake him?" she asks.

"Not yet. I'll give him the morphine at eight and we'll wait for it to work before we inflict any more pain on him." I'm convinced Sin would have faired far better had he been in a head-on collision.

Eight o'clock arrives and it's time for Sin's morphine injection. I wipe his hip with alcohol and make the V like Jamie showed me, looking at my target. The thought of driving this needle into his flesh nauseates me. "I don't know what's wrong with me. I'm normally not squeamish."

"It's the thought of sticking something intae the muscle. It'll pass after ye do it." She places a supportive hand on my shoulder. "When he wakes, he'll be proud of the way ye've cared for him."

I get it. This is my service to him. By doing this, I'm showing him how grateful I am for what he's done for me. His act was one of love and so is this.

"Breck. It's Bleu. I'm going to give you a shot of pain medicine in your hip." I have no idea if he can hear me. I highly doubt it but it doesn't seem right to jab him without telling him what's coming.

I pop the needle into his skin, down into his muscle, but he doesn't flinch, still sedated from the morphine Jamie gave him earlier. Good. "Sleep well, my Breck."

CHAPTER TWENTY-FOUR

SINCLAIR BRECKENRIDGE

I ACHE FROM THE TOP OF MY HEAD DOWN TO THE TIPS OF MY TOES AS I SHIFT IN the bed. I open my eyes—or eye, since it seems my left one is swollen shut—and lift my head, causing my brain to throb. I recognize it as rebound pain from the narcotic. That shit does it to me every time.

I look at my surroundings and discover I was brought home and placed in my own bed. Good. It's the only place I want to be right now.

It's likely late evening based on the amount of sunlight in the room. That means I've slept a long time but it's not surprising. I'm sure Jamie shot me up with plenty of narcotics.

Bleu is sleeping next to me, curled into the fetal position. I can't resist touching her so I reach out and stroke the back of my hand down her face. "I love you, Bleu MacAllister. I'll always do what it takes to keep you safe, no matter the extreme."

She stirs in her sleep so I stroke her face again. I'm aware of how selfish I'm being for waking her but I can't help myself. "Bonny."

She stretches and turns on her side to face me, eyes wide open. She reaches out to touch my face and the sensation is peculiar. It feels fat and numb, from the swelling I suppose. "Breck. You're awake."

"Only just now." She scoots closer, careful to not come too near. As much as I love her touch, I don't think I can stand it. Everything hurts. "Opeing my eyes to see you lying next to me … there isn't a more beautiful sight to look upon when waking." I wouldn't mind it being this way every morning of our lives.

"You left here last night on your way to a meeting with The Fellowship council. How in the hell did it escalate to this?"

I recount the events of last night for Bleu. "So clearly, it didn't go the way anyone expected."

"Obviously," she says.

"Abram is very displeased." That's an understatement. He's mad as hell.

"Why? He got to see you get the shit beaten out of you. He probably popped fresh popcorn while he watched the show." Wow. She's bitter.

"He likely did enjoy it since I burst his bubble by informing him I'd never marry his daughter, Westlyn."

Bleu makes a confused face—wrinkled brow, narrowed eyes. "But she's your cousin."

"Not by blood. Remember Abram was adopted. The brotherhood would accept it, probably happily. Our union would strengthen the brotherhood. That's win-win for everyone, except me."

"He wants you as a son-in-law so he can whisper in your ear."

She gets this completely. "Exactly."

"He would be a total nightmare as a father-in-law."

"Without doubt," I agree.

"I think he finally understood it's not going to happen."

"Good." Her hand finds mine. "Are you in much pain?"

Aye. I feel like I've been run over by a train but I'll never admit it. I don't want her to carry any guilt about my decision. "It's not too bad."

"Liar."

"I've been called worse." I laugh, and then grimace because it hurts like a son of a bitch. "Mmm …," I groan.

"Okay, Mr. 'It's Not Too Bad.' Tell me how I can make this better."

"As much as I dread getting up, I need the toilet and I fear I'll require your assistance." She comes around to my side of the bed. "I'm going to be slow."

"No worries. I have all the time in the world. I'm a kept woman so

I have nowhere to be."

"I'm not sure how well kept you'll be while I'm in this kind of shape."

"We're partners, Breck." She leans down to kiss the top of my head. "You take care of me and now, I'm going to care for you."

She squats down and attaches my blade I wear at home as I sit on the edge of the bed. I then use her for support while walking. "I've got it from here."

"I don't trust your legs."

I don't really want her in here with me when I piss for the first time. I'm expecting blood—maybe lots of it considering the abuse my kidneys and bladder took. I'm afraid she'll freak out. "Come on, Bonny Bleu. You won't even take a piss without closing the door."

"I shut the door because I'm a lady and I prefer you didn't know I have bodily functions. You, on the other hand, use the toilet in front of me all the time. You're not shy so there's no need to start now."

"Don't fight me on this."

She sighs and leaves, shutting the door behind her.

I finish using the toilet and I'm glad she wasn't with me. It was a lot of blood—enough I should probably tell Jamie. I'm not sure that's normal even for what I went through. "All done."

She helps me back to bed and removes my prosthesis. "Can I get you something to eat?"

I was hit in the gut too many times to have much of an appetite. "Maybe something to drink. A Johnnie Walker."

"You've mixed enough whisky with narcotics. I'll get you tea instead."

I smile at her retreating figure. She's going to be a total pain in my ass while I recover. And I love it.

It's been a week since endurance. I'm much better, thanks to Bleu's excellent nursing, so it's time for her initiation into The Fellowship. The ceremony is taking place at my parents' country estate outside of Edinburgh. My mum has gone all out, making it a formal affair. It's the complete opposite of the usual meeting in the conference room with a few witnesses, followed by lots of whisky at Duncan's.

Mum's plans for Bleu's inception aren't routine but they're fitting. Neither Bleu nor our relationship are typical. Her acceptance into our circle is the first of its kind; therefore, her commencement should be as well.

I stand outside the bathroom door and check my watch. "Bonny, are you almost ready? If we leave right now, we'll still be five minutes late."

"Just a few more minutes." Right. She said that ten minutes ago when we should have been leaving.

Fifteen minutes later she comes out of the bathroom smoothing the front of her clothing. "I'm not sure about the dress. What do you think?"

It's sexy—black, fitted, and short. A combination that can never go wrong on my bonny lass. Her hair is pinned away from her face on each side and cascades down her back. Suddenly every minute she spent getting ready, including those that will cause us to be late, becomes worth it. She's breathtaking.

"I've never seen you look more lovely." No one will look at her and wonder why I was willing to go through hell and back.

"Good. Then I'm ready to go."

"Not yet." I take out the box I've been hiding in my jacket pocket. "I have something for you to wear."

I flip the top so she may see the Celtic knot pendant I had made for her. "Oh, Breck. It's beautiful." She takes a longer look and I wait for her to make the connection. "Is that what I think it is?" I smile and she knows the answer. "It matches your tattoo."

"I could've chosen something more feminine—or romantic—but you seemed to really like my Celtic shield. And I liked the idea of us wearing matching ones, even though mine is ink and yours is platinum."

"I love it." She turns and pulls her hair from her neck. "Will you?"

"Aye."

I close the clasp.

She frees her hair and goes to the mirror to take a look. She touches the pendant hanging in the dip of her throat. "It's perfect. Thank you."

Mum steals Bleu from my side within minutes of our arrival. This is about so much more than a Fellowship ceremony for my mother. She's delighted to introduce Bleu as my lass. She too has become quite taken with her. And that makes me happy.

We enjoy drinks and hors d'oeuvres before my father calls everyone out into the garden area. A large tent protects tables covered in white cloths and adorned with lit candles and huge floral arrangements. It looks more like a wedding reception than an initiate ceremony.

"We gather here tonight to receive Bleu into The Fellowship as one of our own. Come forward, Sinclair and Bleu." We join my father on the portable wooden dance floor next to a tall table in the center. It's garnished to match the larger tables throughout with one exception—a dagger.

I purposely didn't tell Bleu about this part. "Liam Sinclair Breckenridge, do you accept responsibility for Bleu MacAllister?"

"I do."

"Take the dagger." I lift it as my father instructs. Without any warning, I grasp Bleu's hand and drag the blade across the center of her palm. She gasps, either in pain or surprise. I'm not sure which. I pierce my own and lace our fingers together so we're palm to palm. Blood runs the length of our forearms, collecting at our elbows.

"Will you have her as your novice and guide her in the ways of the brotherhood?"

"Aye." I squeeze her hand, my eyes locked on hers. "I will have her."

"Repeat after me, Bleu."

My father states The Fellowship decree. It's something I've heard a million times in my life but it's been adjusted to fit these new circumstances.

I only listen to Bleu's voice repeating after my father. "I will be loyal and never betray any of the secrets of The Fellowship. I will never violate the family of another member. I will allow my sisters to guide me in my role. My blood is Sinclair's blood, as his is now mine. From this day forward, we are one family known as The Fellowship. This I solemnly swear."

It's done. Bleu is mine and one of us. I can finally display my affection for her without concern. The next step will be telling everyone I've claimed her. But what I really want right now is to possess her.

Everyone will want to use this time to get acquainted with Bleu, but they'll have to wait. Her declaration is a huge turn-on so I need to get inside her—five minutes ago.

I take her hand and tug. "Come."

"Where are you taking me?"

"Mum had the guest house redecorated after she went home goods shopping with you. It's quite lovely. You need a tour since you inspired it."

"My, my. You're very passionate about home decor tonight." She giggles.

"I'm passionate about something but it doesn't have a thing to do with new linens."

"Is the initiate ceremony always that ... hot?"

I completely agree; it was sexy as hell. "Never. It's always two men with a few witnesses in the conference room. The older member accepts responsibility for guiding the new one."

Mum comes out of nowhere and blocks our way. "Where do ye think yer taking her?"

"Umm ..."

"Aye, that's what I thought ye would say, but ye can turn yerself back around. Dinner is being served and the guest of honor cannae go missing for a shag in the guest house." Cock-blocked by my own mum.

We regretfully return to our table and take our place next to my parents for our catered dinner. We're two courses in when I put my hand on Bleu's thigh beneath the table. I slowly glide it in an upward motion. "I'm not craving leg of lamb. I want these legs with a side of something very special."

"You are so bad." She giggles and pushes my hand away. "You'll get everything you want—later."

I notice her pushing food around her plate but not eating. "Have you found more Scottish food you don't care for?"

"No. It's not that." She scrunches her nose. "It's the medication to treat the ovarian stuff. I'm still having side effects—GI symptoms."

"Maybe you should see a physician here."

"My doctor told me this might happen so it comes as no surprise." She shrugs if off. "I'll consider making an appointment if things don't improve."

When dinner is finished, a band launches into its first set and everyone moves to the makeshift dance floor in the center of Mum's well-kept garden. Of course, I get first dance with the guest of honor. "Is this how every new member is welcomed?"

"Only you."

She's smiling. "I feel very special."

"You should—because you are." I kiss her forehead. I want to tell her I love her but, again, this isn't the right time. It shouldn't happen in front of the entire brotherhood.

"There are a lot of people here. Are they all Fellowship?" she asks.

"Mostly. If they aren't in the brotherhood, they're comrades. They were invited because it's necessary they know you."

"I'll never remember all these people."

"You will in time." I say it as though she'll be around forever but we both know that isn't the case. That'll be a whole new problem to deal with when the time comes. I don't wish to think about it right now. I'm too happy.

The song ends and I'm forced to give up my lass so she may dance and mingle among her new family, leaving my dance card open. Westlyn gets up from her chair and walks in my direction so I grab the closest lass I can find.

"Is this your way of asking me to dance?" Lorna says.

"This is my way of telling you we are."

"Then I guess we're dancing." We sway to the music as my eyes search the crowd for Bleu. I'm not sure I'll ever stop being uneasy when she's out of my sight. "You've surprised me—and every other member of the brotherhood."

"How so?"

"You took a huge leap for Bleu," Lorna says.

"Aye."

"It's nice to know you aren't all heartless."

Is she referring to Leith? "Bleu told me about your feelings for Leith."

"I don't know what you mean."

"I'm talking about you being in love with him."

This time she doesn't deny it. "He doesn't know I exist except to put me on the work schedule."

He used to know she existed because he got into her knickers often. We all did. But I had no idea I wasn't the only one no longer banging her. "You don't shag anymore?"

She looks at the floor, shaking her head. "Not since he walked in on me and you almost two years ago. Things became really weird between us after that."

I knew Leith saw us but he never mentioned it. And I never gave it another thought since all three of us were having fun with her.

"We have a working relationship. That's it—unless he's been on the whisky. He loosens up around me a little then."

How strange. "Should I talk to him?"

"No. He's clearly disgusted by me, so I don't want him to know how I feel."

"But he may feel the same."

"He doesn't. Trust me. He knows he could have me anytime he wants but chooses not to."

Bleu has made me a little more romantic, so I feel like passing along some advice to Lorna. "I'm going to tell you something about men in general. We're selfish, possessive bastards when it comes to our women. We don't want other men having them. If you want Leith, don't sleep around."

"I haven't since that day."

"You haven't had sex with anyone in almost two years?"

She shakes her head. "The look on his face when he saw us—it haunts me. I'm not sure I can ever be with anyone else again."

Is Lorna who Leith was talking about when we were in the ring together? He said I always took everything he wanted. At the time, I had no idea what he was talking about, but now I may.

The song ends. "I'm sorry." I'm not sure what I'm apologizing for. "Let me know if you decide you'd like me to talk to him."

She looks like she may cry. "That'll never happen, but thanks for the offer."

I dance with numerous Fellowship daughters, some behaving as though they're in mourning. I suppose they could feel as though the dream of marrying the future Fellowship leader is dead. But it's the role they're in love with, not me.

I come face to face with Westlyn so I'm forced to dance with her. To avoid her would make the situation more awkward. I take her in my arms the way I have hundreds of times but this dance is different. She was hoping to be my wife, and I've rejected her.

"Are you enjoying the party?" I call it that instead of what it really is. I don't wish to make her feel bad. She's my cousin. We grew up together so I love her. I'd never want to hurt her.

"Everything is beautiful. Aunt Isobel went all out."

"She did. Exceedingly so, I'm afraid."

"She should have. It isn't every day the future leader of The Fellowship volunteers himself to be beaten in place of the woman he loves so she can become part of his world."

"I'm sorry for how this played out." I'm apologizing again for something I don't understand. "I had no idea how you felt."

She looks confused. "How I felt about what?"

"You were planning to be my wife."

"God, no, Sin. I could never marry you. My father is the one who planned on me being your wife. Not me." She leans back to get a better look at my face. "Is that why you've been avoiding me tonight?"

"The very reason."

"No. Dad came up with that. I'm not at all interested in climbing the chain of command. That's all him. I'd probably leave The Fellowship if I had a choice."

"God, I couldn't be more relieved." I adore Westlyn. She grew up tagging along behind me, Jamie, and Leith, so this misunderstanding has been incredibly unsettling for me.

"I'm happy to have that cleared up."

"Me too," I agree.

"I'm very much looking forward to becoming friends with Bleu. I've never been allowed to socialize with anyone not from within the brotherhood."

"She'll be very happy about that. I'm afraid she's been here for months and has no friends—except Mum. I'm sure she'd like some her own age."

"I'd love for you to introduce us later."

"Absolutely."

"I have a confession," West says.

"Aye?"

"I don't plan on marrying a man from The Fellowship."

Oh, shite. "You must know your father will never allow you to take a husband from outside the brotherhood."

"I don't really care what Dad has to say about it."

Are my actions responsible for her decision? "When did you decide this?"

"Years ago. It has nothing to do with you and Bleu."

Abram will never see it that way. Not only have I rejected his daughter as my wife, he'll now blame me for putting this idea into her head. "Do us both a favor and wait a while before you drop this bomb."

"No worries. I have no prospects at the moment. No need to stir trouble yet."

Aye. I have enough problems as it is.

Abram isn't finished with me and Bleu. I'm certain of that. All I can do is lie in wait, bracing for his next move. Because it's coming.

CHAPTER TWENTY-FIVE

BLEU MACALLISTER

I'T'S OFFICIAL. I'M A FELLOWSHIP MEMBER, GOING ON TWO WEEKS NOW. I'm completely and utterly in love with its future leader. I want to be with him forever. Undeniably, this isn't ideal. It's stupid and reckless but it's what I've chosen because I refuse to live without him.

And Harry can never know. He'd die of a coronary before the cancer had a chance to take him.

I'm undecided about my plans for Thane. I only know one thing: I still plan to kill him. But it won't be soon. I'm not ready to force Sin into his leadership role.

Clearly, my original plan has gone to shit. But … shit happens.

I have a dying father four thousand miles away and I'll need to return home to him soon. No exceptions. I spoke to Ellison yesterday and she tells me Harry is declining. It's expected, but I need to introduce the idea of going back to the US for a little while. And I know exactly how I'll do it.

Sin is working in his office. I stand in the doorway and take a moment to admire how handsome he is before disturbing him. He's still wearing his clothes from work, minus the jacket and tie. He's rolled the sleeves of his shirt to his elbows and is wearing his reading glasses. Mmm … I was right. He's hotter than a freshly fucked fox in a forest fire.

His eyes lift from the book lying open on his desk to his computer and he notices me standing there. The lopsided grin I love so much makes an appearance just for me. I covet it, especially when it's accompanied by a single dimple. "Hey, you."

"I hate to bother you. Can I have a minute?"

"I always have a minute for you." He pushes away from his desk and pats the top of his thigh. "Come see me."

I sit on his lap, sliding my arm around his shoulder for support. He pushes my hair away from my face so he can clearly see my eyes. "Everything okay?"

"Yeah. I just wanted to talk to you for a moment about something that's been on my mind."

"Sounds serious." He rubs his hand over my back in a circular motion.

"I'm afraid I don't make a very good kept woman. I'm used to working. Daily yoga and meal planning isn't my thing."

"Okay. I get it—you're bored—and I assume you've come to me because you have a solution?"

"What are your thoughts about me moving my photography business here?" I ask, having no idea what kind of response I'll get.

"Hmm … I don't dislike the idea but I think your services could be better utilized by The Fellowship. Working for the public does nothing for the brotherhood."

I can sort of see where he's going with this. "How might I serve The Fellowship?"

"You're a photographer. We could often use the services of a professional."

I'm liking this idea much better. "You mean you'd have me taking surveillance photos?"

"Aye. It's something we require on a regular basis so I think it's worth considering."

Criminals interest me far more than blushing brides and other people's crying babies. Since I've been trained in surveillance, this will work out much better for me. "I like it."

Now here comes the part about getting me back to the US so I can spend time with Harry. "All of my equipment is stored at my studio. I'll need to make a trip home so I can pack it and ship everything here. I have my aunt's settlement so I can take care of closing the studio for good while I'm there."

"I'll need to run it by Dad but I think he'll be pleased with the idea."

"I wouldn't rouse suspicion since I don't look the part of the typical Fellowship member you'd utilize for surveillance. Hopefully, your father would see me as an asset."

"I agree. And going home would give you a chance to visit with your father and sister. I'm sure you miss them."

"I do, terribly." He can't possibly imagine how much.

"Then we shall get you home." Sin takes off his glasses, putting them on his desk. "I haven't given you the attention you deserve this week. For that, I'm sorry, so I'm going to put this work away until another time."

"Thank you."

"I think we should go out tonight. Maybe invite some friends to go to the casino with us? What do you think?"

That sounds like fun. I haven't been gambling in a while. "I would like that very much."

There are six of us. Sin invited Jamie and Leith. I invited the only two girls I feel like I know at all—Lorna and Westlyn. That sucks for Jamie since Westlyn is his sister but Lorna is in love with Leith, so maybe I'm doing her a favor by bringing them together outside of work.

"What would you like to play first?" Sin asks.

Blackjack is my game. I'm a card counter—but I tell no one. I believe my mother was one as well. Perhaps that's how she fell into the gaming profession. I guess you can say gambling is in my blood.

I don't want to give myself away. "I should probably start with the American roulette table."

Westlyn, Lorna, and I take the seats at the table while the men stand behind us. Sin tosses a pile of bills on the table and the dealer changes them for chips. "I've got the first round."

Damn. He's spotting everyone.

We've never discussed finances but I know how much money Sin has. It was part of my research—to know how much and where his funds come from. He has legit investments that have nothing to do with The Fellowship. He's highly intelligent when it comes to capital so he's a wealthy young man. I'm sure that's another reason all the single Fellowship ladies are so sad to see him take up with the likes of me. I don't love the thought of how many women would like to have him.

I can think of one good thing about Sin substituting in my place for my endurance test. No woman from The Fellowship will ever question his feelings for me. He still hasn't said those words. I'm not sure he ever will but what he did leaves no question in my heart or mind. Sinclair loves me.

Everyone places bets but I go straight for the zero and double zero. It's my favorite wager because the payout is greater. "That's all you're betting?"

"It's a good bet. If either of the zeroes hits, it'll pay well." I'm not going to place stupid bets simply because I'm not using my own money.

Lorna is clueless about what she's doing. She's placed several wagers that will cancel one another out so I turn to Leith behind me. "You should help Lorna. She has no idea what she's doing."

"Lorna makes her own decisions." He brings his whisky to his mouth and tosses it back.

"She doesn't understand the rules of the game. Her bets don't make sense and the dealer isn't going to tell her the difference."

"Then she shouldn't play games she doesn't understand." Leith can be cold toward Lorna at times. I never noticed him being that way with the other girls at the bar. I'll need to ask Sin later if he knows what Leith's problem is.

I don't fare well at the roulette table so I decide it's time to head over for some blackjack. "I've lost enough here. I'm going to try my luck at cards. Want to come with me?"

"Aye." We sit side by side. "Do you know how to play?"

I avoid a direct answer. "You try to come closer to twenty-one than the dealer without busting?"

He seems satisfied with my understanding.

"Good luck," the dealer says.

The first cards dealt are low so I assign them a value using the hilo strategy. Low numbers are more beneficial to the dealer but the good news about pulling low ones is that my odds increase for higher ones, which benefits me. For every low number played, the percentage of high cards in the remaining shoe increases.

I choose to stay while Sin increases his bet. "You shouldn't have done that. You're gonna bust."

"We'll see." He sounds so cocky.

The cards are dealt and it plays out exactly as I predicted. "Dealer wins."

"Told you," I say.

"You lost too."

I did but that won't last after I count a few more hands. "I lost the minimum, unlike you."

"You have to spend money to make money."

"Or you watch and bet wisely," I argue.

"All right, lass. Show me how it's done." And that's exactly what I do with the next dozen hands. My stack of chips grows while his diminishes. "You're a natural."

Yes, I am. And he has no idea why.

I win four more hands and see I'm gaining the attention of the pit boss. We need to roll.

I lean over to kiss the side of Sin's face and whisper, "It's time to leave, Breck."

"But you're doing so well." Now isn't the time for him to argue.

"I don't want to keep you out too long. You have to work in the morning." I push my chips in to exchange them for larger ones. "Let's cash out and go home."

"Sin, you have quite the blackjack player with you tonight." Oh, shit. The pit boss knows who Sin is. I don't see this going well.

"This is Bleu MacAllister," Sin introduces. Now he knows who I am as well. "Bleu, meet Todd Cockburn."

"Hello, Bleu. It's a pleasure to meet you."

We're in a casino. He'll refuse my hand if I extend it so I offer a smile and nod instead. "The pleasure is all mine."

"We missed you at Bleu's initiate ceremony," Sin says.

What?

Todd shrugs and gestures at his surroundings. "Someone had to be here running this place."

A dealer from across the pit approaches. "Mr. Cockburn, I'm sorry to interrupt you and Mr. Breckenridge, but we have a problem."

"Duty calls," Todd says.

Sin is wearing a teasing grin.

"This casino is Fellowship?"

"Aye." He laughs.

"I was ready to dash out of here because I thought I'd been discovered."

"For what?"

"Card counting—as if you didn't know."

I look at the dealer and she smiles. "It took a while for me to catch on." She looks at Sin and shrugs. "The lass is quite good."

"Yes. She's quite good at everything she does, I'm afraid."

CHAPTER TWENTY-SIX

SINCLAIR BRECKENRIDGE

BLEU IS GOING HOME. I WON'T SEE HER FOR TWO WEEKS. I'M NOT SURE HOW I'LL handle being without her for so long since we haven't spent a day apart in three months.

We said our goodbyes last night—all night long. There were many times I considered telling Bleu the things on my heart. I. Love. You. They're three simple little words—but I couldn't bring myself to say them.

Work has robbed me of the time I'd prefer to spend with Bleu. That's why I'm taking the afternoon off to be with my lass. Her red-eye flight doesn't depart until almost midnight so we'll have several hours to … say goodbye again.

I'm already in the shower when I hear her come into the bathroom. I expect her to join me at any minute—but she doesn't—so I grip the handrail and peek around the tile wall.

She has taken off her gown and is standing in front of the mirror naked, looking at her body. "Admiring yourself?"

"No." She laughs and twists, moving her hand to her hip. "I was wondering what a Celtic shield like yours would look like right here."

She wants matching ink? "Stunning—that's how it would look."

"You'd approve?"

"Of course."

She comes into the shower with me, putting her arms around my body from behind. "I know I told you a hundred times last night but I'm going to miss you like crazy," she says.

"I'll miss you too, my Bonny Bleu. I mean that." I can tell her I'll miss her but why can't I man up and spit out the words I so desperately want to say?

I still have tonight. That gives me all day to think about the perfect way to broach the subject.

"Will you be seeing your doctor while you're in the States?" She mentioned making an appointment. I hope she does because I'm very concerned about the way the diabetic medication makes her feel.

"I doubt I'll be able to get in to see her on such short notice. You usually have to have an appointment months in advance."

"If you can't, I'll make sure you get in with the best doctor here when you come back." She's let this go on for months. She should have already been seen by someone.

I turn and wrap my arms around Bleu. There's nothing better than the feel of her wet body pressed against mine. "I wish I had time to make love to you in the shower but I don't. I have early court this morning."

"No worries. We'll take advantage of the time we have before I have to go to the airport."

It's five o'clock and I'm on my way out the door when Heather stops me. "Mr. Breckenridge. I'm so glad I caught you. I have a message from your uncle. He wants you to come by his office."

"Now?"

"Yes, sir. He said it was an urgent matter."

No fucking way! If I rushed home, I might have four hours with Bleu before she has to leave. I don't want to waste that precious time with Abram instead of being with her in our bed.

I dial Abram's number. "I got your message but Bleu has a red-eye, so I'll be in a rush to get her to the airport." Not the whole truth. "Can we reschedule for the morning?"

"Absolutely not. It's pertinent you see me before she leaves." I doubt that. "Trust me, Sinclair. You're going to want to hear what I have to say."

"I'll come for ten minutes." That's all the time I'll allow him to steal from Bleu.

I can walk the distance between our offices in the financial district in about fifteen minutes, but I'm in a hurry so I catch a taxi instead. Abram's secretary is still there when I arrive. "Mr. Breckenridge will see you."

"Thank you."

I stand in the doorway of Abram's office. He's combing through a file spread wide across his desk, appearing completely engrossed—or obsessed. I tap on the door to gain his attention. "I'm here."

"Aah … Sinclair. Come in and take a seat, my boy."

He hasn't called me his boy in years. He's absolutely giddy, so I don't expect this to be good. "I can't stay. I'm in a hurry."

"Yes. I hear our dear Bleu will be leaving the country."

"Only for a couple of weeks. She's going home to retrieve her photography equipment and visit her family. She's not seen them in months." Why am I explaining this to him?

He gestures for me to come inside. "You make me nervous standing around like that. Come in and sit."

I do as he asks. "I said ten minutes. You're down to eight."

"Then I shall get on with it," he says. "It has recently come to my attention that someone has been meddling in my business, so to protect my interests, I inventoried my vulnerabilities."

I already know where this is going—Bleu. "This again? Really? Why are you unable to let it go?"

He tosses several photos across his desk in my direction. "Take a look for yourself and you'll understand why."

I pick up the stack of photos—all of Bleu dressed in an iconic uniform I recognize. In one, she's standing next to a sign: FBI Academy. Quantico, VA. The others clearly display her accepting a diploma and then posing with it while giving a thumbs up. "Where did you get these?"

"The home of Harold MacAllister, her father." He scatters the photos and scours through them. "This is an interesting story. It becomes more and more intriguing the deeper you dig." He holds up a picture of Bleu with a man, both dressed in FBI uniforms. "You see, it turns out Bleu followed in her father's footsteps—being a part of the FBI is a family trait."

I'm numb. It's a fucking blow to learn Bleu's been lying to me all this time, but my brain can't make the connection. The States shouldn't have any kind of interest in anything we do. "The FBI can't touch us."

Abram gets up and goes to his liquor cabinet. He pours two whiskies. "I don't give two shits about the FBI. However, I care a lot about Bleu claiming to be a photographer from Memphis, Tennessee, when the evidence tells us otherwise."

There has to be an explanation, one that explains why Abram is wrong and I'm not in love with a woman who has betrayed me. "I don't know, but I intend to find out."

"It's not your job to find out anything. Leith is the one who originally let her slip in when he hired her. That's a mistake he'll pay for, but it was you who brought her into your bed and made her part of this family. It's your responsibility to take her out."

He isn't suggesting I safely send her home. "You want me to kill her."

"I want you to make good on the promise you made." I know the exact one he's referring to. I said I would be the one to do it if she turned out to be something different than she claimed to be.

"I remember but ..." I love her.

"After the first betrayal, there is no other." I know the motto well. Many brothers have died for far less. "You know there's no other way —absolute and unwavering loyalty to you and The Fellowship. You must demand that from any woman in your life."

I see the evidence but I refuse to accept it. "There has to be an explanation."

"She has betrayed you and The Fellowship. She can never be trusted now. She must die."

I can't do it. "I love her. She's mine. I've claimed her."

"Do you love her enough to die in her place?" I do but killing me wouldn't save Bleu and it would never satisfy Abram. He's thirsty for her blood.

"Listen very carefully, Sinclair. Bleu played the part of the perfect woman for you—because it was her job. That's why she was so easy for you to love, but none of it is real," Abram says.

I thumb through piles of photos of Bleu and see a woman I don't know. "Everything was a lie—a figment—right in front of my face, and I didn't see it." What does that say about me?

Abram leans back in his chair, his fingers interlaced, hands clasped. "From the heart's point of view, this must feel like an immense betrayal. But for Bleu, it was just business. She was here doing a job she was hired to do and she was damn good at it. Don't knock yourself too badly. Think of it as a lesson well learned."

"I don't know how to kill the woman I love."

"Quickly—it's the only way. Before your heart, or dick, has time to interfere."

"I'm losing my lass, the only one I've ever loved."

"Your heart is telling you to mourn the loss, but the truth is that your lass was never real. She didn't exist." Try convincing my heart of that.

"I understand she made you fall in love her. That's why I'll overlook you killing her quickly and painlessly."

He's right. Again. But for the life of me, I have no idea how I'll kill this woman I love so dearly. I can't imagine a darker sin.

I'm sitting on the sofa in the pitch-black dark when Bleu comes through the door. "Sin?"

"In here," I call out.

"I thought the storm might have knocked out the power." She walks over to the lamp and switches it on. "Why in the world are you sitting in here with the lights off?"

"I'm listening to the rain."

She notices the drink in my hand. "And you hear it better in the dark while having whisky?"

"Aye, it clears my mind." I'm relieved she came back. Although her luggage is sitting by the door, I thought she'd figured out I'm on to her and fled. "You weren't here when I got home."

"I left a note telling you the zipper on my suitcase was broken." She walks over to the coffee table and picks it up, showing me. "I had to run out and get a new one before the store closed."

She comes to me and sits in my lap. Her hand cradles my face. "You don't seem your usual self. What's troubling you?"

I have to kill you because you've betrayed me—and it's breaking my heart. "I'm going to miss you terribly, Bonny Bleu."

She entwines her fingers in the back of my hair. "We have a couple hours. Let me take your mind off it."

She brings her mouth to mine and kisses me slow but hard. "Mmm … I love when you taste like whisky." She sucks my bottom lip. "I want you to take me to bed and make love to me."

Kill her quickly—before my heart or cock has a chance to interfere. That's what I'm supposed to do, but I can see right now that's not going to happen. I'm not ready to squeeze the life out of her. "Lead the way."

CHAPTER TWENTY-SEVEN

BLEU MACALLISTER

SIN KISSES MY MOUTH AS WE WALK UNTIL THE BACKS OF MY LEGS MEET THE BED. He goes to his knees and presses his face to my abdomen. "I don't know how to do this—how to let you go."

I stroke his hair. "You act like it's forever. I'll be back in two weeks —fourteen days—think of it that way."

He puts his hands beneath my dress and slides them up the back of my thighs. He finds my panties and drags them down my legs. I step out of them and shoes at the same time, kicking both to the side. I pull my dress over my head and toss it to the floor. My bra comes off last and I'm left standing bare and vulnerable before this man—with my heart in my hands, offering it to him.

He presses his lips to my belly and places a kiss there before moving downward. He moves his nose back and forth, dragging it over my smooth groin. "You always smell delicious."

He places his palm against my stomach and urges me to the bed. I sit back and he pushes my feet up and apart so my heels are flat on the mattress. He loops his arms around my thighs from behind and spreads me wide. He's done this enough that I know what's coming, but it doesn't stop me from jerking when his mouth touches me. It's still like the first time. "Ohh … Sin."

I trail my fingers through his hair while his tongue glides up and down my center in a torturously slow rhythm. My body rocks with the motion of his mouth until his tongue switches to a faster, circular movement. The waves of pleasure in my pelvis slow momentarily but return with a vengeance when he adds his fingers, gliding them in and out of me. "Aah …" Everything in my groin buzzes with pleasure. A moment later, the sweet torture begins—the pulsation of contractions, mixing with the warm euphoria spreading throughout my entire body all the way to the tips of my curled toes. Bliss.

Complete and utter ecstasy—that's what Sin gives me every time we're together.

He stands and strips while I watch the show from the best seat in the house. When he's as bare as I am, he crawls over my body until we're face to face. He traces my bottom lip with his fingertips. He gazes at my eyes, studying them, as though he's memorizing every fleck of blue and gold.

His body nestles between my legs and he enters me gently. He's moving slowly, never taking his eyes from mine. I touch his face, cradling his scruffy cheek in my palm. He leans into it and places his hand on top of mine, pressing it harder against his skin. He squeezes his eyes shut, as though he's savoring my touch. They're still closed tightly when he tenses and groans, thrusting himself deep inside me. I feel the light quivers of his body inside mine before he goes completely lax over me.

He lies motionless between my legs while remaining inside. I trace my fingernails up and down his back, bringing goosebumps to the surface. I love doing that to him.

"Into me … you see." He opens his eyes to look at me again and I'm overcome with an emotion I've never known. My heart feels as though it might burst from happiness, and I don't want to contain it any longer. "I love you, Sinclair."

I go motionless when I feel the cold barrel of a handgun pressed firmly beneath my chin, my head extended upward, painfully so. "What are you doing?"

"After the first betrayal, there is no other."

I have no idea what he means. "What are you talking about? I haven't betrayed you."

"Who. The. Fuck. Are. You?" he yells.

Oh, shit! What does he know?

"Hands behind your head. Now!" I slowly do as he orders.

"Breck, whatever you've uncovered, it doesn't matter. You know the real me." He shoves the barrel into my jawline so hard, it's digging into my skin.

"I thought I did." He bites his lower lip and shakes his head. "Tell me, Bleu. If you play the role well enough, does it become real?" His voice cracks on the last word. He's hurting but I don't forget who is holding the gun to my head. This is Sinclair Breckenridge. He'll kill me if he believes I've compromised him or the brotherhood. I have zero doubt about that.

Say what you have to say to sell it. "Ask me again who I am."

He does as I tell him. "Who are you?"

"I'm your Bonny Bleu, the one in love with you."

"Says the woman with a gun to her head," he sneers. "You'll say any-fucking-thing to keep me from blowing your brains out right now."

"Fuck! Why can't I do this?" He squeezes his eyes shut and I move my hand to his, the one holding the gun. I slowly push it away from my face.

"Because you're not a monster."

He rises and sits back, resting the gun against his thigh. He uses his free hand to fist his hair. "You're a fucking FBI agent."

"I was. Past tense. I quit." I need that gun out of his hand. "I'm not sure I can talk about all of this while you're still holding that. It's more than a little distracting, considering you were holding it to my head threatening to kill me only a minute ago." I gesture toward the nightstand. "Do you think you could maybe put it over there while we talk about this?"

"No sudden moves, Bleu. I mean it. You know what I'm capable of." He hesitates for a moment and then places it on the nightstand. "Who are you working for?"

"No one."

"You're lying."

"I'm not. I'm here for me." It's finally out there. "I came to avenge a murder. Your father shot and killed my mother."

"Abram was right again. You are Amanda Lawrence's daughter."

"The world thinks I died that night. That isn't the case, as you can see."

"My father didn't kill your mother. He loved her."

"You're wrong. I was there. I saw him. And when he was finished, he held a pillow over my face until I stopped fighting. He thought I was dead."

"If you'll stop and think about it, you'll realize you're confused."

He's relaxed so I make a move for the gun. I'm surprised when he doesn't try to stop me. "Both hands on top of your head. Slowly move to your back on the other side of the bed."

He smiles while doing as I ordered.

I reach under the mattress and retrieve the handcuffs I'd hidden for a time such as this. I toss them onto his chest. "Handcuff yourself to the headboard."

He shakes his head while doing as I've told him. "I as good as placed that gun in your hand myself."

I know. Sinclair Breckenridge would never be so careless.

"Why haven't you killed my father since that's what you came to do? You've had countless opportunities, yet you haven't."

I don't answer as I go through the clothes on the floor. I find what belongs to me and I begin dressing.

"Because you fell in love with me," he says.

I'm in my panties and bra with my dress in my hands. "I did. And it ruined everything." I pull my dress over my head and step into my shoes, careful to not take the gun off Sin.

"I fell in love with you too."

"Says the man handcuffed to a bed."

"You aren't going to kill me, so I have no reason to lie."

I go over to sit on the edge of the bed, the gun pointing at Sin. "You're right. I'm not going to kill you, but I am going to leave you handcuffed here so I can get a head start before the brotherhood comes after me."

"I have things to say to you."

I'm not sure I should listen to this. Even with his hands bound over his head, Sin holds the power to hurt me in so many ways. "I don't have time. The brotherhood will be after me. I need to get out of here."

"Please, don't go yet. No one is on his or her way. Give me a few minutes. That's all I'm asking."

It isn't safe to do so, but I'm dying to know the things he wants to tell me. "Be quick."

"I love you like a fucking lunatic. It's going to kill me to watch you walk out the door but I understand why you must do it. It isn't safe for you to stay. I want you to go until I have time to figure out how to handle this with the brotherhood. I'm going to make it okay with them and after I do, I'll come for you."

He has no idea who he's dealing with. I can't be found if I don't want to be. "You don't know me. I'm a trained chameleon. I'll change my colors when I walk out that door."

"Because you're an agent?"

Yes. "You'll never see me again. I'll disappear without a trace."

"Is that a challenge?" he asks.

"Sure. We can call it that if you like."

I grab my purse from the chair and retrieve the keys to the handcuffs, leaving them on the dresser. "I'll text Jamie to come over and release you when my plane pulls away from the jet bridge." I pull the bed sheet up so he won't be naked and exposed.

"Thanks." He laughs.

I shouldn't but I sit next to him on the bed and lean down for one last kiss. I'm not stupid so I'm holding the gun to his chest, pointing right at his heart. "I'm going to kiss you but one hinky move and you'll literally be the heartless bastard everyone believes you really are."

I lower my mouth to his and press a featherlight kiss against his lips. "I love you, Sinclair Breckenridge. It's going to hurt like hell to never see you again."

I give him a final kiss and walk toward the door. I open it and look over my shoulder at the man I love one last time before I walk away from him forever. I touch my lips and hold out my hand to him. "We both know I can stay or I can survive, but not both."

I knew this day was coming from the start. But never in my wildest dreams did I imagine it feeling like this. We're very much like a flame in the wind. We danced and burned brightly but one large gust and we're extinguished.

"I'm going to fix this, Bonny. We will be together. I only need a little time to make it happen."

I shake my head. "You told me you wanted to know the rest of our story. Well, this is how it ends."

To be continued …

The Next Sin
to be released on February 9, 2015

One Last Sin
to be released on March 23, 2015

ABOUT THE AUTHOR

GEORGIA CATES

Georgia resides in rural Mississippi with her wonderful husband, Jeff, and their two beautiful daughters. She spent fourteen years as a labor and delivery nurse before she decided to pursue her dream of becoming an author and hasn't looked back yet.

For the latest updates from Georgia Cates, stay connected with her at:

 @georgiacates

 georgia.cates.9

www.georgiacates.com

authorgeorgiacates@gmail.com

THE Beauty SERIES

EA T RO AI
OO

EA T RO
S RRE ER
OO

EA T RO O E
OO

Aussie winemaker Jack McLachlan and American musician Laurelyn Prescott agree to a three month relationship while keeping their true identities secret.

A heartbroken Laurelyn Prescott returns to Nashville to pursue her music career and finds the success she's always dreamed of. Jack Henry McLachlan spends three months searching for his beloved but their reunion doesn't come easy. Will she be able to see beyond the glitz glamour and visualize a life that includes him?

Life for Jack Henry and Laurelyn is beautiful until their post-wedded bliss is cut short when his dark past springs into their present happiness. He wants to shelter Laurelyn but keeping her untainted by his previous life proves impossible when yesterday's sins insist on returning to haunt him. Will it be possible for them to find happiness in their forever with a past like his?

Going UNDER SERIES

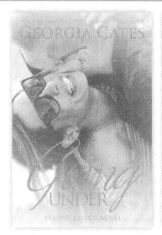 

THE VAMPIRE AGÁPE SERIES

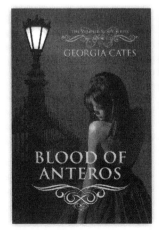 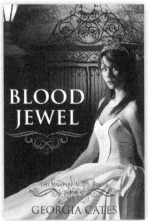 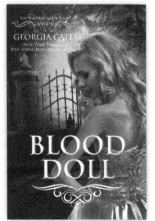

Made in the USA
Charleston, SC
06 January 2015